I0672406

Accounts of a Killing

by

Michael Davies

© Michael Davies

July, 2009

Accounts of a Killing

All Rights Reserved

Copyright © 2009 Michael Davies

Reproduction in any manner, in whole or in part,
in English or any other language, or otherwise,
without the written permission of the copyright holder is
prohibited

This is a work of fiction.
All characters and events portrayed in the book are fictional.
Any resemblance to real persons or events is purely
coincidental.

For information address: mickiedaltonbooks@lycos.com

First Published in 2009 in Australia

ISBN: 978-098-18087-6-5

First Printed In Australia

Published by The Mickie Dalton Foundation
NSW
Australia

www.mickiedaltonfoundation.com

They say the measure of a man is in
the quality of his friends

To Bob and Carmel Comley, friends
for many years and who make me
confident of my quality as a result

Other Books by Michael Davies

The Nightmares of God
The Janus Conspiracy
A Friendly Killing
Helix Dreams
Dreamkill
Ready, Steady, KILL!

For the Young Adults (12-18)
The Many Worlds of Mickie Dalton
The Many Galaxies of Mickie Dalton
The Many Universes of Mickie Dalton
The Strange World of Mark and Anna

For the 8-12 age group
The Julie Malloy Gang and the Smugglers
The Quest for the Locket
The Secret of Yuri Kirilenko
The United Nations and the Extra-Terrestrial
The Secret of Charlotte's Cello
The Star of the Yshan Kings
The War of the Yshan Empire
The Star of the New Yshan Empire
The Red Fog of Time
The Mysterious Recorder and the Door to Elsewhere
Prisoners of the Picture

For the Little Ones (3-5)
Mary's World

And in non-fiction
The Business School Approach to Writing Your Novel

Prologue

Four people sat round a large table. The room was pleasant, well-furnished, lined with rich brown wood. The atmosphere was calm, relaxed.

"Which brings us to the subject of Garry Barton," said one. "I suspect we have all been waiting for this moment to arrive."

Some moments of conversation followed, some questions, some answers, some tension to modify the general air of decisions already reached. Finally, one of them brought the issue to a head.

"The matter of Garry Barton is now on the table," he said. "Does anyone wish to make any suggestions, or add a comment?"

He looked at each of them in turn, tapping his gold pen against his lips. Finally, one of them spoke for them all.

"We have him killed, of course."

All four nodded.

Garry Barton would be killed.

Chapter 1

"In my opinion, you have less than three years to live," Garry Barton said to the group. A stir of amusement and an angry snort erupted from the four people seated around the large boardroom table.

"Come on, Garry," Jack Conway said pleasantly, and smiled. "I know we've heard some outspoken things from you in the past, but this is a bit steep, even for you!" Well-groomed silver hair on top of a lean, aristocratic face completed the image of affluent elegance, and authority sat comfortably in every line of his body. Conway was of the Bostonian School of Superiority and had evidently graduated Magna cum Laude. He was the only one in the room to have retained his jacket and a gold cuff link with a heavy blue opal provided a gaudy splash of color next to the dark pinstripe of his suit. His other hand remained on the arm of his chair, hidden under the edge of the table.

Garry returned the smile. The chairman of Porter, Allen & Conway was a man for whom Garry had a great deal of respect. "Sorry, Jack," said Garry. "Far from being a bit steep, I think I may even have understated the case. Unless you bring PAC into the modern age of technology, I seriously doubt your capacity for survival."

"That's bullshit!" The explosion came from William Trent, head of the audit department. His thick spectacles began to slide and he pushed them back up with the forefinger of his left hand, an action that was almost metronomic in regularity and frequency. It was always accompanied by a severe squint, as if protecting his eyes from the probing of the finger. The lenses distorted his cheeks, providing lines of reducing images of pink skin inside the black frames. Full lips and fleshy jaw showed a man who rarely stinted himself.

Garry looked calmly at the large man glaring across the table at him and smiled. "Can you be a little more explicit, Bill?" he said, keeping his composure. Trent had long since lost the power to intimidate Garry, though others still suffered from the audit partner's blunt manner. At six foot five, with bulk to match and a voice that could shake windows, Trent was an overpowering personality. He stood up now to exert that massive presence.

"You're damn right I'll be explicit!" he said loudly across the boardroom table. The three other seated executives flinched. "I've had it up to here with your determination to spend this firm's money as if it was going out of style! We're regarded as the best audit firm in the city and we do very nicely, thank you, without all these silly toys you insist on buying!"

The noise and the threatening bulk could have overwhelmed Garry. In the past, it had done so. As he had done before, Garry used an old trick he had learned as a boy, of imagining the other man naked, and the thought of the gross, flabby body immediately dissipated the fear.

Garry smiled gently at Trent, and the angry man obviously was further irritated by Garry's refusal to be threatened. "Anybody else feel that way?" Garry asked calmly to the table in general.   Trent remained standing, looking at each of them in turn, daring them to disagree with him. He was unsuccessful.

"Bill, please sit down, you're blocking the sun!" The lightly mocking voice came from the left side of the table. Stephen Petheram always made a joke about other people's size, almost laughing at his own fragile five-foot four-inch stature that sometimes made him look like a youth in adult company. He was barely in his mid-thirties, but power and authority sat well on him, despite his diminutive size. Strong, dark features under gleaming healthy hair reflected confidence, aggression and a limitless energy that kept two shifts of secretaries fully occupied covering his sixteen-hour days.

"Garry asked you to be specific and you weren't," continued Petheram. "Merely blasting at him won't get the answers." He turned his handsome face towards Garry and smiled. "So Garry, why don't you be specific instead, while Bill collects his thoughts?" he said. "In what way are we so dangerously lacking?" His light blue eyes sparkled with internal amusement.

The little guy is probably the brightest man I have ever met, thought Garry. He wondered why Petheram devoted himself to running the Insolvency Department of a mid-size accounting firm when he could make a fortune practising law.   Petheram was a qualified attorney, and for all his lack of height, he was a powerful personality who could take over a roomful of noisy people without raising his voice.

Garry smiled back at him in gratitude. "Just look at the place, Stephen," he said, waving his arm in a general sort of way to indicate the three floors of PAC's offices. "You have certainly come a long way in the last five years, I grant you. You have at last installed a proper network of all your personal computers and your own internal accounting systems are adequate, if not quite current. But the reason I can say that is that I was the one who installed the network and located suitable systems for you three years ago and look at the battles I had with most of you to achieve that! But there are some other problems resulting from your delays in upgrading to keep current and they're costing you thousands every year."

Petheram nodded, as Garry knew he would. The two men had conducted this conversation before, and Petheram had deliberately given Garry the opportunity to get a real point in before the young consultant launched the rest of his criticisms.

"And not only are the systems not quite current," Garry continued, "you haven't done anything to bring the work flows and operations in line with the systems requirements as I recommended when I did that installation. It means paperwork is travelling too far and spending too much time being reviewed at too many levels. This reflects in our fees, and that makes us less competitive. Now, in the consulting department, we have created a far more efficient work flow and we therefore get our bills finalised and out to the client much quicker than the rest of the firm. Our cash flow is therefore faster."

"Yes, but you're in the computer business. People expect you to use all that hi-tech stuff! Accounting just doesn't have the need for that level of sophistication."

The voice was almost a whisper, but the power of the personality behind it could not be disguised. Garry looked down to the woman at his right. Bridget Newman was thin, all bone and grey, her eyes a cave-mouth black under hooded eyelids. She sat upright, her hands flat on the table, and she appeared to be studying the veins on their backs with intense interest. She was dressed immaculately, a severely cut black skirt enhancing the expensive silk of the high-necked blouse. Round the collar hung a small Wedgwood medallion, the purity of the white profile contrasting with the royal blue ceramic background in a pattern unchanged in over two hundred years. Newman ran the tax department with a quiet, sarcastic management style that terrified her subordinates but kept them loyal with high salary levels and a training program second to none in the industry.

Like a praying mantis, thought Garry. Of all the people in the room, this woman was the only one who could threaten his composure. He swallowed and forced his voice to remain calm and regular. "Really, Bridget? You can't see where improved support staff productivity would help? You can't see where project management systems would speed up your assignments enormously? You can't see where an on-line system for billing would improve your cash flows?"

She raised her head to stare at him. Garry felt a moment of panic but looked back firmly at her, gazing into her deep black eyes that always seemed to be hiding terrible secrets.

"You may be right," said Newman. Her voice was hardly above a whisper. "But I still haven't seen why this is going to destroy the firm in three years, as you claim."

"Nor can anyone else! That's why I say again, you're talking rubbish and I don't know why we listen to you!" Trent resumed the attack. He had sat down again but he leaned forward in his seat and glared at Garry.

Garry fought the impulse to shy away and stared back. "Well, Bill, good timing," he said firmly. "Because you're the worst culprit and the major cause of our imminent death, so maybe it's time we addressed the matter of the audit department."

"How dare you talk to me like that!" Trent banged a heavy fist on the table. "Who the hell do you think you are?" His face was dangerously red and veins stood out in his neck. For a moment, Garry seriously thought Trent was going to come round the table and physically attack him, but Conway interceded.

"William!" he snapped. "That will do! We listen to Garry because I ordered it. We've had good cause to value his contributions in the past, and the rule at this meeting is everyone has the right of free speech, regardless of their position, so sit down and let him explain!"

Garry felt the high-tension electricity crackle in the room. Trent slowly leaned back in his seat, still glaring at Garry. An audible sigh of relief drifted around the table.

Garry kept his eyes firmly on Trent's, refusing to be intimidated. "So, let's look at the audit function within PAC," he said. "I agree that right now, Bill can point to a decade of uninterrupted growth followed by the last three years during which we have maintained at least a flat level of earnings, even though the audit market has had all the volatile excitement of a Koala bear on Valium."

"I'm glad you accept that," growled Trent. "At least it means you can see beyond your nose." He subsided in the face of a sharp glare from Conway.

"But I've completed an interesting study recently that might cause you some concern," continued Garry. He touched a key on his laptop computer and that woke up the device from its hibernation. It was connected to the overhead projector that hung on the ceiling and the screen on one wall came alive. He saw the sudden glare cause a few eyes to blink, then he pointed at the screen which now displayed rows of figures. "Through some devious means, a lot of telephone calls, and studies of a few companies' financial statements, I've been able to compare our costs of doing an audit to some of our competitors'."

He pulled an electronic pointer from his shirt pocket, pressed the button which lit a red laser beam and pointed it at the top row of data. "You will see," he said, "that for similar-sized companies requiring equivalent audit teams, the cost of a PAC audit of a company's accounts relative to the client's receipts is more than fifteen percent higher than anyone else's."

The room was silent. Garry looked at each of the four partners, who were staring at the screen. Trent drummed his fingers loudly on the table.

"The cause of that increased cost is the extra time we use to complete a significant number of our audits," said Garry. He switched off the projector and turned back to the table.

"Those figures are garbage," grated Trent. "How do we know you didn't just make them up?"

"If you want to believe that, then there's little I can do," replied Garry. "But I got the figures by calling a lot of people, including my counterparts in other audit firms, and the systems directors at several companies that were audited recently. It wasn't difficult."

"If I understand you," interrupted Conway, "you're saying that we cost more than our competitors because we take longer?"

Garry nodded. "And we're less effective too. We don't get as deep into the clients' accounts..."

His words were violently cut off by Trent.

"That's enough!" he bellowed. Trent's face was red again. Garry felt a wave of anxiety for a second, sensing the violence in the man. If Trent lost control, Garry seriously doubted if the other three could stop him.

"I've heard you spout garbage before, Barton," raged Trent. "But this is beyond the limits! How dare you insult my professional competence?"

Garry stared back but felt his strength wilting in the face of Trent's barrage of fury. He was saved by an unexpected source.

"William," said Newman, lifting her head from her constant study of the backs of her hands and looking directly at Trent. "The only one who sees it as an insult is you. Unless Garry has made up those figures, they reveal a serious problem. I for one would like to know about that problem."

Her sibilant voice sliced through the anger in the room and dissipated it. Garry let out a long breath. In fact, his statement really had been an attack, because the problem was directly one of Trent's making. Reinforced by Newman's support, he looked firmly back at the huge man on the other end of the table.

"There is only one reason why we take longer and achieve less than our competition, Bill," said Garry, "and that's because the only computer audit systems we use are as old as Noah and seriously limited in effectiveness."

"Rubbish!" Trent's face was tight with anger.

"Let's keep this objective, William," said Conway, leaning back in his chair. "Garry, how many of our competitors use computer audit systems which you would consider to be up-to-date?"

"All of them," retorted Garry flatly.

"And does that cause a problem?" broke in Petheram. "Other than the time and cost of conducting the audit?"

Garry nodded, knowing full well that Petheram had again acted as straight man, feeding Garry a chance for a decisive response. "A massive one," he answered, keeping a wary eye on Trent whose furious eyes and drumming fingers said he was ready to explode again. "It means that, for an increasing number of our clients, we're paying far less attention to the major commercial engine within the client's organization."

"I don't understand," said Conway. "I'm an old-fashioned accountant and I've not worked as an auditor for thirty years. What exactly do you mean?"

Garry thought for a few moments. "Suppose you were called in to conduct an audit on a company with very old-fashioned ways of doing business," he said finally. "Your team examines in details the cash position, the state of the building, the quality of the staff, all that standard stuff. You study all the accounts receivable, the accounts payable and the general ledger, but you ignore the room full of clerks working in the accounts section who produce all the data you've been studying. You don't look at how they process the data, what they do with it, how they control the flow of papers and guard against loss or fraud. What sort of audit would that be?"

"A lousy one," replied Conway with a small smile.

"Right," agreed Garry. "Our audit teams examine every aspect of the business. They look at printed output and reports and all that, but we only take samples of the customer's computer transaction for auditing. That was fine ten years ago, but the modern systems are so powerful that they can audit the entire computer files in less time than we take to review just a sample."

"Let's ignore for the moment the question of how we service a customer with these audit packages," said Conway. "First, explain to me what a computer audit package actually does." He looked at Trent with an apologetic smile. "Forgive my ignorance, Bill, but as I said, it's been a long time since I conducted a client's audit."

His soft words lessened the tension considerably. Garry moved away from his position at the slide projector and took a seat next to Petheram, to Trent's right.

"Bill, please correct me if I say anything wrong here," said Garry with a small smile to the audit partner. Trent grunted and said nothing. Garry turned back to the table.

"In a standard audit," he began, "the auditor is required to confirm that the accounts being presented are a true and fair representation of the company's position. I believe that is the correct phrase?" He turned to Trent for confirmation, and the big man eased a little at the obvious deference to his expertise. He nodded back at Garry who continued.

"Now in manual situations, we can actually look at how the accounts or other data are prepared and check that the processing is correct," he said. "But when the processing is done within the bowels of the electronic beast, you can't physically watch it. That's what a computer audit system does. It tracks the electronic processing."

He paused and looked around the table for confirmation that they were all following him. "Now, as I said earlier, the systems which were first introduced were relatively slow and we did the traditional audit process of taking just a sample of transactions from the client's computer file and testing them. But given the massive increase in the power and speed of our little laptop computers, we can run analyses of all of the transactions for the entire year, a hundred percent of them, not just a sample. So while with the earlier systems we could miss some fraudulent transactions or just errors, now we can check everything in less time than the old systems took."

He paused for a moment and realised everybody was following him, though Bill Trent was looking increasingly disturbed as he obviously knew where Garry was heading.

"The problem which we have, and which is rapidly increasing, is that we use an obsolete computer audit package which takes only samples for testing. Our competitors are using the latest in what is known as CAAT, Computer Assisted Audit Techniques and they therefore conduct a far more intensive audit in less time than we do. We therefore run the serious risk of missing something in the client's business that might later come back and bite us on the bum."

"Is that true, Bill?" asked Petheram. "We're using out-of-date audit software?" Garry knew very well that Petheram already knew the answer. He and Stephen had discussed that particular point only the day before.

"It's true," admitted Trent. "But that's hardly a problem. We're still performing in accordance with the rules."

"That may be true," replied Garry. "But the fact remains that our competitors are doing a much more professional and comprehensive job than we are. And our clients are not dim, they will soon recognise that fact if they haven't already done so"

"Which means they could be seeking new quotes from our competitors?" asked Conway.

Garry nodded. "Which almost undoubtedly means we'll lose the client at some stage," he said as gently as he could.

"Bill, what are you planning to do about that?" asked Petheram.

Trent shook his head in anger. "I have no information that any clients are planning such action," he said tightly. "I think Barton's making it up."

"I doubt that," said Petheram. "But why have we stuck with the old systems? Why haven't you acquired these CAAT things?"

"Because we don't need them," Trent said, pushing his spectacles back up his nose, his face become more red as his obvious anger got greater. "We manage our audits perfectly well, and the huge improvement that Barton is blathering about doesn't exist. It's just not worth spending tens of thousands on new software."

"Is that it, or are you simply frightened of the extra learning curve that you'll need to climb to become familiar with more complex systems?" asked Garry, feeling a little combative in the face of Trent's anger.

"Crap!" retorted Trent. "You don't know what the hell you're talking about."

Garry shrugged. He was confident of his facts and Trent's hostility was having less and less effect on him. "I'll circulate the series of press clippings, business reports and extracts of books which describe the latest series of CAATs. They'll be on your desks by this afternoon. Read them, and you can't fail to see that continuing with old software and obsolete laptop computers for our audit staff is a path to bankruptcy for us."

A moment of silence hovered over the table, broken by Conway. "Is that a true and fair representation of the situation, Bill?" he asked, a slightly mocking smile on his lips. Trent glared at him and offered no response.

"Then I have to ask you, Bill," continued the chairman, "just why are we not using more advanced computer audit packages?"

"Because I'm not convinced they're reliable, fully tested, or even work properly," replied Trent. There was an air of defiance in his voice. "And that's the view of the partner in charge of computer audit."

"But didn't Garry say all our competitors are using these things?" Newman's voice had an edge.

"They're not worth it." Trent's tone was final and the three other partners around the table looked astonished.

"But, William," said Petheram, "you've just referred to our computer audit partner who is surely an expert in these matters. Is this the view of George Elliot?"

"Yes it is," barked Trent. "George and I agree with each other entirely on this."

"But this still puzzles me," said Newman. "Does that mean all our competitors who have spent tens of thousands, maybe hundreds of thousands on new hardware and software are all wrong and only you and Elliot are right?"

"I think the answer is something different," broke in Garry before Bill could answer. "I think the answer lies in the fact that George Elliot learned these original packages in his early days and has not been able to update his thinking on the subject."

"Remember who you're talking to here," said Trent in anger. "George is a partner and you're not. He's far more experienced than you are."

"In accounting, yes," agreed Garry. He was in his own professional area now and felt confident taking the attack to Trent. "But as a computer technician, George hasn't climbed out of the pouch yet."

"Rubbish! You're being offensive." Trent was getting red in the face again but Garry detected discomfort and embarrassment as well as anger in the large man.

"Let's compare, shall we William?" said Petheram with a gentle smile. Garry knew that Petheram was enjoying the conflict. "Garry, just what is your experience in computing?"

"An honours degree in computer science from Sydney University," replied Garry. "Then ten years with major computer suppliers both in England and the States, ending as a Systems Manager in a large software house here in Chicago. I completed a Master's in Computer Science at Northwestern just before joining PAC four years ago."

"And do you know what George's experience is?" asked Petheram.

"It's not relevant," said Trent loudly.

"I think it is," replied Stephen in a voice that allowed for no dispute. "Garry, do you know?"

"George attended a general computer course at Illinois State University fifteen years ago, as part of his degree in accounting" replied Garry. "He has never worked as a professional computer programmer or analyst. He did a one-month course in computer audit seven years ago when he was a manager, and you promoted him to computer audit partner a year later."

"That's it?" Newman looked up at Trent. "We made him a partner based on that experience?"

Trent appeared to be under great stress. "We had no computer expertise at all in the firm," he mumbled. "We had no way of evaluating his experience."

"I still don't understand," broke in Conway. "If it's George's function to introduce computer audit techniques and develop our expertise in them, why is he not doing so?"

"Because he doesn't believe the other available packages are any good, that's why," said Trent, his anger rising. "I've already told you."

An expectant silence rang round the room.

"I think there's a different reason," said Garry. "I think that in the country of the blind, the one-eyed man is king."

"Garry!" Conway lost his air of studied relaxation and sat up sharply. "Are you saying that George is suppressing the level of computer knowledge within PAC simply to protect his position as the firm's expert?"

"George learned a single computer audit package when he did his course seven years ago," said Garry. "It was the package we've been using ever since. George knows that package well, but that's the limit of his knowledge. All the other packages require an understanding of advanced computer techniques. George has never learned such techniques and has made certain nobody else has, either. And it's worse than that. The fact is, for fully effective use of these audit techniques, even the average auditor must now have enough comprehension of computer technology to operate as a competent systems analyst. George hasn't got it and seems unwilling to acquire it, neither for himself nor for his staff."

"You'd better be able to support that statement." Trent started to rise from his seat again.

"No sweat," replied Garry, staring firmly at the red-faced giant. "Each of your audit managers has been scheduled this year to go on advanced computer audit training programs. I know, because I helped arrange them at their request."

"You did what?" Trent rose fully to his feet.

Garry ignored him, looking instead at Conway. "And George Elliot cancelled each of those courses," he said. "I know that too, because those six managers came to me practically tearing their hair out in frustration."

"That's a lie!" snapped Trent. "You're a damned liar, Barton! Jack, this is going too far. I demand an apology."

Conway looked briefly at his partner but said nothing.

"Ask them and find out for yourself," replied Garry.

"I don't need to ask them! I know you're a liar!" Trent's rage subsided to be replaced by contempt. He leaned back in his seat with his arms crossed and stared out of the window.

"Garry, you indicated to me a few days ago, that your consulting team does detailed examinations of computer systems," said Conway, changing the topic rapidly.

"Yes, I did," replied Barton. "And that's another sore point. I win a fair amount of work in that area, especially in the areas of business continuity, disaster recovery planning and crisis management. But we could do a lot more if the auditors would take us in on every major assignment to support the audit work."

"And Bill," said Conway, looking at Trent, "why don't you invite the consultants into your audits?"

"They're not accountants," retorted Trent. He spoke quietly, but Garry could see his hands trembling. "I can't take the risk of having non-professionals involved."

Garry took a deep breath and controlled his own anger. "And that brings us to another matter, just as critical and perhaps the main reason why we're becoming obsolete. I spent some time reviewing the professional institutions of the accounting profession. One thing really interested me. The international practice members groups now talk about the audit of senior management processes, not just the auditing of accounts. To do so requires exactly the same processes that management consultants employ, understanding of the client's management style, goals and aims, organisational structure and culture. There are techniques to interviewing top management. This is something that is part of my daily process, but I can't see where any of your auditors ever go into this area of reviewing companies' top management operations."

"Because we're auditors of accounts, not goddam bullshit consultants," shouted Trent.

"But according to the profession leaders, you have to be both. It impresses me that they have accepted this as part of the requirements." Garry was feeling confident now. He had made the major point and he could see it had scored with some of the people in the room. "And that's why you should be using my department," he continued. "We can fill that gap until your people have developed the extra skills."

Petheram spoke up again. "It seems to me, Bill that the result of your attitude is that the client is denied a true evaluation of his business, possibly operating at serious risk if he has no disaster recovery plan and this partnership is denying itself income."

"I'm not sure which is worse," said the thin woman across the table. "We risk censure on one count and lose money on the other."

Trent stared rigidly at the far wall and said nothing, but his discomfort was evident to Garry.

"And all this is the reason Mister Barton believes we'll be dead in three years?" Newman's contempt was obvious, a sudden switch in her attitude that left Garry confused. Had she not apparently been condemning Trent a moment ago?

"Primarily, yes," he answered, trying to withstand her bleak stare at him. "But these things simply represent a deeper problem within the firm."

"And what might that be?" There was a dangerous edge in Newman's voice.

"It seems to me that you are too deeply committed to audit as a cash cow in this partnership," replied Garry. "Now, I know that your own department is highly profitable, and Stephen runs a most lucrative insolvency practice too. But you ignore the fact that audit is actually a stagnant business sector, as evidenced by the figures of the last few years. You seem to believe that audit will always bring in the main cash revenue, and you ignore the consulting business completely."

"And rightly so," said Trent. "From what we've just seen, you people cause too much trouble."

"William, that will do," cautioned Conway. "Garry, why do you think so? You have several people in consulting, you all make good money. What's the problem?"

"Why isn't my boss on this Management Committee?" asked Garry. "What sort of message does that send to the consulting department?"

"Andrew Whittaker isn't even an accountant," responded Trent. "What the hell does he know about running an accounting practice?"

"Could an accountant run a wholesale hardware distribution firm?" asked Garry.

Trent looked confused. "Of course he could," he replied.

"Why?" asked Garry. "How could an accountant know anything about hardware distribution?"

"Because as accountants, we get into every aspect of a business," said Trent sharply. "We learn the widest set of skills because of what we do."

"But you have just said that you do not get into top management practices, nor evaluate corporate goals and objectives, corporate culture, or any of the business policy elements of your clients." answered Garry. "In the last five years, Andrew has turned around a chemical production firm and saved it from bankruptcy. He's revised the operations of a cable-making company and increased their profits significantly. He's implemented management procedures in a sugar mill that saved them from failing, and he's done a wealth of similar jobs, just as I have. Now, you're telling me he couldn't provide valuable management skills to this committee?"

Trent muttered something under his breath and turned to stare out of the window.

Garry continued his attack. "And as a systems designer, I've designed and installed computer systems for every type of application, from accounting through materials requirement planning. How could I do that without a deep understanding of the management principles involved? How can I know less than you do about the same things?"

Garry looked around the room. The four partners' faces were blank.

"Now the strange thing," continued Garry, "is that you all seem unconcerned by the idea that Andrew and I can effectively manage a company for a time and do a turn-around, or give that company top-level management advice, all in the name of this partnership, but you won't allow us to assist the partnership itself."

"I didn't even know you were doing work like that," said Trent. There was almost grudging respect in his voice.

"We've been doing it for years, Bill," answered Garry. "What you've just said may well represent the most dangerous weakness in the place. You don't even know what one division of the partnership is doing. Have you never been interested enough to ask?"

Trent stared at the wall again, and Garry sensed the growing hostility from him as well as from Newman. He looked at his watch and was startled to see it was nearly ten in the morning. The meeting had begun at eight, and he had a lot of work to do.

Seeing the movement, Conway stood up. "I think that's it for today," he said with a smile to each of the others in turn. As they stood and the men collected their jackets, Garry walked out and descended two flights in the fire escape stairway to the sixteenth floor where the management consulting department operated.

Andrew Whittaker occupied a corner office. The heavy-set man behind the desk looked up as Garry walked past the door.

"How did it go?" Whittaker asked and coughed loudly.

Smothering his distaste, Garry entered the office, waving his hand in front of his face. The smoke almost blocked the view of Lake Michigan and some of Chicago's buildings. "I need hazardous duty pay to come in here," he said, not entirely joking. He took a seat across from Whittaker's desk.

Garry's boss stubbed out the cigarette he was smoking. "It's my only vice," he said and coughed once more. "So how did the morning session go?" he asked again.

"I think I lit a few fires," replied Garry with a reflective grin. "Told them the partnership had three years to live."

"You said *what?*" Whittaker stared at him, alarm in his face.

Garry settled back in his chair. "I pointed out the serious obsolescence of office automation in the place, and how it was harming our productivity," he said. "And I was a bit hard on Bill Trent for not using modern computer audit packages."

"You're chancing your luck with that guy," replied Whittaker. "He looks like an elephant and he's got a memory to match."

"I know," agreed Garry. "But how are we ever going to move him if we ignore the problem?"

"It's not your function to develop computer audit in the firm," said Whittaker. "It's George Elliot's job."

"Elliot's a bloody turkey," snapped Garry. "He's had a free ride with this firm for five years now. When is somebody going to expose him? He's a fraud! Back home, we'd call him a bludger!"

"Turkey or bludger, he's also a partner," said Whittaker in some anger. "You should be more careful about what you say."

"Oh, you mean shut up and let the firm die?" retorted Garry. "Just what sort of professional ethics are those?"

"Don't you think you've gone beyond your responsibilities with this?" asked Whittaker in a tone of some conciliation. He leaned back in his chair with a look of concern on his face.

"Possibly," agreed Garry. "When Jack Conway first asked for my technical briefings to the Management Committee, I suppose he had in mind more a series of presentations on what's happening in the world of information technology."

"That's right," said Whittaker. "But you seem to have gone out of your way to point out the firm's failings. I've had a lot of complaints about it."

"Really?" Garry was surprised. "That's the first time you've mentioned it. From Bill Trent, I suppose?"

Whittaker nodded. "Of course," he said. "And maybe this is a good time to reconsider what you're doing."

"Why?" asked Garry in some dismay. "Isn't what I'm doing aimed at the firm's benefit?"

Whittaker looked uncomfortable, and stared out of the window. "It's the classic consultant's dilemma, I suppose," he murmured, more to himself than to Garry. "Telling the client uncomfortable truths can get us into trouble."

"And often has done," added Garry.

Whittaker didn't seem to hear him. "The trouble is," he continued, "you weren't hired by the Management Committee to tell them what the firm needed to maintain its competitive edge. You were asked to provide information on the state of technology today, without providing any judgements on how the firm fails to measure up."

"What's that got to do with it?" asked Garry. "I have as much a vested interest in this partnership's survival as you do. How can I avoid pointing out weaknesses when they fall into my area of professional competence?"

Whittaker finally looked at Garry. "Because you're using up time that otherwise should be charged out to clients," he said. "And because you're causing confusion among the partners. The normal consultant-client ethics don't apply here."

Garry was seeing a side of his boss that he had never seen before, and he felt distressed. "Andrew, doesn't it worry you that we're so backward, technically?"

Whittaker shrugged. "The firm keeps making money," he said. "In time, we'll take the steps to invest in more current technology."

"By which time we may have lost our customers," Garry added. "And aren't you concerned that they don't seem to think you should be on the Management Committee?"

"Not really," replied Whittaker. "We're doing okay in the Consulting Department. That keeps me busy enough."

Garry heard the dissatisfaction in Whittaker's voice. "But you'd really like to be on the committee, wouldn't you?" he asked.

Whittaker shrugged, and looked longingly at his cigarettes. "It's not that important," he said.

Sensing the rising tension in his boss, Garry changed the subject. "Are you officially instructing me to stay away from criticisms of the firm's technology investment?" he asked.

His boss looked at his hands, out of the window and then back to Garry. "I can't do that," he replied. "You have to do what seems best. But I am telling you that this path can get us both into difficulties."

Garry rose to his feet. "I've got work to do," he said, and moved to the door.

"Something you should think about," said Whittaker, reaching for his pack of cigarettes. Garry stopped and turned to him. "Always remember that professional partnerships are closed societies," continued Whittaker, extracting a cigarette and looking at it with an expectant air. He took out a lighter and looked up at Garry. "In the end, they tend to stick together against the outsider, regardless of the truth of the situation."

"You think they'd kill the messenger rather than listen to the truth?"

"It's possible," said Whittaker, striking his lighter.

"That sounds like a warning," said Garry.

"It is," said Whittaker, lighting the cigarette and drawing a luxuriously deep breath.

Garry looked hard at his boss for a second, and walked out.

After an hour of concentration at his desk, trying to schedule his team of ten consultants around a number of projects, Garry was interrupted by the telephone. Not entirely switching his mind off his problem, he picked up the phone.

"Garry Barton," he said, his eyes still concentrating on the chart of activities on his computer screen.

"I thought we might have lunch," said the well-educated voice in his ear. Jack Conway's suggestions usually came in this mild manner.

Garry tuned in fully to the voice on the telephone. "Sounds like a splendid idea," he said. "Somewhere hugely expensive, I assume? Or am I supposed to be buying?"

"My club," replied Conway with a ghost of a laugh.

"I'll come to your office at twelve," said Garry.

"I'll be expecting you," Conway replied and hung up.

Garry felt a little more cheerful at the invitation. The parting from Whittaker's office had left him feeling uneasy. Conway's lunch invitations were regular events, usually once a month and Garry had always enjoyed the affairs. The discussion was normally an informal continuation of the briefing sessions Garry had been giving the Management Committee for the past six months, while Conway explored specific questions for his own information.

Suppressing the worries about the discussions with his boss, Garry returned to the scheduling matrix on the computer screen.

* * * *

At a few minutes before noon, Garry switched off his computer, put on his jacket and walked up a couple of floors to Conway's office. As he rounded the corner, he saw Conway through the open door to his office putting the cap on his gold pen and closing his desk calendar. His desk carried little but that calendar. There was no computer terminal.

Conway smiled as Garry tapped on the door frame. "Exemplary timing," he said, and rose to his feet. Garry stood aside to let Conway leave his office and followed him to the elevator doors. The chairman pushed the call button with his left hand, while the other hand was placed firmly in his pocket. The elevator was almost full, so no discussion took place on the way down, or until they had threaded their way out of the building lobby into the outdoors.

Michigan Avenue was full of pedestrians on this fine day in July. Tourists mixed with locals, walking up and down the sidewalks, staring into the fine shops and at each other. Garry and Conway made small talk as they worked their way through the crowds to the tall building that housed Conway's exclusive and old-fashioned club.

Again, the elevator was full, this time with affluent, middle-aged males, all at least fifteen years older than Garry. Only one pair of men engaged in conversation, speaking in soft tones as the elevator rose. Garry caught a reference to a possible denial of admission of evidence, and assumed they were attorneys.

The elevator emptied as it reached the thirtieth floor and the door opened to the lobby of the club. As they waited for the line of members to be seated by the attendant, Garry looked around him.

The view of Lake Michigan was superb. Two walls of windows sparkled in sunshine and Garry could see the expanse of royal blue spotted with the bright colors of many sailing boats. He felt the panorama lacked the contrasts and color of Sydney Harbour, but was pleased with the view as a backdrop to lunch. The carpet was deep, the walls were decorated with large paintings framed in ornate gold, and the gleam of the white tablecloths competed with the lake for brightness. The room smelled of money, old and new. Garry felt relief that the bill for the lunch was Conway's responsibility.

After a few minutes, they were led to a table in the corner by the window. The two men took seats across from each other and picked up menus. Garry knew from previous events that Conway would normally discuss nothing serious until the meal had been ordered and drinks served.

"Your usual, Mister Conway?" murmured the waiter. Conway nodded, not looking up from his menu. "And you, sir?" asked the waiter.

"A dry sherry, please," answered Garry. "Straight up." The waiter nodded and moved away.

"That was quite a bombshell you dropped this morning," said Conway, unfolding his napkin and draping it across his knees with his left hand. His right had already taken cover under the table. Garry wondered if he would ever have the courage to ask Conway how that hand had been so damaged. The scars were ugly. Conway looked around the room then turned his eyes to Garry.

"I thought that was my role," replied Garry nervously. Conway's opening comment had been more direct than usual and had come unexpectedly early.

"It probably should be," agreed Conway. "But it wasn't what we intended when we invited you to make these technology presentations. Though, to be fair, we had no real idea what we intended at the time."

"And as usual, I gave my client more than he expected," replied Garry.

Conway nodded and smiled. "Indeed you did. And in the process, you seem to have unsettled one or two of us."

"Including you?"

"No, not me." Conway shook his head. "I have always understood your commitment to upgrading the practices of this partnership, and I have valued your submissions."

"So it's Trent, of course." Garry was feeling uneasy. He knew his work had been useful, and he felt frustrated at the obstructionism of the large audit partner. "And anyone else?" he added.

Conway gave him a sharp look. "You think there might be?"

"I don't know about Bridget Newman," replied Garry.

"Who does?" Conway's smile was tiny. "But you may well be correct. Bridget's motivations and values are little understood."

The conversation was interrupted by the waiter's return with a tray. He placed a large glass in front of Conway and gave Garry a smaller glass of dry sherry. Both men picked up their glasses.

"Your good health," said Garry and sipped his sherry.

Conway nodded with a small grunt of agreement, took a large gulp of his Manhattan and smiled. "That cleans away the morning very well," he said.

They both placed their glasses back on the table as the waiter returned with his order pad.

"The fillet of sole," said Conway.

Garry nodded. "The same," he said, and the waiter moved away again.

"Regardless of the personal difficulties caused to your partners," Garry said, resuming the discussion, "I believe that the firm is dangerously lacking in professional competence in audit, its main cash cow."

"And I agree with you," said Conway. "I also agree with the other comment you made this morning, that we have ignored the management consulting side of the firm, to our cost."

"Then what's the problem?" asked Garry. "You're the chairman, you have the Conway name. Considerable power lies with you. You could initiate corrective action immediately."

Conway shook his head. "It's not that easy," he said. "The days are long gone when a Conway or a Porter could deliver a command and have it treated as if it had been brought down from the holy mountain.

My grandfather ran the place like that, but times have changed."

"To your everlasting regret, of course," said Garry with a smile.

Conway echoed it. "Naturally. We Conways are born to command. However, society has forced changes in the old feudal system. My partners actually dare to speak their minds and even disagree with me on occasion."

"Disgraceful," said Garry. "A good whipping should cure that."

"Unfortunately," said Conway in a dry tone, "whippings can not be administered to anyone above the rank of Audit Senior."

"Just as well," said Garry. "Otherwise I can't imagine what your Management Committee would order for me. Hanging at the yardarm or keelhauling, I imagine."

"It does worry me." There was no humor in Conway's face. "The anger I see in William Trent is troublesome. And as I said, I cannot pretend to know what goes on in Bridget's dark mind, but I see little evidence of warmth to your ideas."

"Jack, is this the second warning of the day that I've had?"

"You've had one already?"

"Indeed. Wreathed in curls of ancient smoke from the bowels of hell."

"Ah! Andrew Whittaker says the same thing, does he?"

"I think there's some tension in Andrew," replied Garry. "For all his professed nonchalance on the subject, I believe he feels slighted not to be on the committee. With some justification I think, as well you know."

The arrival of the waiter carrying lunch punctuated the discussion. The two men remained silent as the plates were laid on the table. Garry took a long drink from the glass of cold water that had been poured as they sat down. He was worried by Jack's words, and on top of the discussion with Andrew, his uneasiness was growing.

After sharing out a selection of vegetables from a tray, the waiter departed, and for a few more moments, both men tackled their meals in silence.

Finally, Garry spoke. "Are you telling me to back off from the problem of the firm's policy or lack of it, on automation of the audit process?" he asked. He pushed his plate aside, his appetite gone.

"I can't make such decrees," replied Conway. He took a mouthful of his cocktail. "Nor am I convinced that such a move is in the best interests of the firm."

"Well, that's something, at least," said Garry. "It's nice to know that you believe I may be of value to your partners."

"I have always believed that, Garry," replied Conway. He put down his knife and fork, his right hand disappearing under the table. "My worry is whether it's in the best interests of Garry Barton."

"I appreciate the concern," replied Garry. "I'm a very good management consultant." Conway nodded his acceptance of that comment. "But my strength is also my weakness," continued Garry. "I can't work in the manner of many in my profession, which is to tell the client what he wants to hear. That's simple fraud in my book, though I'm well aware that a lot of the big firms do precisely that. I have to tell the truth as I see it."

"And people are notoriously ill-equipped and unwilling to hear the truth," murmured Conway. "Which means you take a lot of abuse as part of your job."

"Exactly. But you know me. Do you think I can back away from this problem?"

"Not a chance." Conway picked up his knife and fork again and sliced a fillet from his plate.

Garry took his glass and drained the sherry. He paused while the waiter returned and refilled his water glass then drained that as well.

"Which seems to provide us both with a problem," said Garry. "I will continue my attack on the firm's weaknesses as I see them, and in turn will be assailed by the forces of darkness in the shapes of Newman and Trent."

"And my problem?" asked Conway with a faint smile.

"Your problem is how much of a leash can you put on those two, and how far you wish to protect me in order to pull the firm along the path I'm recommending. It seems to me you agree with my position, but supporting me against two senior partners will give you a crisis of your own."

"The consultant's analytical ability shows itself again," said Conway. He was no longer smiling.

"I can't help you, Jack," said Garry, seeing the distress in the chairman's eyes. "This is where you have to justify the multi-million-dollar income. It's your decision and yours alone."

For a few seconds, Conway stared silently at the table. Then he reached for the bowl of tartar sauce and spooned some onto his plate. "I was seven years old when my father first brought me to the office," he said.

Garry recognized Conway's need to change the subject. He was happy to go along with it, and the new topic was fascinating. He knew nothing of Conway's history. "That was in the old offices in Kenilworth?" he prompted.

Conway nodded. "Old man Conway had founded the firm just a few years before. He and John Porter had worked their buns off and built up quite a practice, then they bought a smaller practice from Joe Allen and it went on from there."

"What sort of man was your grandfather?"

"A tyrant." Conway's eyes lit up with amusement. "But that old bastard knew how to build a business. I tell you, an hour after I'd come into the building, I decided to change my career plans, I was so impressed by him."

"At seven?" Garry grinned, pleased with this moment of ease with the chairman. "What did you want to do before?"

"Join the navy," replied Conway. "Pearl Harbor had just happened and my father had enlisted as a navy pilot. The old man was furious and proud at the same time. And when Jack Senior didn't come back from Midway, somehow I was expected to take his place."

"I didn't know," said Garry.

Conway shrugged. "It worked well. When the old man retired, Porter's son took over as chairman. I married his daughter, and that sort of sealed the dynasty."

Garry said nothing, waiting to hear the rest.

"So you must understand," continued Conway. "The firm has been my life since I was seven. There's nothing I won't do to protect it." He picked up his glass and finished the cocktail. "Nothing," he said, and looked sharply at Garry.

"I understand," said Garry and took another drink of water. The intensity in Conway was a new revelation to him.

*　*　*　*

For Garry, the next two weeks were furiously busy, though that was not unusual, nor was the fact that for much of the time he was out of his office.

For the first two days of the first week, he worked at the offices of a hardware distribution firm in Evanston where he had two consultants analyzing and documenting the computer requirements for a new order-entry and inventory control system. Reviewing the work of his subordinates, offering support and counselling for their occasional frustrations and irritations and sketching out the shape of the eventual report took several hours. Several more hours were spent with the company's executives, listening to their problems and making his own evaluations of their needs.

On Wednesday morning, he set off to visit a large law firm where two more consultants were conducting a detailed technical evaluation of the disaster recovery planning requirements for computer systems that the attorneys had recently upgraded. As he drove down Michigan Avenue, he received a call on his car phone.

He pressed the "send" button on the telephone and left it in place so that his hands remained free.

"Neil Murray just phoned from Mid-West Dynamos," said his secretary. Her voice echoed from the tiny speaker by his right knee.

"And what does Neil say?" asked Garry. He had enjoyed the assignment he had done a year ago for the forty-year-old president of the company that made components for a variety of electrical appliances. Garry had located and implemented some sophisticated accounting packages and Neil had expressed his delight with the results.

"He wants you to call him as soon as possible," replied his secretary. "Do you have his number?"

"No, better give it to me," replied Garry. He scrawled the digits on the small notepad attached to his windshield for just such purposes. Some moments later, as he came to a stop in traffic, he called Mid-West Dynamos. Although Murray was out, his secretary was able to set an appointment for Garry for the following morning. Feeling pleased at the prospect, Garry drove on into the city for his meeting at the legal firm.

*   *   *   *

"Business is splendid!" said Neil Murray in answer to Garry's question. "We're taking over Acheson Electricals in Milwaukee, and things are booming."

"And that's where you want my help, I suppose?" Garry settled down in the chair across from Murray at the small coffee table in the president's office.

"Right," agreed Murray. "Achesons have got a lousy computer system, no production planning or anything, and we'll need to get them up to speed quickly."

"Your own systems will need upgrading too, in that case," replied Garry.

"You know damn well they need upgrading," replied Murray with a laugh. "You told me that a year ago."

"So you want to install something that will do the job for both companies?"

"Just as you recommended," agreed Murray.

"Great!" said Garry with enthusiasm. "I've got an excellent young consultant with just the right experience. I can assign her immediately."

"No," replied Neil with an emphatic wave of his hand. "Not a young consultant, excellent or otherwise. You."

"Neil, my fees are ridiculous!" protested Garry. "It will cost a lot less if you let one of my junior people do the main work, and I just supervise and ensure the final quality."

"Screw the fees," replied Murray. "We're rich enough not to worry about a few thousand here or there. I want the job done properly, and I want you to do it."

Garry sighed in mock resignation. "Well, what I can say to that?" he asked with a grin. "If you can give me an office and a laser printer, I can prepare the proposal letter right away and have it to you in an hour or so."

"No problem," said Murray. "My VP of Finance is away this week and his office is empty. There's a laser printer on his computer. Use that."

"Great!" replied Garry and stood up. He picked up his laptop computer that went everywhere with him.

"That way," said Murray with a wave at the wall to his left. "If I'm not here when you're ready, leave it on my desk."

Garry nodded and walked out. In the next office, he reconnected the laser printer to his own laptop, and set to work. An hour later, he had completed a six-page proposal document, several sophisticated charts showing the stages of the assignment, and had estimated a fee of eighty thousand dollars. He watched the highly professional production wheeze its way out of the printer, reflecting that only a few years ago, he would have needed several days, a secretary, a professional artist and a print shop to accomplish what he had just done alone in one hour. He signed the last page, stapled the document pages together and returned to Neil's office. The president was still there, and he smiled as Garry walked in and dropped the paper on the desk.

Murray scanned quickly through it. "Okay," he said.

"That's it? Just like that?" Garry was amused.

"Sure," replied Murray. "I'll have my financial man look it over when he gets back, but the job's yours. When can you start?"

"Three weeks," said Garry. "I have to reschedule some projects to get free for it."

"Fine," replied Murray. "I'll send the contract over next week."

With handshakes, the two men parted, and Garry walked out to his car, feeling delighted with the morning's work. He looked forward to telling Andrew Whittaker about it.

* * * *

By the end of the second week, not having returned to the office at all, Garry drove home from a visit to an office equipment company in Waukegan, feeling weary but satisfied.

Life's bloody good, he mused to himself. *I have a nice town house in Wilmette, one of the prettiest places around Chicago. I have a fairly comfortable car, the income is pleasant and I seem to be doing well at PAC. There's got to be partnership somewhere in the near future. No particular lady in my life, but that will surely change soon, it usually does. Tomorrow, I'll take the wind-surfer out at Wilmette beach. Sunday I've got a ticket to Wrigley Field to see the Cubs. Tonight, I'll have a sushi oink-out at the Japanese restaurant near the townhouse.*

All in all, he decided, not a bad picture for a young Australian lad born to working-class parents in the suburbs on the west side of Sydney.

Greg and Cassie Barton had never expected any more of their son than leaving school at fifteen, following Greg into the cable-making factory and marrying a local girl. But he'd astonished them by winning a scholarship to Sydney University. The mandatory world trip for which all Aussie kids hungered had been made when he graduated, and the cultural confines of Australia had simply become too tight. England had been fun for a few years, and he had fallen in love with the pubs, the culture, the countryside, the puckish humor and more than a few women. But America was where it all happened, he had decided. He overcame the bureaucratic procedures to get his residency, settled on Chicago, and decided that was where he would stay. Two return trips to Australia had confirmed his decision. Lovely climate, magic beaches and magnificent wine, none of these made up for the massive scale of operations that were the norm in the USA. One day, perhaps he would return to Australia, but for now his home was here.

"Yes, life's a bloody doddle," he said aloud, pressing the automatic garage door opener as he turned into the driveway.

Chapter 2

The first tremors of the storm hit him on the Monday morning when he returned to the office, and within two hours, his life was a wreck.

Andrew's office had been empty when he came in, but Garry had a meeting arranged with one of the senior audit managers, so he went straight upstairs. Clive Carter was about the best of the managers, Garry thought as he reached the audit section floor. Carter had been enthusiastic about using the consulting team to assist in the audit of one of the firm's larger clients, and this meeting was intended to finalize the details. But when Garry reached Carter's office, the door was closed.

Garry turned to the secretary sitting nearby at her desk. "Clive's earlier meeting running late, Rosalind?" he asked.

She looked confused. "He doesn't have a meeting that I know of, Garry," she replied.

"Then perhaps he's on the telephone," suggested Garry.

The woman shook her head, looking down at her console. "He's not on the phone," she said.

"Let me call him, then," said Garry and moved round her desk. She slid away a little to let him get to the desk, and Garry was conscious of her perfume as he picked up the phone. *The next girlfriend had better come along fairly soon,* he thought to himself as he punched the number for Clive Carter. The phone was picked up immediately.

"Carter," said the voice. Garry could also hear Clive speaking a few feet away in his office.

"Garry Barton. I thought we had an appointment."

There was a moment of silence at the other end. "I had to cancel. Sorry." Carter seemed hesitant.

"Sorry? That's it?" Garry was irritated.

"Garry, I can't..." began Carter but Garry cut him off.

"I'm coming in," he said firmly. "I refuse to talk to somebody by telephone when I'm ten feet away." He slammed down the handset and walked round to Carter's office. He opened the office door and walked in to see Carter standing behind his desk.

"For Christ's sake! Close the door," said Carter.

Garry complied. He sat down in the plain leather visitor's chair across from the desk and looked up at the young man. "What's up?" he demanded.

Carter sat down, flexing his hands as if he had cramps in them. He was a fair-haired man, about Garry's age, and the look of anxiety on his face did not suit the pleasant features. "Trent canceled the assignment," he said. "I went in to see him last week about the final details and he just said it was off. No explanations."

"Is that all he said?" asked Garry, feeling anger rise in him.

Carter shook his head. "No. He also said that there would be no projects of any sort where the consultants worked on audits. He was furious. I'm not supposed to be talking to you."

"I see," replied Garry, beginning to understand.

"Garry, what the hell is all this about?" asked Carter. "I've never seen Trent like this before."

"I offended him by telling him he should use more advanced computer audit packages," said Garry. "It looks like he wants to hide his head in the sand rather than admit the future has already come."

Carter sighed and relaxed back in his seat. "He's really impossible. We've all tried to raise the issue before and he gets rabid on the subject."

"Clive, why do you stay here?" asked Garry. "This has to be hurting your professional standing by being so backward. Any of the big firms would surely be glad to have somebody like you."

Carter shook his head. "It's not that easy, Garry. Five years ago I could have moved, sure, but the job market is too tight right now. Nobody's hiring at my level. And anyway, if I keep my nose clean, I'm probably looking at a partnership in another couple of years. I can't throw that away."

"No, I suppose not," agreed Garry sadly. "This morning, I had the same thoughts of a partnership as you. That's obviously just gone down the bloody drain."

"You think so?" replied Clive. "This will blow over, surely?"

"Not a chance," said Garry. "This is only the tip of the iceberg. I may not even have a job by the afternoon."

"That's crazy! How can they fire you?"

"Let me count the ways," answered Garry, and stood up. "Good luck, Clive. You're one of the better ones around."

Carter stood up, shaking his head in disbelief. "Let me know if you see an opening anywhere else for me," he said.

Garry nodded and walked out, leaving the door open. On an impulse, he walked along the corridor to the office of another audit manager, Anne Bertolli. Anne had been particularly upset when the computer audit training program had been cancelled and had expressed serious worries about her career prospects.

"Got a few minutes?" he asked as he leaned in at her office.

She looked up at him and Garry could see the distress in her face. "No. Go away, Garry," she said. "You've caused me enough problems as it is."

"What?" Garry was shaken. Anne was normally a friendly person who always seemed ready to discuss business with him. "What problems?"

"You should know," she replied sharply. "I've had George Elliot screaming at me all week."

"George has? What about...?" Garry stopped, realizing why. "Has George been acting up again about those computer training programs?"

Anne took out a handkerchief and blew her nose. "Come in and close the door, please," she said. Garry moved inside and sat down across from her desk. "Last week, Elliot suddenly came in here and demanded to know why I had lied to you about those courses," she said.

"Lied to me? You never lied to me."

"According to George, I did. He said he never canceled the courses, but that I forgot to go on them."

"And did you agree that you forgot?"

"Not at first." Anne looked shamefaced. "But after half an hour of abuse while George got increasingly hysterical, I finally agreed that I'd forgotten."

"That's not like you, Anne."

"It's not like me, it's not like the others either, but we've all accepted the blame."

"All six of you? You've all admitted you forgot to go?"

"Afraid so. Elliot and Trent have been hammering at all of us, and we finally caved in. We still have to work here."

"Anne, I'm really sorry."

"It's not your fault, Garry," she said with a sigh. "I just wish I could find somewhere else to go, but the job market is too tight right now."

"That's what Clive said just a few moments ago."

"Clive took the heat, too."

Garry stood up. "I don't know how much longer I'll be here," he said. "Probably no more than a few days. If I see an opportunity for a top audit manager, I'll let you know."

"I wish you'd do that, Garry."

Garry's anger had reached a point where he was prepared to take on anything. Rapidly, he walked round to Trent's office to see another closed door. Trent's secretary was watching him with a nervous expression.

Garry looked at her. "Is he in?"

"He's in, Garry, but he said he was not to be disturbed."

"Anyone with him?"

She shook her head then came to her feet as she saw Garry's intention. "Garry, please!" she called out, but he ignored her and opened the door.

Trent was hunched over his desk, reading a file of papers, and his face showed astonishment as Garry strode in. "What the hell are you doing here?" he shouted and rose to his feet, towering over Garry.

Fighting down the fear, Garry quietly turned, closed the door in the face of the frightened-looking secretary, and sat down. "Why have you canceled consultant involvement in the audits?" he asked.

Trent remained standing, and folded his arms. "Because I don't want a bunch of meddling amateurs working with professionals," he said offensively.

"Bill, there's nobody else in this room who has to be impressed," said Garry. "That sort of crap is beneath you, and you know it. There are no meddling amateurs in my group."

"They don't understand audit, so as far as I'm concerned, they're amateurs." Trent was staring out of the window, not looking at Garry.

"You're really terrified of all this, aren't you?" returned Garry, feeling calmer now.

"Terrified? Yeah, I'm terrified of idiots like you screwing up our work," replied Trent, turning his eyes from the view with a smirk.

"No, you're terrified of the future and incapable of seeing that's it's already here," said Garry. "And you're prepared to kill the firm rather than accept your mistake."

"The partners decided that your stupid forecasts are the things hurting the firm," said Trent, still smirking. "Typical consultant blue-sky craziness."

"What the hell are you defending, Bill?" asked Garry. He was astonished at Trent's persistence in following this line of aggression. He knew that the big man was intelligent enough to recognize reality. "You go to the accounting conferences, you attend the continuing education programs. You know, and all your managers know, that we're behind the times. Maybe I didn't tell you the situation with the tact and diplomacy that I should have used, but is that enough reason to stick your head in the sand?"

"Look, Barton," rasped Trent. "The decision's been made. Keep your consultants out of my affairs."

"And is this ruling to be followed by all the departments, or have you decided this all on your little lonesome?" asked Garry.

Trent's face went red and he leaned over his desk. "Listen you..." he began then stopped, obviously realizing there was no point in becoming abusive. The battle was already won. He stood upright. "Get out," he said, and pointed at the door.

For a second, Garry stared at him, then shrugged and stood up. Ignoring Trent, he walked out and closed the door behind himself. Feeling crawling worry about what else the day would bring, he returned to his office.

Whittaker was bent over his desk as Garry walked by, the standard cigarette in his fingers and the cloud already smoking up the view. He looked up, saw Garry and gestured at him. There was nothing friendly about the gesture, and when Garry came in, Whittaker didn't put out his cigarette as he had always done in the past in deference to Garry's distaste for the habit.

"I had some meetings with the Management Committee last week," Whittaker said without preamble. "You won't make any further presentations to them."

"I see," replied Garry. "The truth has become too hard for them to handle, has it?"

Whittaker glared at him. "Your version of the truth is garbage," he answered loudly. "This firm is doing very well without your rabble-rousing and scare-mongering."

"That's interesting," said Garry. "A couple of weeks ago you agreed the partnership was backward. Now you've changed your mind. What's happened? Have they agreed to give you a place on the Management Committee if you toe the line?"

Whittaker refused to meet his eye. "It means I've got serious difficulties with you," he said, ignoring the question. "I can't assign you to work with our clients when the other partners know you can't be trusted."

"Can't be..." Garry took a deep breath. "For the last four years you've trusted me well enough, and I've earned you a lot of money."

"Well that's over," snapped Whittaker. He took a cigarette out of the packet on his desk and lit it. Garry stared pointedly at the half-smoked one lying in the ash tray. Whittaker snatched up the cigarette and stubbed it out angrily. "I expect to have your resignation on my desk by lunch time," he said.

"Resign? I have no intention of resigning," replied Garry. He was pleased to see the irritation on Whittaker's face.

"Why not?"

"Because I want you to fire me," replied Garry. "So that I can bring an immediate law suit against you and the firm."

"You'll get nowhere with that action," replied Whittaker and took a deep draw of his cigarette.

"Really?" replied Garry. "Let's see. I've been here four years, and each year I've had a superior performance evaluation. They're in my files, and they're signed by you. My salary has risen by well above cost of living increases, and I've been promoted to being a director and your second-in-command. I've brought in well over a million dollars a year of new business each of the last three years. And so now you fire me? What do you think a good attack attorney would make of that in a courtroom?"

Whittaker was visibly shaken and Garry smiled. "Have they given you a seat on the Management Committee, Andrew?"

Whittaker looked away. "That's got nothing to do with it," he mumbled.

"So much for consultant's ethics, eh?" said Garry. "It didn't take much of a bribe to corrupt yours, did it?"

"That's enough," blurted Whittaker.

"No it's not," retorted Garry. "What sort of cowardice was it to wait till I was out of the office for a few days to arrange this little coup?"

"That will do!" Whittaker shouted. "You and I have nothing more to say to each other. Go and write your resignation."

Garry rose to his feet, and looked down on the man he had once admired so much. "I'm not resigning, Andrew. So as far as I'm concerned, I've got work to do on behalf of the firm."

He walked out of the smoke-filled office and returned to his own desk. Despite his words, he knew his career with PAC was over, and he felt sadness. Only three days before he had been so satisfied with his future, and in the space of a morning the whole thing had collapsed. He stared through the window and wondered what to do. He considered writing his resignation and getting the whole thing over and done with then rejected the idea. At least he could still get another month's salary by hanging on, and if Andrew did fire him, he was pretty sure a lawsuit could be the way to go, though he was aware it could take months, and be very expensive.

As Clive Carter had said only a short while before, the job market was sluggish, and he felt worried about being out of work. His depressed musings were interrupted by the telephone.

"I would like you to come and talk to me, if you could," said the educated tones of Jack Conway.

"Are you sure I won't infect you?" asked Garry sarcastically.

He heard a light laugh at the other end. "I am immune."

"I'll be right up," said Garry and replaced the telephone. As he walked to the elevator doors, he met two of the firm's partners waiting for the elevator. As Garry arrived, they stopped talking and turned their backs on him. The movement sent a small wave of pain through him. His life at PAC was definitely over.

Conway was seated at his desk and he smiled as Garry walked in. He gave a small wave at the door and Garry hid a smile as he closed it yet again. *Like living in a police state,* he thought.

"You've had a busy two weeks while I've been away," he said directly to Conway, not giving the chairman time for any opening pleasantries.

Conway raised an eyebrow. "I am truly sorry about all this," he said.

Garry gave an irritated gesture. "Don't be sorry," he said forcefully. "Just tell me what happened."

Conway looked taken aback, but nodded. "Trent began a major lobbying exercise the Monday after that last meeting," he began. "I was in New York for most of that week, which is probably why he chose that time. When I got back the damage had been done. With Newman's support he has managed to convince enough partners that your presence is damaging the firm."

"And by bribing Andrew Whittaker with a place on the Management Committee, he got my boss to go along with it?"

Conway nodded, looking pensively down at the desk surface. "It was too far gone for me to counter," he said. "The first thing I saw was a letter signed by most of the other partners requesting that Andrew be appointed to the Committee. Bill had obviously sold them against you."

"I've already told Whittaker I won't resign," said Garry with defiance. "You're going to have to fire me and face the consequences."

"So Andrew said in a rather panicky conversation with me earlier on," said Conway. "That would not be a good move for either of us. A law suit would be ruinous for you and poor public relations for us. It would do severe damage to morale in the firm as well."

"That's your problem."

Conway looked at Garry and leaned forward on his elbows, the left hand covering the scarred thumb of the right. "I think we can arrange a peaceful separation," he said softly. "How much were you earning with us, Garry?"

"A hundred and fifty grand, plus bonuses."

"Which brought it too..?"

"Last year? A hundred and seventy five."

"Then if you will stay around till lunch time," said Conway, "I will have two things prepared. One will be a statement that your departure was by mutual agreement, and that you will take no legal action against the firm for it. I'll have Stephen Petheram prepare that. On signing it, you will receive the second item, a certified check for one hundred and seventy five thousand dollars. I then hope and expect that you will give Andrew your written resignation, we'll part company, and as far as you and I are concerned, still friends."

Garry stared hard at Conway, trying to control the beating of his pulse. A year's salary? That would certainly ease the transition to unemployment and give him time to seek alternatives. It was an astonishingly generous settlement too, one that seemed to indicate a strong current of guilt.

"I agree to that," he said.

"Good," said Conway and stood up.

Garry did the same. "Your problems aren't over," he said. "Killing the Prophet of Doom doesn't deflect the incoming missiles."

"I know," said Conway with a rueful smile. "But I hope that your ideas will become acceptable before the thunderbolts strike us."

"I hope so, too" said Garry. "At least a few of you know that the missiles are coming. Despite all this, I don't want to see PAC fail."

"Nor I, obviously. My name is on the shingle."

"Call me when the documents are ready," said Garry. "I have a resignation to write."

Conway nodded, and Garry walked out and back to his office.

When he sat down, his first thought was to compose a letter of resignation as promised. But another thought struck him. He switched to his personal details file on his computer, checked a number, then punched the buttons on his phone.

"Neil Murray, please," he said when the receptionist at Mid-Western Dynamos answered. Murray answered on the first ring. It was a characteristic of the man that appealed to Garry, that the young president did not keep a secretary as a shield between himself and the world.

"G'day, Neil, it's Garry Barton."

"Hey, Garry," said Murray. "I was just talking about you."

"In terms fit for human consumption, I trust?"

Murray laughed. "Indeed," he replied. "My VP of Finance and I have just reviewed your letter and we have the contract ready to send off."

"Well, that's what I called you about," said Garry, feeling a mix of nerves and excitement about his next move. "I've just been fired."

"You've what?" Murray's shock was evident. "What the hell for?"

"Internal politics," replied Garry. "But it gives you a choice to make."

"What sort of choice?"

"You can still hire PAC to do the job," said Garry. "In which case you get the security of the firm's name and all that, but you don't get me. Or you get me on my own."

"You'd do it? As a private contractor?" Murray's voice was sharp.

"Yes. I'll reduce the fees, of course."

"Screw the fees, I told you that before," replied Murray. "It was you I wanted for the job then, and that hasn't changed. Who needs a bunch of audit partners to review something they don't understand anyway?"

"Yes, but Neil," protested Garry, "some of that money was allocated for just that purpose. It wouldn't be right to charge you for it."

"Look, Garry," said Murray. "Start the job, charge us the fees. This way I reckon you've got a better chance of staying in business on your own, and we can use you some more. Okay?"

"If you say so," said Garry, a smile starting to form. "I'll start Monday."

"Summer hours are seven-thirty to four-fifteen," said Murray. "Go to bed early on Sunday. I expect consultants to be on time."

"Yes, sir!" said Garry, and replaced the telephone. He sat stunned for a moment. With his separation from PAC and a job already lined up, he would get over two hundred thousand dollars on resigning! The morning horrors were fast dissipating and he wondered if he should strike again while the iron was as hot as it seemed. He thought about the assignments for which he had submitted bids recently but for which no contracts had yet been signed. Conway's legal agreement to take no action against the firm did not cover this situation, nor did his personal employment contract with PAC.

There was a company in DeKalb, about sixty miles west of Chicago, who had tentatively agreed to have PAC do a complete business continuity plan. It was a complex job specification, covering the resumption of business in the event of any catastrophic incident that would shut down operations. Garry had done several such exercises in the last two years and felt he was a reasonable expert. The company made toys, model railways and hobby kits for model boats and aircraft, and was highly profitable. Garry had proposed to have one of his junior consultants do the work while he managed it and ensured the final job was up to standard.

He picked up the phone and called the financial controller with whom he had dealt when he had developed the job description some months ago.

"This is Garry Barton at Porter, Allen & Conway," he said when Angela Rayburn answered.

"Hello, Garry," said the middle-aged woman who handled the company's financial affairs. "What's going on?"

"Angela, I have a matter of some delicacy to discuss," he said.

The woman laughed. "That sounds intriguing," she said.

Garry smiled to himself. "That assignment for the disaster recovery plan," he continued. "Have you decided when you want us to start?"

"Sort of," she said. "We conditionally decided last week at our Operations Committee meeting to start the beginning of September. But we do have a problem, which is why it's conditional. We feel the fees are way too high, and we were going to call you to discuss the matter."

"I have a suggestion," Garry said.

"You're going to suggest you do the job as a private consultant at a reduced fee," said the woman as a flat statement, not a question.

"Angela? How did you know?" Garry was almost breathless.

"Garry, I'm not dumb," replied Angela. "PAC's been doing our audit for ten years and we've been getting unhappy with the quality of the work. The last time you were out here, the question of computer audit came up and I could see it bothered you. Clive Carter told me it was a source of conflict between you and Trent. It was only a matter of time before you left them, and Clive's already called me this morning about the blow-up."

"Ah," said Garry, lost for words.

"You had set the fees at a hundred and ten thousand," said the woman. "What's your proposal?"

Garry hadn't even considered the question, and cursed himself for being unprepared. He groped rapidly in his mind then decided it didn't really matter. He was already set for several months of high income. The fee was unimportant, but he might as well aim at a reasonable amount.

"Sixty thousand," he said firmly

"I'll make the contract out in the name of Garry Barton. What's your address?"

"You mean, you accept?"

"Of course!"

"Angela, that's fantastic!"

"Not it's not," she replied. "It's good business. And Garry?"

"Yes?"

"From your point, it's about time too. I always thought you were wasted, working for those shnooks."

Garry gave her his address, then sat back in his chair and laughed softly. From the wreckage of his career a few hours before, he was suddenly a self-employed consultant with two contracts worth a hundred and forty thousand dollars, and a further hundred thousand and seventy five thousand as blood money from PAC. And despite his intended peaceful departure from the firm, it was a warming thought that he had already given PAC a bloody nose by snatching away two clients.

He turned back to the computer, carefully composed the blandest possible resignation letter and printed it out on his laser printer. He signed it, placed it in an envelope and slipped it into his jacket pocket. It was not yet time to hand it to anyone.

Feeling the finality of his actions, he switched off the computer and began disassembling it. It was his own machine, purchased when he joined PAC as the firm had not been willing to buy one for somebody who was not an auditor. The original packing boxes were in one of the storerooms, and he collected them and carried them back to his office to repack the delicate items. Nobody came near him while he did this, and later on, he found more boxes and packed away his private books and other possessions. As he was unhitching his framed picture of an aerial shot of Sydney from the wall, the phone rang.

"We have everything ready," said Conway.

"On my way," replied Garry.

"This contract states that you will take no legal action against the partnership for any reasons related to the terms of your departure." Petheram's youthful face was expressionless, and he would not meet Garry's eye, but Garry sensed the embarrassment the young partner was feeling.

"In return for your written resignation and your signature on this document," continued Petheram, "I will give you this check for one hundred and seventy five thousand dollars."

"Let me see both," said Garry. He reached over the desk and took the two copies of the legal document from Stephen's hand. Carefully, he read the half page of typing and could see no fault. It was written in simple, straightforward language. "And let me see the check," he added, holding out his hand.

Petheram passed the certified check to Garry who again examined it with care. It was made out to Gareth Joel Barton, and the number of digits was almost overwhelming. Carefully, Garry kept the check within easy reach and pulled out his pen. He signed both copies of the document Petheram had given him, and passed one of them over the desk. He reached inside the breast pocket of his jacket and took out the envelope with his resignation, also passing that over to Petheram. The young man opened it, read the document carefully and nodded at Conway.

"Everything is in order," said Petheram.

Garry put the check and his copy of the agreement into the envelope that had held his resignation letter and stood up. "Thank you, gentlemen," he said, and extended his hand to Conway who took it cordially.

"Good luck, Garry," said Conway.

"And to you, Jack."

Ignoring Petheram, Garry walked out.

Taking the elevator down to the lobby, he walked into the bank next door where he had a checking account, and deposited the check into it, noting with pleasure the raised eyebrows of the teller. Immediately transferring forty thousand to a savings account to cover the tax liability, he looked at the balance with affection. Feeling cheerful, he returned to his office.

The office assistant had already loaded the laser printer and all the boxes on to a trolley and Garry accompanied the young man down to the lobby again where he called a cab. An hour later, he was home, carrying boxes into his townhouse, feeling enormous excitement and amazement at what had happened on this extraordinary day at work.

He took a can of beer from the fridge and stood in the middle of his lounge room.

"Stone the bloody crows," he said to the silent room. "Life really is a doddle."

Chapter 3

The atmosphere in the boardroom was tense.

"My understanding is that Barton had arranged those assignments before he had even signed the agreement," said Petheram. He looked pale, and the anxiety in his face was evident.

"Then we sue the bastard!" said Trent loudly. His face was flushed a dangerous pink. His pushed his heavy glasses back up on his nose.

"Unfortunately, William," said Conway. "The agreement did not cover such action, nor did his original employment contract."

"Well it damn well should have," retorted Trent angrily. "That's stupid!"

"Such clauses exist only in partnership contracts," said Petheram defensively.

"Let's not worry about shutting the barn door, William," said Newman casually. She was sitting bolt upright, studying the backs of her hands laid out flat on the table. "I'm more concerned about the alacrity with which both clients took Barton's proposals. Andrew, is there a warning to us in that?" Her tones were icy in their softness, and Whittaker looked uncomfortable.

He shrugged and tried to look unconcerned. "He proposed about sixty percent of the fees to Cambridge Modeling than we had originally proposed. Hard to ignore that sort of cut."

"Yes, but I believe that Mid-West is paying him exactly the same fee as the original proposal." Newman's tones were even more frigid. "That's a lot harder to ignore. Barton has taken away a hundred and forty thousand dollars from us."

"Plus the money we paid him to shut up. I still think that was stupid!" said Trent, glaring across the table at Andrew Whittaker.

Whittaker looked steadfastly at the tabletop. "It's a hell of a lot cheaper than a law suit," he muttered. "Stephen said we'd have had difficulties with a charge of unfair dismissal."

"Gentlemen," said Newman. The room fell silent. "You're losing sight of the problem. We have to determine whether Barton will take any further consulting work away from us. Andrew, your thoughts?"

Whittaker shrugged his shoulders. "Not for a long time," he said. "He's got enough work to keep himself busy for a year. But at the fees he can charge, it will be hard to compete if he has another go at any of our clients. However, unless he hires people and goes for it all out, he can't do too much damage."

"I'm not so sure," broke in Petheram. "Young Garry has a lot of ability and even more energy. It would be a mistake to underestimate him. Hiring people and going flat out to steal our business is exactly what he could do."

"He's not that good," sneered Trent. "I don't know

what you're all so scared about. The man's been lucky, but he can't do anything to a firm of this size."

"And what if he tries to influence any of our clients against us and gets them to move their audits?" asked Petheram.

Trent banged the table with his massive fist. "I'll break his goddammed neck if he tries anything like that!"

"That will do," said Conway sharply. "Let's not allow this discussion to degenerate into violence. But the point has been raised, Bill. What if Barton raises questions in a client's mind about the cost and quality of our audit work? Are you confident that George Elliot is performing technically competent work in that field?"

"Yes I am," insisted Trent defiantly.

"And is there any reason to believe that our fees are unnecessarily high, as Barton suggested?" persisted Conway.

"Absolutely not!"

"Then I must ask you, Bill." Conway still looked uncertain. "What about those six managers who were supposed to attend computer audit training? What happened there?"

Trent was angry. "That was their fault! They were advised of the courses that George Elliot arranged, not Barton, and they simply forgot to attend. I'll be disciplining all of them."

"All six managers forgot?" Petheram was looking curiously at Trent. "That seems quite a coincidence."

"I don't care how it seems," said Trent, glaring at Petheram. "They forgot, and they admitted it!"

"And what of those cost comparison figures Barton presented?" replied Petheram, unaffected by Trent's angry stare. "Don't they prove that we're less efficient than our competitors?"

"No they don't," replied Trent. "I examined those figures myself. Barton made a number of invalid assumptions. The figures were exaggerated. So was his claim that we could lose audits. I talked with the Vice-Presidents of Finance at several companies and nobody seemed to have any plans to look elsewhere."

"So we are not at risk with our level of audit technology?" asked Conway. He tapped his pen on the table in a gentle rhythm.

"No we are not," replied Trent.

"I truly hope so," replied Newman. "For all our sakes. Andrew, I suggest you keep an eye on what Barton's doing, especially at our clients' offices."

"Me?" asked Whittaker. "He's working at audit clients, and you and Stephen both do work for those clients as well. It will be easier for your people to keep an eye on him."

Newman nodded. "That's true," she said. "Stephen, you and William should instruct your people to watch out for Barton when they're at Mid-West or Cambridge. I'll do the same for mine. Find out what he's doing and report back to us."

A small echo of agreeing grunts replied to her orders.

"In that case," said Conway. "I suggest we move onto the next item on the agenda."

* * * *

Newman closed the door behind her as she

entered her office. She loved her solitude and the presence of other people was always a distasteful element for her.

The fools! she thought to herself, sitting in the armchair by the coffee table. *Why were people so slow and stupid all the time?* Her entire life, she had wrestled with this question. As a child, she had been frustrated by her parents who could never understand why she wanted to spend her days reading books in her room rather than playing with other children. By the time she was ten, she had exhausted the books in her parents' house. She began to haunt the local library, spending all her time reading, consuming four, five, even six books in a weekend. She could not recall a single occasion of truly communicating with her parents. To her, they were simply the irritatingly shallow people she was forced to live with.

Accounting had appealed to her from the start. Taxation had been an obvious choice as a specialization. The complexity of the problem, the delight in defeating smaller minds than her own by the application of infinite care and logic, and the financial rewards resulting from the exercise made it to her, the finest game in town.

There was no other game, either. At school, she had been as she was as a child. Her colleagues had nothing to offer in the way of social or intellectual stimulation, and she ignored them. Her isolation was not a problem, but a reward. There was no joy in waiting for their plodding minds to reach the conclusions she had reached in the beginning, and certainly no entertainment in their endless discussions of sex and sexual conflicts. She developed a massive contempt for all other humans, thinking of them as "cattle-people" in her own mind.

Just once, she had met someone who seemed to match her intellect. She was twenty years old when she encountered a graduate student of physics during her first year at Northwestern, and found herself talking to him. Over subsequent weeks, the friendship, her first ever, had grown as she explored his mind, finding a breadth of knowledge equal to her own, and a scientific, analytical skill that possibly exceeded her own. For the first time, she looked at herself in the mirror one night, and studied the image carefully.

She was thin, that she had always known, having carefully disciplined her eating habits all her life. The discipline had been easy anyway, as food held little attraction or interest for her. The constant bleatings of other women about excess weight were another of the silly obsessions of the cattle-people. Her face was interesting, she felt, feeling a rush of enthusiasm for this unusual exercise. Not beautiful, certainly, but she had good features and exceptionally black eyes, framed by jet black hair. She thought about the man who was, for the moment, considered a friend. Phillip Wareham was in his late twenties, probably quite handsome, she decided. She had never thought about any male this way before. All the others had always seemed so coarse, so silly, so obsessed with puerile activities of sport, sex and cars.

She made the deliberate decision to have sex with Phillip Wareham. The idea appealed to her as another piece of research to be followed through with care, examination and learning. A week later, she maneuvered the situation to the point where it could happen. She went to his apartment to borrow a book he had recommended. He offered her a drink, and she accepted, seeing the possibilities of alcohol. Three drinks later, they were together on the couch and she moved close to him. From then, events followed the series of feints, explorations and tactical moves that she had expected. Finally, they moved to the floor and the main encounter began.

She experienced it with cold examination, and discovered that the activities held no excitement for her. They seemed very silly, in fact. The fine mind in the head above hers was now preoccupied with basic and somewhat animal-like stimuli, and to her, this diminished him seriously. The physical sensation was a mixture of some pain and occasional mildly pleasant twinges, and she could see nothing that would merit a repeat performance. She was relieved when it was over, and she moved to the bathroom to clean up. It was the end of the friendship with Phillip Wareham, and the last time she ever considered another human being to be her equal.

Newman brought herself back to the present with a small shake of annoyance for wasting time thinking about the past. Yet again she was surrounded by fools. While she had a slight appreciation and respect for Petheram's intellect, she felt he was far too young to be in his position. Trent was a loud-mouthed boor, and why he persisted in defending that village idiot George Elliot, she had no idea. Elliot was a simple-minded ass, she had decided from the first meeting with the newly appointed computer audit partner. She knew very well that computer audit techniques were in common use in the industry and that the rate of technological change had made the earlier systems obsolete, and the only reason she had attacked Barton for his advocacy was that she had felt Barton was gaining too much prestige in the firm. His arrogance had irritated her.

But she saw the problem created for the firm, and she realized that she was the only person who could solve it. Somehow, modern audit techniques had to be introduced into the firm without damaging Trent, whom she believed to be a competent if journeyman partner without the imagination to do it himself. Conway was too much the old-fashioned gentleman of an era long past. The firm needed a new force at the top. To become that force was the target she set herself. Meanwhile, she would lead those three fools by the nose until she had them where she wanted them.

Newman opened a client's tax file, pressed the buzzer on her desk for her secretary who would know that fresh coffee was required, and switched her disciplined mind from the difficulties of PAC to the coldly numerical problems of her client.

*   *   *   *

Garry found the life of a self-employed businessman tougher than he had ever expected. There always seemed to be conflicting demands on his time, and he learned to schedule himself carefully. It was not too bad the first two months, as he was able to concentrate entirely on the assignment at Mid-West Dynamos, but even then, he was working ten or twelve hours a day, reaching home too weary to do anything but throw off his clothes and fall into bed.

But when the second assignment at Cambridge

Modeling began at the beginning of September, the stress grew heavier. Slowly, he learned to plan for two to three weeks ahead and allocate the time between the two organizations, and ignore the times when he felt he should switch to handle a problem at the other client.

When the fees began to roll in, he saw the advantages of being self-employed. At the end of August, he paid in twenty thousand dollars to his bank account, and the following month, nearly thirty thousand. In mid-September, the size of the check he wrote out to the Internal Revenue Service for his quarterly tax payment was astonishing to him, and he contacted a one-time tax manager from PAC who had since formed his own small accounting and tax consulting partnership. Garry realized he needed specialized assistance, and the knowledge delighted him.

All through the Fall and early Winter he worked steadily, taking no more than a Sunday afternoon off to watch the Chicago Bears play football on television. He found he was averaging over eighty hours a week, and there was no time to think about anything else but keeping up with the pressure. At Christmas, he did little but catch up on sleep and rest, lying in a dopy snooze for most of the day, rousing himself only to eat something and to make some telephone calls to his parents and friends in Sydney. He was far too weary to feel any of the loneliness that a Christmas alone could cause.

Two days after the New Year, he realized his physical condition was poor. His belt was feeling tight and he was more out of breath carrying groceries from the car than he should be. He packed a bag and drove to the health club in Evanston that he had joined a year before.

Garry lay back on the bench on which he had been doing sit-ups, gasping in pain. His stomach hurt and his breathing was heavy, and he fell back against the leather padding with a sigh. *This is not good,* he decided, forcing himself upright. Recovering his breath, he idly tuned in on one side of the conversation a young man talking on his mobile phone a few feet in front of him.

"Dammit, Aiden, this is a hell of a time to discover you're not coming!" said the man. He was fairly short and muscular in build, with red hair and strong features. He was dressed in tennis shorts and shirt and holding a squash racquet. His expression seemed irritated to Garry. "I had the court booked for a whole hour," he continued. "What's caused it?"

The man listened intently for a few moments, then spoke again as Garry raised himself to his feet and stretched. "Well, I suppose you can't be blamed for that," said the red-haired man. "These things happen. Okay, Aiden, we'll try and do it again next week."

As he replaced the telephone, the man caught Garry's eye. "I don't suppose you play squash, do you?" he asked. "My pal's been held up at work, and I've got a court booked."

"I've done a bit," replied Garry. He had played competitively at university and maintained his game with occasional matches at this club. "Are you any good?"

"Nah!" said the young man with a grin. "Strictly swing-and-a-prayer stuff myself!"

"Well, in that case, we might give it a go," replied Garry, warming to the open friendliness. "Got a spare racquet there?"

"Sure, no problem. It's court three."

"Let's do it."

For a few moments, they smacked the ball against the far wall to warm up, each quietly trying to assess the other one's game. After a minute or two, Garry suspected with amusement that his opponent had been lying about his expertise as much as he had himself, judging by the adroit wrist-flick and unexpected speed off the wall that he achieved.

"Ready?" Garry asked, received a nod and the game began.

After ten minutes, Garry was quite certain that both of them had been completely dishonest about their abilities. The game was fast and furious, long rallies of varying speeds and mad dashes up and down the court, and before long, a small crowd of spectators had built up on the rows of seats outside the glass wall behind them. Garry took the first set with his favorite shot, a viciously fast forehand that hissed along the right wall, slammed into the wall an inch above the line and hurtled back into the back corner, never more than half an inch from the side wall.

"Great shot, you swine!" gasped the other, the grin wide across his face. Garry leaned against the wall, laughing.

Before starting the second set, they walked up to the far wall where they had left their towels, to wipe some of the sweat away.

"You know, you can get coffee without caffeine!" said the young man with a grin.

"You can talk!" replied Garry. "You're like a bloody kangaroo on speed!"

"I must admit, I've played once or twice before," said the other, and buried his laugh in his towel.

"Me too," said Garry, and they started the second set.

They ran out of time before they could complete the match, and the next pair of players was standing by the door as they fought out a long rally. Finally, the red-haired man caught Garry out of position with a looping shot into the back-hand court, and the ball dropped dead in the corner. Breathing hard, they collected their towels and left the court, smiling in some embarrassment at the applause from the watchers.

"A drink, definitely a drink," gasped Garry, and led the way to the bar by the indoor pool. Collapsing on the metal chair while the other man did the same, Garry signalled the barman. "A beer?" he asked the other and received an enthusiastic nod. Garry mouthed the words to the barman and received a gesture of acknowledgement.

"Garry Barton," he said, realizing that he had not given his name before.

The other man laughed. "Peter Haywood," he said. "Glad to meet you, even if you do play a nasty game of squash."

"Much like yours," agreed Garry, and busied himself with a vigorous wiping away of sweat with his towel.

"What's a Garry Barton?" asked Haywood.

Garry chuckled at the style of question. "It's a management consultant," he replied. "It mainly does work in information technology. How about you?"

"I'm an accountant," replied Peter.

"A pity," said Garry. "I'll try not to hold that against you!"

Haywood laughed. "What have accountants done to you? That sort of response is usually reserved for lawyers."

"I used to work for a firm of public accountants," replied Garry. "I was singularly unimpressed by them and we eventually parted company when they insisted on remaining in the previous century."

"Who were they?" asked Haywood with a wide grin. "Sounds like somebody I know."

"Porter, Allen & Conway," replied Garry. "I hope you don't have any friends there."

Haywood shook his head in sympathy. "No way," he replied. "Anyone who would be a partner at PAC would hardly be a pal of mine."

Garry's interest was aroused by that flat statement, but further comment was put off by the arrival of the barman with two large glasses of beer.

"Another two of the same," said Garry to the barman. "These won't last long." The barman nodded with a smile and moved away. The two men each took a glass and drank deeply.

"God, I can feel it hissing on the way down," said Garry with a happy sigh. Peter Haywood simply waved a hand in agreement. Both glasses were nearly empty when they were back on the table.

"What's the accent, Garry?" asked Haywood. "It sounds English, but not quite."

"Australian," replied Garry. "I grew up in Sydney, but I lived in England for a few years before coming here about ten years ago."

"That explains the kangaroo reference. So who are you working for now?"

"Me," replied Garry, and picked up his beer glass.

"Self-employed? The only way to go," said Haywood. "Especially after working for PAC. What exactly do you do?"

"I've got two jobs running that are pretty representative," replied Garry. "One of them is to develop a detailed business continuity plan for a hobby shop that builds stuff and distributes all over the States. The other is for a manufacturing company. I'm finding new software for their manufacturing and planning operations and for a company they've just bought, and I'll get new computers for them and set up a network. I also do a lot of strategic planning for information technology."

"Interesting," said Haywood thoughtfully. He drained his glass and waited as the barman returned and placed two new glasses on the table. "How busy are you?" he asked, when the barman left.

"Right now, it's a bloody zoo," replied Garry. "This is the first time off in months. But I'll finish both jobs by March and I'll have to get down to some serious marketing."

Haywood leaned forward on his chair and placed his elbows on the table. "I've got a real nice practice," he said. "There's just three of us partners, and we've got about thirty staff. Charlie Levin does the tax work, and I do the audits with Micky Ashley. But a lot of our clients keep asking us for assistance with their computer systems. Only last week, one of them asked me about what to do if their offices burned down and took out their computers. So far, we've had to apologize and tell them we can't help them, and that gives me a pain in the butt."

"It would," said Garry, feeling a wave of interest in where this conversation was going.

"Is that the sort of thing you'd tackle?" asked Peter.

Garry nodded. "Exactly that sort of thing."

"Then it sounds to me," said Haywood, leaning back again and reaching for his beer glass "that you and my bunch should get together and talk. And soon."

"That's how I see it," said Garry with a wide grin. "Just who is your bunch and where are you?"

"We're called Haywood, Levin and Marsh," replied Haywood. "I formed the firm six years ago with Charlie Levin and Greg Marsh when we were senior managers with one of the big accounting firms, just after all the large mergers started. We figured partnerships would be few and far between as all those big bastards began joining up to become even bigger bastards, so we jumped ship and started our own operation. It's gone very well."

"Greg Marsh is the other audit partner?" asked Garry.

Haywood shook his head. "We lost Greg two years ago. He died in a road accident when he was on vacation. About a year ago, we made our best audit manager a partner. Micky's done great, but none of us has the experience to handle consulting, certainly not in computer technology."

"And where do you hang out your shingle?" asked Garry.

"In the West Loop," replied Haywood. "On Randolph Street almost at the ramp to Interstate 94. We've got a whole floor of one of those renovated buildings there."

"Sounds convenient. When do you suggest I come and visit?"

"Can you give me a call tomorrow morning?" asked Peter. "I'll check with them when I get back to the office, and we'll try and set it up for tomorrow afternoon, if that's okay with you."

"Sounds good," replied Garry. "Let's get cleaned up and perhaps you can give me a card or something when we're both ready."

"Right." Haywood drained his glass of beer and stood up. "To the showers!"

Following his lead, Garry followed him to the changing rooms and took a long hot shower, all the time feeling the excitement of big things about to happen in his life. Forming an association with an accounting firm which could provide a captive client base was surely the best way to operate, he thought. He could save weeks of marketing effort when he was ready to take on new clients.

Dressed in jeans and a sweater, he walked out into the lobby to find Peter Haywood waiting for him. The other looked a lot different, wearing a very smart, dark blue suit, crisp white shirt and military-style blue and white-striped tie. With the red hair, the combination was quite colorful.

"Sorry I'm late," said Garry. "Got lost in my own thoughts."

Haywood smiled and extracted a business card from his billfold. "No problem," he said. "I settled the bar bill, so we're going to have to play again. I wish I could stay and talk, but business calls. I'll talk to you tomorrow."

"Good," said Garry, reaching into his bag and finding one of his own business cards. He had ordered them printed a few days after leaving PAC. "Thanks for the game."

"Hah!" laughed Haywood, looking at the card and storing it away in his billfold. "Next time we'll book the court for two hours and I can thrash you!"

"In a pig's bum," retorted Garry, and they parted as if they had been friends for years.

Chapter 4

The lobby of the offices of Haywood, Levin and Marsh was small and pleasant. Deep red carpet, pale cream walls and comfortable leather armchairs made a welcoming environment as he gave his name to the elegantly dressed woman at the reception desk.

"Yes, Mister Barton," she said with a warm smile. "Mister Haywood is just on the telephone. If you could take a seat, I'll tell him you're here as soon as he finishes his call."

Feeling oddly at home in the lobby, as if the location would soon be familiar to him, Garry took a seat in one of the armchairs. For a few minutes, he listened as the receptionist answered incoming calls with a courteous and musical voice that impressed him. A few moments later, his squash partner of the previous day appeared from behind the wall leading to the main offices.

"Garry!" said Peter Haywood with a wide grin. "Great to see you. Come on through to the boardroom. The others will be here soon."

Standing up, and feeling delighted to see Peter, Garry shook hands and followed him through to the area behind the receptionist. The same colour scheme extended to the corridor that led to several offices. Large windows gave a light, open sense to the area, and Garry decided he liked it. The boardroom was in the corner, and Garry followed Haywood into it. The boardroom table was ash blond wood, highly polished, with six chairs around it.

"Coffee?" asked Haywood. "We keep coffee brewing facilities in here to help us through the panic-stricken days."

Garry grinned, and moved to the small sink and coffee machine on one wall. "Never known to refuse good coffee," he said, and waited while Peter poured the aromatic brew into two mugs with the letters HLM printed in bright blue around them.

"Sugar and stuff in the bowl," said Haywood and took a seat at the end of the table. Dropping a spoon of sugar into his mug, Garry followed him, sitting to his immediate left.

"Good location," he said, taking a sip of coffee.

"Almost perfect, isn't it?" agreed Peter. "We're five minutes walk from North Western station and ten from Union Street. And the rents are way below anything inside the Loop. We've been here for five years now, and I think it was the best move we could have made."

"Tell me about your other two partners," said Garry. "Charles Levin, and Micky Somebody."

"Micky Ashley," said Peter with a smile. "Sure. Charlie's the Tax guy. He's got twelve people in there, and they have the west section of the office." He waved generally in front of him. "He's about our age, and as I said, he and I and Greg Marsh were all managers together when we opened up this place. Charlie's one of the brightest minds you could meet. He's also an attorney, which is pretty useful."

"And Micky Ashley?"

"We made Micky a partner just a year ago..." began Peter, and was interrupted by the door opening. The man who entered was tall, over six feet, and slender in build. Jet black hair over equally black and heavy eyebrows provided a setting for a face that would stand out in a crowd. Dark brown eyes glowed with humour and a wide, full mouth seemed to carry a half smile.

"I'm Charlie Levin," said the newcomer and extended his hand.

Garry stood up and took it, feeling the friendliness emanating from the man. "Garry Barton," he said.

"Welcome to our slum," said Charles. "Peter said you have skills that might help us." He moved to the coffee pot and poured himself a mug, then walked round the table to sit across from Garry at Haywood's right.

"And vice versa," replied Garry.

"That would be good," replied Levin. He turned to Peter and asked "Is Micky coming in?"

Peter nodded. "Yes, but you know Micky," he said with a grin. "Being on time is an alien concept to young Ashley."

"Ah, the joys of being the junior partner," said Garry, remembering the haggard looks that new partners seemed to wear for their first year at Porter, Allen & Conway. "No doubt this guy is a useful dogsbody and whipping boy for you two?"

Peter looked amused. "You might say that," he replied and exchanged a smile with his partner. "Do we beat up on Micky too much?"

"Nowhere near enough," retorted Charles. "Ashley needs constant abuse to be kept in line."

"He's the other audit partner, you said?" continued Garry.

"Er... yes," said Peter. Garry was minutely intrigued by the amusement that was floating in the air. He tried to ignore it.

"I assume you have some reasonable computer audit packages in use?" he asked.

"We have an excellent system," replied Haywood. "We've found that we can complete the average audit in just over half the time it used to take us. And we can do remote audits from our desks when the clients give us the access, so that saves huge amounts of time and money as well."

"And all your auditors are trained in these packages?"

"Trained and accomplished," replied Peter. "Every one of our people is equipped with a lap-top computer the day they join us and they use the system from day one."

"Excellent," replied Garry with a small sigh. "Not at all like PAC."

"We're very different from PAC," said Levin with a laugh. "We have a local area network of personal computers in the place, and everybody has a PC on their desk. We insist on electronic mail, no paper memos, everybody uses the electronic calendars so we can see where everybody is without leaving our desk, and we can schedule meetings easily."

"And document control management and all that good stuff?" said Garry hopefully.

"All that good stuff," agreed Charlie.

"How do you go with top management process audits?"

"That is still a problem," replied Peter. "I know that the international standards recommend that, but frankly, our people are still a bit inexperienced for working at the boardroom level."

"I can understand that with small firms," said Garry. "But it may be something I can help with. It's the stuff of life for me."

"That would certainly expand our auditing role," said Levin with a look of interest. "It's something we've been discussing in recent months."

Before Garry could reply, the door opened. A woman walked in and Garry forgot about computerised audit systems.

He felt his pulse pounding and his throat dried up. He dimly heard Peter Haywood speaking, but he was mostly conscious of calm hazel eyes studying him seriously. He simply could not have imagined the effect this woman was having on him. Never in his life had he been so affected simply by an aura of feminine warmth such as she seemed to exude. He stood up and felt sweat behind his knees.

The woman was of middling height, with trim lines and a face of calm serenity with a hint of amusement at the world's follies. Dark hair fell in gentle waves to her shoulders. She wore a dove-grey business suit with a light blue blouse open at the neck.

"Micky, this is Garry Barton," said Peter Haywood from many miles away. "Garry, this is Michelle Ashley, and I'm sorry we left you in the dark for so long."

"Good morning," she said without smiling, not offering her hand. She moved round the table and sat next to Charles Levin, across from Garry.

"Hello," said Garry, feeling his voice rasp in his throat. He cleared it hurriedly and sat down again.

"I asked Garry to come and visit us," began Peter, "because he appears to have skills that complement this practice. Garry does high level work in information technology, and also disaster recovery planning, which seems to have become a hot topic recently with several of our clients."

"I'll say," said Levin. "Everywhere I go these days, people are saying how worried they are about the risk of losing their computer systems to some catastrophe. The Chicago flood triggered that, and the World Trade Centre made it worse."

"How many of those sorts of projects have you done, Garry?" asked Haywood.

"Quite a few in the last three years," Garry began and then coughed to clear his throat again. He was painfully conscious of Micky Ashley watching him, and felt a wave of embarrassment. He was sure she was laughing at him. "And I'm in the middle of another one for a company in DeKalb."

"And you concentrate on restoring the computer facilities?" asked Levin.

Garry shook his head. "That's how it began," he said. "But an earlier job developed into a plan for covering total loss of the business premises, manufacturing facilities, warehouse, everything."

"And what about pure information technology work?" asked Peter. "Tell us a little about those sorts of jobs."

"I've done most things," replied Garry, still sensing Micky's eyes on him. He struggled to keep his voice under control. "But over the years, straight-forward computer acquisitions and software packages have become completely stock standard work and few consultants get involved any more. So while I still do that occasionally, I've moved away from that and any work involving technology work such as network design, because that was never my strength. I've moved far more into the disaster recovery, business continuity and crisis management planning and these projects are almost my entire business."

"And what does that entail?" Micky asked in a soft, yet clear voice. Uncertain if it was a good idea to look at her, Garry turned his head in her direction and took a deep breath to try and control his emotions.

"A number of workshops with staff at all levels to define the priorities of systems, functions, products and so on," he said. "Then it's mostly a matter of developing details action plans for everybody for what to do in a variety of disaster scenarios. It includes rebuilding systems in alternate locations, places for people to work, which systems and functions get re-established in what order, and so on. If the company makes or distributes actual physical product, I look at alternate sources, emergency warehouses, all that sort of thing. It's mostly just common sense, but it has to be documented and be available because when the disaster strikes, it's possible to forget your own home phone number, so everything has to be laid out in fine detail."

She said nothing, but wrote some lines in a small notebook.

"I'd say there were two immediate possibilities we could talk about," said Haywood. "One of our clients called the other day saying he was most unhappy with his computer installation. It seemed to be horribly expensive, and nobody had a good word to say about the benefits of it. That in your range, Garry?"

Garry nodded. "I do quality assurance reviews like that," he said. "The client may not always like the answer, though."

"Why's that?" asked Levin with a small laugh.

"The problem may not be the system," answered Garry. "It could be the people using it."

"I see." Levin looked thoughtful, nodding slightly as ideas seemed to run through his head.

"The other one," continued Haywood, "is a pharmaceutical company in Lombard. They're one of those worried about the plant burning down. They've had some bomb threats from religious fanatics recently too, because they own a genetic engineering company in California. Some of their products are life-saving drugs that absolutely have to be delivered when called. Their computer systems and all other operations are vital."

"I've done work with pharmaceutical companies before," said Garry. "I understand their particular problems."

"Then I suggest we set up appointments for you to visit both of them," said Peter with a wide smile. "This really could work out very well."

"What about the logistics and financial arrangements?" asked Charlie. "A commission basis, straight fees, or what?"

"I'm more concerned about keeping our clients happy and still with us," replied Haywood, "rather than making money out of extra assignments."

"I have a suggestion," said Garry. Three sets of eyes turned to him.

"Go ahead," invited Haywood.

"Any work I get as a result of an introduction to one of your clients, I pay you fifteen percent of the fees I bill," began Garry. "In return, I would like only the use of an office here, if you have one available, so that I can maintain communications with you on the client's affairs. I suggest that we do no more than that for the first two assignments so that we can decide whether we like each other or not."

There was a muted chuckle from the two other men, but Micky showed no change of expression. Garry felt depressed at the evidence of her coolness to him, but continued. "If this relationship looks workable," he said, "I could introduce you to some companies that aren't clients of yours. If they decide to move their audit and tax business to you, I get five percent of their fees for say, the first year."

There was a moment of silence. The three partners exchanged glances and seemed to come to a rapid agreement.

"Sounds okay to me," said Haywood. He received nods of agreement from Charles and Micky. "There's an office the other side of mine that we've been using as an extra meeting room," he continued. "You can take over that. Meanwhile, both the clients I suggested are going through audits, so setting up meetings will have to wait a couple of weeks. But I know that Micky had a couple of similar calls recently. So Micky, why don't you take Garry along to your office and give him all the details? Then if Garry decides he'd like to handle the jobs, set up a meeting for him with the clients."

Garry felt a small lurch in his stomach at the thought of spending time alone with this woman. He stood up and looked across the table at her. She didn't look back, but instead nodded at Peter.

"I'll do that," she said, and began to walk out of the boardroom.

Garry reached over and shook hands with the other two. "I'll talk to you after I'm through with Micky," he said to Peter. Haywood nodded with a small smile, one that was echoed by Levin, and Garry wondered if the effect of Micky Ashley had been that obvious. Slightly embarrassed, he walked out and followed Micky, conscious of her graceful walk and the trail of delicate perfume she left behind.

She led him along the corridor and into an office that had flowers on the desk and two colourful paintings on the walls. The window looked out over the interstate freeway, and the room was light and airy. Micky sat down behind her desk and watched Garry as he took a seat across from her. She made no move to take out any files or documents. Instead, she looked at him with a hint of amusement. It was the first sign of any expression Garry had seen.

"You present me with a problem, I think," she said, breaking the awkward silence.

"I do?" Garry was confused, and feeling young and gawky. He realized he had been staring at her mouth, fascinated by the curve of her tiny smile.

"I could hardly miss noticing the impact I appear to have had on you," she said. Her eyes remained steadily on his. Garry felt a wave of anxiety run through him.

"I didn't realize you'd seen it," he said, sensing his jaw tighten.

Her smile widened and her eyes lit up. "Seen it?" she said. "Garry, it practically jumped across the table and assaulted me!"

Garry cringed in embarrassment. "I'm sorry I was so obvious," he replied. "It was clearly a one-way thing with no effect on you at all."

Her gaze softened. "That's not entirely true," she said. "Believe me, this has never happened to me before, and I could hardly fail to respond to it in some way."

"And have you responded?" A small starburst of excitement shot through him.

She smiled again. "Garry, let me admit that you're an attractive man. A woman would be insane not to like the idea of seeing you react the way you did."

"And are you insane?"

"No."

The word hung in the air between them like the echoes of a Chinese gong. Garry found he was holding his breath and let it out carefully.

"But as I said, you give me a problem," she continued. "In fact, two problems. The first is the obvious one. I'm engaged and I expect to get married fairly soon."

Garry tried to hide his disappointment. For a few moments when she had confessed her awareness of an attraction between them, he had thought she was signalling something positive. She had just doused that effect quite thoroughly.

"And the second?" he asked.

"A common problem," she replied. "You and I are

going to be working together in this small business. Getting involved would be a disaster. These things never work out."

Garry fought for self-control, recognizing the truth of her words. He smiled at her. "Then I suppose I have a choice," he said. "I can walk away and not see you, and suffer from that and the loss of business, or I can suffer here and make a lot of money in the meantime."

She laughed out loud. "Rich and suffering is definitely better than poor and suffering," she agreed.

They looked at each other for a few moments then she broke the spell. She opened her file drawer in her desk and extracted some manila folders.

"These two companies have both called me in the last few days to ask if we can give them some help with computer problems," she said. "These are my notes on the conversations. I told them I'd get back to them soon, but I was a bit lost as to what to do." She looked up at him with a smile. "Then you came along and you seem to be the answer to these problems and the cause of some new ones."

Garry returned the smile, feeling more confident that he could handle the situation with her for a while at least. He took the files from her, noting that her hand was slender and beautiful. He opened the first one, seeing that her writing appeared to be firm and clear. It matched her style, he thought, reading through the details on the yellow legal-pad pages.

The company was a small distributor of office products, with both a retail outlet and a small wholesale distribution operation. Their needs appeared to be standard and Garry was certain that any one of several software packages written for personal computers would handle the requirements. He closed the file and looked up at Micky to see her watching him with that same clear, calm gaze with which she had studied him earlier.

"Why don't you call this..." he referred back to the file. "Jim Forster, and let me talk to him. I think we can give him some names of companies that can help him without any need of our assistance. No point in trying to charge fees if it isn't necessary."

She nodded and consulted her Rolodex file, then picked up the phone. She must have dialled a direct number, Garry assumed, because she spoke immediately to her client. "Jim," she said. "It's Micky Ashley. I promised I'd get back to you on that computer question."

She smiled as the speaker on the other end responded, then spoke again. "I'm going to put you on to Garry Barton," she said, looking up at Garry. "He's a top consultant working with the firm."

She handed the phone over and Garry took it, touching her hand as he did. He felt a small shock at the contact, and she seemed to feel the same, because she sat back with a small flush on her face.

Concentrating on the business matter before him, Garry turned his eyes away from her, and spoke into the phone. "Good afternoon, Jim," he said. "This is Garry Barton."

"Hi there!" said a cheerful voice. "Micky said you could help us. What's this going to cost me?"

"Nothing," answered Garry with a laugh. "Not for my time, anyway. I'm just going to give you some names of people who have the systems that would help you. I suggest you look at a few of these. You can call me if you have any difficulty, but I doubt that you will."

"Well that sounds pretty good," said the other man.

Garry reached inside his briefcase and extracted his diary, turning to the list of computer hardware and software companies. "Okay, Jim, try these," he said, and read out six names and telephone numbers. "I'm quite sure all of them have solutions for you. Based on the volumes of data I see here, you'll need three personal computers, and link them in a local area network with one, maybe two printers. Those volumes are quite small."

"You're sure?" Forster seemed cheerful, but needed reassurance.

"Call me when you've picked the system you want," said Garry. "I'll come and have a look at it for you and probably get you a discount."

"That's great! I'll do that, and thanks a lot. Put me back to Micky will you?"

Garry grinned and returned the phone. Again, their fingers touched and she stared down at her desk with a tiny smile on her lips.

"Yes, Jim?" she said, then grinned and looked at Garry. "Yes, he does seem to know what he's doing. Glad we could help."

She replaced the phone. "Neither of us is going to get rich if you do all your assignments that way," she said, smiling.

Garry returned the smile. "Goodwill and marketing," he said. "Let's have a look at the other one."

He sat back and opened the second folder, conscious of her gaze on him, then became interested in the problem in the pages before him.

The company manufactured adhesives, resins and agricultural products and had some complex data storage requirements for individual formulations and manufacturing instructions. Raw materials control was obviously a problem, also. A phone call would not solve this one, Garry knew. He closed the folder and looked at her. She was writing a letter with a black fountain pen, and her concentration seemed total.

"Micky?" he said, realizing with a small shock that it was the first time he had called her by her name. She looked up.

"This one needs a visit," he said and returned the folder to her desk. "Can you call them and arrange it for next week?"

"Sure," she said, and picked up the phone. Garry watched her with pleasure as she asked for Cliff Potter, the company's financial director according to the notes Garry had been reading. She exchanged a few social words then told him about Garry.

"Just hold on, I'll ask him," she said into the phone, then cupped her hand over the mouthpiece. "Tuesday afternoon, two o'clock?" she asked. Garry nodded, and she returned to her conversation.

"That's fine, Cliff," she said. "I'll give him the address." She replaced the phone and wrote some lines on a sheet of notepaper.

"The address," she said, and slid it across the desk. Garry collected the paper, slipped it into his briefcase and stood up. Micky did the same and for a moment they looked at each other.

"I'd better be going then," said Garry. She nodded and looked back at him. "I'll call you after I've spoken with them," he continued, feeling a little foolish, turned and walked to the door.

"Garry," she said as he opened it. He turned back and looked at her. "I'm very conscious of what's happened," she continued. "And much as I'd like to, I can't ignore it. Please, let's both be careful."

Garry took a deep breath. "We'll just have to see what happens," he said.

Her voice was soft. "Yes, I think so," she said.

*   *   *   *

To avoid thinking too much about the events of the previous week, Garry spent the wintry weekend in front of his computer, putting the finishing touches to the details of the disaster recovery plan for Cambridge Modelling. The complexity and mass of detail kept him well occupied, and the only time he took off during the day was to watch the Chicago Bulls play a game on television on the Saturday afternoon. He stayed in that night, somehow feeling unwilling to go out to a show, or a blues bar, or even to take in a movie. Instead, he worked till after nine, watched an hour of an Italian opera on the Bravo channel on television, drank rather too much scotch, and went to bed feeling giddy.

Sunday, he had a lengthy breakfast at the pancake house in Wilmette, drank several cups of coffee and returned to his computer by ten, staying there almost without a break until five before he relented and took the rest of the day off. Somehow, he had kept Micky Ashley out of his mind to some extent. But on the Sunday evening, it was hard to watch the television and he found himself losing most of the plot lines of the gormless comedies and blood-soaked movies that performed pointlessly for his attention. His thoughts kept returning to Micky.

He went to bed early and slept soundly, waking up to a cold and blustery Monday morning. He left early for the ninety-minute drive to DeKalb and Cambridge Modelling.

"It's ready for testing," he said to Angela Rayburn.

She beamed at him across her desk. "A month ahead of schedule," she said. "That's splendid!"

"Some of the telecommunication problems were simpler than I had estimated," replied Garry. "We can test the plan next week, and I'm pretty certain everything will work well."

"Good," said Angela. "Then let's talk about something else." She opened her desk drawer and took out a file, opened it and extracted a letter. Garry was able to see the familiar logo of his old employers, Porter, Allen & Conway on the letterhead.

"I just had this letter from PAC," she said, looking down at the sheet of paper with an expression of distaste. "They completed the audit three months ago, and we paid the bill for that. It was a hundred and twenty thousand, which I thought then was too much."

Garry took a deep breath. He knew what was coming and the excitement ran through him like spring rain.

"I wrote to William Trent," continued the woman, looking up at Garry, "and I expressed my concerns that the audit had taken too long, cost too much and seemed to ignore any reviews of operational issues. In reply, I got this letter a couple of weeks ago."

She looked down at the single sheet again, and a look of irritation crossed her face. "Trent told me that PAC follows the highest standards of auditing procedures," she continued. "He said that some elements of computer audit techniques were inappropriate for our organisational structure, so no reduction in the fee is possible. In fact, the fee will increase next year, by six percent."

She looked up at Garry. "What did he mean by inappropriate? I couldn't understand that."

Garry laughed in sympathy. "What it means," he said, "is that George Elliot only knows one obsolete audit system which he learned some years ago and is seriously limited compared to the modern systems. But he's frightened of adopting the more advanced techniques and so he's keeping his staff from doing so as well"

"You mean we're paying excess fees because Elliot doesn't know what he's doing?" Angela had never seemed to Garry to be an emotional woman, but she looked angry now. She lifted up the PAC letter and glared at it, as if it was the face of George Elliot.

"That's about it," agreed Garry. "One of the main problems that caused my dismissal was the fight we had about computer audit. I told them they were out of date and priced too high, and they chose to get rid of me rather than hear about a possible problem."

"That's disgraceful!" Angela replaced the letter in the file and shook her head in dismay.

"I agree whole-heartedly," said Garry with a cheerful grin.

"This group you've joined up with," she said, replacing the file in her desk draw with a definitive and somehow final slam as if she were consigning PAC to the archives of her company's history. "Could they do a computer audit on our systems?"

"Extremely well," replied Garry, confident that he was speaking the truth. Haywood's operation had simply smelled of professionalism and competence. The wave of excitement grew stronger as he thought about what was to come.

"Then I'd like to talk to them," said Angela.

"Can I use your phone?"

She nodded, and moved the phone across the desk.

Garry picked it up and dialled. "Good morning, Monica," he said when the receptionist at HLM answered. "Let me talk to Peter, please."

As Garry waited, he knew that PAC had done its last audit of Cambridge Modelling.

Cliff Potter had been drinking at lunchtime and his red nose and poor skin indicated that it was not for the first time. The smell of bourbon from his breath mingled with the chemical smells from the factory, giving Garry some concern about his health should he win an assignment at this client of HLM and have to work there for some weeks.

"What do you think?" asked Potter after an hour of discussion on the factory's data processing problems. The noontime tippling did not seem to have dulled his mind.

"You need a computer upgrade," replied Garry. "And you need a proper system for your order-entry and inventory control requirements. What you've got now is somewhat primitive, if you don't mind hearing the fact."

"It's why you're here. What'll that cost me?"

"About a quarter-million, all up. The hardware upgrade is easy enough, but any package will require some modifications. Your requirements are a bit unusual."

Potter grunted. "And could you help us get all that?"

"Of course. It will cost you twenty-five grand for my time."

"Okay. Let's do it."

Garry controlled his surprise. "Just like that?"

"Sure," replied Potter. "You've proved to me you know what you're doing. We need the systems. Let's do it."

"I'll drop a contract off to you in the morning," said Garry, feeling a rush of exhilaration.

Potter shrugged. "If you want to," he said. "As far as I'm concerned, we've got a deal."

They shook hands, and Garry got another wave of bourbon.

"That's great!" said Micky Ashley. Her voice was slightly distorted through the tiny loudspeaker of Garry's car phone. "You'll let me have a copy of the proposal?"

"Of course. I could give you a more personal proposal, too."

The speaker was silent for a moment. "Garry, you're making things difficult for me," Micky said.

"I know. Do you eat Japanese?"

"Everything except the boots and cameras," she replied.

Garry stifled a snort of laughter. "There's a very nice Japanese restaurant near my home in Wilmette," he said. "Great sushi."

"Yes, I know," she replied. "Craig and I have been there a few times."

Ah, thought Garry. Micky had slipped the knife in very neatly. He tried to ignore the small pain. "Have dinner with me there tonight and celebrate?"

"No, Garry. You know I can't."

"Okay. I had to try."

"I know." Her voice seemed a little cooler.

"Transfer me to Peter then, please," he said.

He heard only a click as she pressed the disconnect button to transfer the call.

Peter was more enthusiastic. "Hey, Garry! This is hot stuff!" he exclaimed. "I'm going in to see Angela Rayburn on Thursday. I'm going to propose ninety grand for the audit."

"That's thirty thousand below their last bill," replied Garry. "And a lot less than the next one would have been. Can you do it for that?"

"Hell, yes!" replied Peter. "And make money on it too!"

"Well, Angela will probably fall all over you and smother you," said Garry, grinning to himself. He slowed down as traffic built up on the Eisenhower freeway into Chicago. It was four in the afternoon, and the outbound lanes looked like an elongated parking lot.

"Is she young, single and gorgeous?" asked Peter. "I'll settle for merely gorgeous."

"She's fifty-something, very smart and elegant," said Garry.

"Okay, I'll settle for the contract. I'm a married man, anyway. Where are you?"

"About two miles out on the Ike."

"Coming into the office?"

"Yes I am. I need to prepare the contract for Cliff Potter."

"You got that job?" Peter sounded delighted.

"Naturally! I'm a genius, remember. And with my accent, how can I lose?"

Peter laughed loudly. The sound stretched the capability of the loudspeaker that rattled and squawked. "You have an unfair competitive advantage, I have to agree," he said. "Have you got any more PAC clients we could steal?"

Garry drove for some seconds in deep thought. *Why not?* he thought. He owed PAC nothing, and there would be no legal constraints on him if he played the game carefully. "If I had," he finally said, turning his head slightly to the microphone above the car door, "would you have the staff to support them?"

"Not yet," said Haywood. "But what a nice problem to have. We'd need two more managers and some other support staff."

"I know a couple of managers at PAC who could be approached."

"Are they any good?"

"Good as they come," replied Garry. "They'd need training in your computer audit packages, though."

"Not a problem," said Peter. "You get the clients, I'll hire the staff and train them."

"Sounds reasonable. What about a drink?"

"How soon can you get here?" Even above the noise of the heavy traffic around him, Garry could hear Peter's laugh.

"About half an hour."

"Well, don't just sit there. Pedal to the metal, my man!"

Garry chuckled and pressed the disconnect button.

* * * *

"So in two days, you've won a twenty-five thousand dollar job with one of our clients, and probably got us a new audit worth ninety grand?"

"Not a bad week's work, is it?" Garry smiled at the look of pleasure on Peter's face. In only a few days, Garry felt he had made a life-time friend.

"I'll say!" Haywood took a deep breath and reached behind him to a cabinet. The door swung open to reveal a line of bottles and a small refrigerator. "What'll you have?" he asked, pulling out a bottle of Teachers scotch.

"That," replied Garry.

"Good choice," said Peter and took a pair of glasses from the cabinet, turning round to place them on the desktop. "Anything in it?"

Garry shook his head and watched as Peter poured two generous helpings of the fine amber fluid, and passed one over.

"Your great health," said Garry and took a sip.

"Financial and physical," retorted Haywood and took a deeper gulp. "We've both done well out of this arrangement so far."

"Let's hope I can keep this up."

"I've seen enough already to believe you will," replied Haywood. "So as soon as the other two clients I mentioned the other day are free, I'll set up meetings for you."

"Sounds wonderful. We could both make good money out of this venture."

"Indeed." Haywood was staring into his glass. Remembering how he had done the same when talking at the squash club, Garry decided he could expect a decision from Peter. He was not mistaken.

"There's a spare office next to mine that I suggested you use when you were here last week," said Haywood, gesturing to his right. "Why don't you take it over permanently?"

Garry was silent for a few moments.

"A problem?" asked Peter.

"Yes," replied Garry. "A problem."

"Of course. The lovely Miss Ashley."

"Was it that obvious?" Garry felt embarrassed.

"It was. Hard to ignore that rampant passion exploding all over the boardroom."

"So what should I do?"

"Move in anyway." Peter drained his scotch and reached for the bottle. He carefully poured a small amount into his glass.

"I don't want to cause you any problems," said Garry.

"Garry, the sort of problems you're causing this firm, I want a lot more of," said Haywood, and sipped his scotch.

"Yes, but..."

"Shut up and have another scotch."

"Yes, sir," said Garry with a grin and watched as Peter added a few drops to his glass.

"Let me tell you about the adorable Micky Ashley," said Peter and leaned back in his chair.

"Will it help?" Garry stood up and removed his jacket, hanging it over the other armchair in the office. He looked out of the window and saw the traffic on the freeway almost at a standstill. There was no point in leaving to go home just yet.

"I think so," replied Peter.

"Okay. Begin." Garry sat down and picked up his glass. For all his casual air, he felt intense interest.

"Micky's thirty-two," said Peter. "She was married in her early twenties, but her husband was killed in a car crash after only a few months."

"That's horrible. Is she going to marry this Craig character?"

Peter looked astonished. "You know about Craig?"

"She dropped it on me when I asked her out to dinner earlier on."

"You asked her... You've got balls, Barton, I have to admit."

Garry shrugged. "Nothing ventured, nothing gained, and all that stuff."

Haywood leaned back in his chair and sipped his glass thoughtfully. "Craig Hampton is a lawyer with one of the big legal firms. Corporate stuff, very boring. I've met him a couple of times, and frankly he's a wimp."

"That's crazy! How could a woman like Micky be engaged to a wimp? Is she really going to marry him?"

Peter tapped his whiskey glass with one finger. "She certainly makes all the appropriate noises to that effect," he said. "But they've been together over two years, and no real arrangements have been made. Certainly no date has been set that I know of."

The information made Garry feel a little more cheerful. "It sounds pretty silly to me," he said.

"And to everybody else," replied Peter. "Probably any shrink worth a dime would give you a valid reason, but it's always seemed to me that keeping an endless engagement going is a pretty good way of insulating oneself from the realities of marriage and also from being single, both at the same time."

"So you think there's a chance there, do you?"

Peter chuckled and swung himself forward to lean his elbows on the desk, looking Garry directly in the eye. "I was talking with Charlie last night on this very subject," he said. "We agreed that you'd be a much better man for Micky than the wimp. So we think you should go for it."

Garry nearly choked over his glass then laughed out loud. "Do I need your collective consent to this?"

"No, but it helps." Peter's grin was wide and cheerful.

"Rude bastards, the pair of you!"

"True. Not like any public accountants in your previous experience?"

Garry smiled at him. "Not at all. Maybe if there had been, I'd have had a kinder impression of you lot."

"Always glad to help the professional image," said Peter, looking at his watch. "Doing anything for dinner?"

"Thought I'd have some stuffed wombat and a fricassee of koala bear ribs."

"Sounds disgusting. Come home with me. Pauline wants to meet you, and my three-year old daughter wants to ask about kangaroos."

Feeling relaxed, Garry picked up his briefcase and followed Haywood out of the office.

Chapter 5

The gleam of the morning sun off the waters of the lake reflected off the silver teapot on Conway's desk and speckled the walls with brightness. Colonies of ice-floes on the water looked like small fleets of boats. They seemed to be holding the chairman's attention.

"So what's the damage?" Conway asked, turning his eyes back to the room. His words broke the stasis in the room, and all eyes turned to Trent.

"We've lost the Cambridge Modelling audit," said Trent. "Our fees for next year would have been a hundred and twenty-seven thousand. And Neil Murray has already advised us that he'll be switching his audit to Haywood, Levin and Marsh for the next financial year. With his take-over of Acheson's, his fees would have been over a hundred grand."

"So we've lost about a quarter-million in audit fees after this year?" Conway's voice was quiet and calm. "I recall that this committee had agreed Barton would be unable to affect our audit base. What happened?"

"We didn't foresee that he'd join up with another accounting firm," replied Petheram. "I suppose when we saw him set up his own private operation, the idea that he'd go with anyone didn't occur to us."

"Very short-sighted of all of us, it seems," said Conway. "And what about consulting fees, Andrew?"

Whittaker shifted in his seat as the eyes of the room focused on him. "No more than since we last spoke," he replied. "Barton completed the assignments at Cambridge and Mid-West Dynamos, and I understand that his other work is with HLM clients."

"Well, that's a relief, I suppose," said the soft voice of Newman. "That might keep him too busy for a while to interfere with us."

"And has the Tax Department lost clients, Bridget?" asked Conway.

"Not yet." Newman's eyes remained focused on her lap. "But as the financial year ends, I will be at risk with those clients who have switched their audits. It would be logical that some of them will move their tax business over as well."

"And you, Stephen? Any damage?" Conway looked at his most junior partner who sat slumped in his chair like a schoolboy.

"None," said Petheram. "Insolvency work isn't linked to the audit base. The courts assign the jobs. But of course, if PAC's seen to be a loser, the courts will start to reconsider us."

"Both our audit losses have been to HLM," said Conway. "Just what business factors led to their decision, William?" His voice was dangerously calm.

"They quoted fees at seventy-five percent of ours," said Trent. His heavy face was directed at the floor and his body looked rigid with tension.

"And how does HLM keep its rates so low?" Conway was still calm.

"Their overheads are a lot lower than ours, I imagine," mumbled Trent

"Yes, I imagine that too," said Conway. "Their office costs would be very much less than ours. But rents alone will not account for a twenty-five percent drop in costs."

Petheram joined the attack. "I was told that HLM uses advanced computer audit packages which can handle just about any system. They all use laptop computers with software that lets them connect into their clients' systems. Charlie Levin tells me it saves a lot of time and money."

Trent flushed red. His spectacles slipped down his nose and he pushed them up again. "George Elliot says that's ridiculous," he said, his throat tight with anger. "Those packages are not widely accepted in the industry and the procedures are highly suspect. Nobody uses them."

"Manifestly untrue," replied Petheram. "HLM is evidently using them most effectively."

Newman spoke before anyone else could. "Gentlemen, I think we have lost sight of the problem," she said. "Rather than fight over judgements and opinions, we have to decide what we're going to do about this situation. Does anyone have any ideas?"

Silence hovered in the room.

"Nobody?" continued Newman. "Well, it seems to me that the choices of action fall into three categories."

She had got their attention.

"Go on, Bridget," said Jack Conway.

She smiled a brief flicker of a smile. "The first option is to do nothing and hope the problem will go away," she said, and raised her hand immediately to stifle Trent's objection before it left his mouth. "Clearly, that has little merit," she continued. "I believe that Barton has tasted blood and will probably want more. The problem is to prevent a feeding frenzy. We must do that either by circumventing HLM or somehow stopping them. The second option is therefore to cut our costs to meet HLM's and trust to client loyalty to retain the business. I doubt we can do that without acquiring computer audit packages similar to those used by HLM, and I believe that such a course of action would be unacceptable to our brethren in the audit department."

She raised her head from her lap and looked across at Trent. "They might have to do some very hard work to learn new techniques in which they do not believe anyway," she said. "That would cause such stress that we might lose some of our partners, and we couldn't handle that pressure now. Mind you, in the long run, I wonder if that might not be the best path."

The tension in the room rose by several points.

Newman smiled again. "So that leaves us with some ways of stopping HLM," she said. "Does anyone have any ideas?"

Silence blanketed the room.

"A couple of options present themselves," Conway said after a few moments. All eyes shifted toward him. "They may sound drastic, and will not appeal to you, but I must ask that you let me finish before you speak." Nods and grunts around the room signified assent.

"It's clear that Barton is out to make a point with

us," continued Conway, "and we have to accept that he has well and truly made it. Regardless of what some of you may believe, he has proven that everything he said at that Executive Meeting was correct. Therefore, I suggest that one option is for us to swallow our pride and invite Garry back to join us as a partner of the firm."

The group emitted a collective gasp. Andrew Whittaker jerked with dismay. Trent folded his arms tightly over his chest as if to keep himself in check. Conway looked briefly at him with some contempt in his eyes.

"But Garry is not stupid," Conway continued. "And he will know that such a gift from us will be loaded with conditions. I doubt he'd accept. The other option is the more sweeping suggestion to propose a merger with HLM. Now I invite your comments."

The room was silent in astonishment. Petheram broke it. "Do you believe HLM would consider it? They probably think they're growing fast enough as it is."

Conway shrugged. "I suggest we try it and see."

Trent finally burst under the pressures within him. "If that bastard comes back here, it's over my dead body!"

Conway looked at him without expression. "We may just have to pay that price, William," he said.

Trent's face went white, and he sat back in his seat. Petheram gave him a quick look of sympathy then turned his eyes to the view of the lake.

"The other alternatives," continued Conway, "involve some sort of persuasion of HLM to cease their attacks on our client base, as Bridget suggested.

Stephen, perhaps you could work with our attorneys to explore the legal pressures we could bring to bear on them."

Petheram nodded. "We probably have no basis for a legal action, but it's possible that the threat of an extended suit would cause them to reconsider the financial problems."

"I'm in favour of another approach," growled Trent. His face had regained its colour. He squinted as he pushed his spectacles back up his nose. The room turned to him. "Take out Barton," said Trent, "and you remove the driving force behind HLM."

Silence held the room for a few seconds.

"Just what the hell are you suggesting?" asked Petheram, his voice rising a notch in astonishment.

"I'm suggesting that we tell the little bastard that he'll get a couple of broken legs if this keeps up, or even worse." Trent glared defiantly round the room, and his face flushed as a few chuckles broke out.

"And just how would you arrange such a thing?" asked Petheram with a grin. "Will you do it yourself, or will you take out a contract with some local thugs?"

"That's enough!" rapped Conway, for the first time in the meeting raising his voice. "I'm astounded that you could even think such ideas! It's obvious that you've run out of constructive solutions. I suggest that we all return to our work and think about sensible approaches to the problem."

The four partners rose and left the office, leaving Conway sitting in his chair looking blindly at the ice on the lake.

* * * *

Petheram didn't go to his own office. Instead, he followed the hulking shape of Bill Trent as he stamped back along the corridor to his office. Trent turned as he was about to open his door, and looked with some surprise at the diminutive figure of Petheram.

"Got a few minutes, Bill?" asked Petheram, his smile and charm establishing a link across Trent's hostility. Nodding, Trent opened his office door and walked in. He took the seat behind his desk, ignoring the more convivial armchairs around the coffee table in the corner.

Petheram tried to ignore the absence of friendliness in the room and took the chair across from the desk after closing the door behind him. The windows offered a city view, and the magnificent Chicago skyline held his attention for a few moments. "I'm sorry, Bill," he said, turning his face to Trent. "I hadn't meant to sound scornful about the idea of tackling Barton. It came as a bit of a shock, that's all. It threw me."

"Forget it," said Trent. His tone was abrupt, still not forgiving.

"You took a bit of a reaming out from Conway, there," continued Petheram. "I didn't think it was deserved."

Trent grunted and relaxed his hunched shoulders a little. "It's just the idea of that little jerk coming back as a partner that got me," he said. "After what he's done to us..."

"There's no chance of that," replied Stephen. "I'm more worried about the other stuff that's going on."

"What stuff?" asked Trent.

Petheram shifted in his seat. "Mainly, it's Bridget," he replied. "She's beginning to frighten me."

"How?" Trent was intrigued. The idea of Petheram being frightened by the dark presence of Bridget Newman surprised him.

"She's starting to have too much influence," replied Petheram. "I think Jack's losing his control a bit. And I don't know that I like the idea of Bridget in charge of anything outside the Tax Department."

Trent let out a long sigh. "Now there I agree with you. It's been worrying me for some time."

"Yeah, she threw a real bomb at you this morning," said Petheram. "I wonder how long before she moves on me?"

"Why should she?"

"Any time I disagree with her, that would be reason enough."

"I suppose so," said Trent. "But on the other hand, she may be the best thing for keeping Jack on the offensive. If we really have to get down and dirty with Barton, I'm not sure Jack could do it. It's like a war. Sometimes you need a leader who can take the hard decisions."

Petheram nodded. "Do you really think we'll have to go that far?" he asked.

"You tell me. Will your legal efforts have any result? You've already said there are no real grounds for action against HLM."

Stephen sat back in his chair and looked out of the window. "You're right," he said. "It's only the threat of court costs that might work. We have no real legal standing."

"And so then what?" Trent leaned forward on his desk. "What can we really do, Stephen?"

"We might all have to swallow our pride, Bill," replied Petheram. "Especially you and George Elliot. You have to consider getting in some more advanced computer audit skills."

"Dammit, I know that!" snorted Trent. "I lost my cool a bit too much there with Barton. He's such a snot-nosed jerk!"

"He's arrogant, I agree," replied Stephen. "But you mean you really agree with him?"

"Partially," admitted Trent. "But I also have to defend my partners. I know that Elliot's a bit behind the times, but I was still hoping he'd start to do something productive. But I couldn't stand there and let my department be dragged through shit by Barton."

"He could have been a bit more tactful about it," agreed Stephen. "I wish to Christ he had been. He's a good operator, whatever you think about his personality."

"I suppose so," agreed Trent. "But we're stuck with it now. And I'll bet this firm to a pinch of coon-shit, we're going to have to get pretty hard-nosed about the situation."

"You were serious about a warning to Barton, weren't you?" said Petheram. "That wasn't a joke?"

"You bet your life it wasn't a joke," snapped Trent. "One thing I've learned is that people are frightened about their physical safety. I'm serious. If we beat up Barton, he'd have second thoughts about taking any more of our clients."

"You'll never get Jack Conway to see it that way," said Petheram thoughtfully. "But you know, I wouldn't be surprised if Bridget did."

"And what about you?" demanded Trent.

Petheram spent a few seconds looking out the window. "The idea scares the hell out of me," he said, finally. "I've never seen violence as a means to an end. It always comes back to haunt you."

"So we turn the other cheek, and stroll our way into bankruptcy?" Trent's tone was cutting.

"Of course not. We have to fight to protect the firm, but we can surely do it by legal means."

"I hope so. I'm looking at ways of increasing our audit productivity, and if comes to the crunch, George Elliot's out on his ear. But what if nothing works?" Trent slammed his hand on the desk in frustration. "Dammit, Stephen! I'm a family man! I've got three kids at private school. My wife spends money like it's going out of style. I've just added a quarter-million bucks of extensions on the house. I know we earn good incomes, but we live a pretty tense existence working this way, always under pressure to earn more, increase profits, cut costs. We've damn well *earned* this life-style. I'm prepared to do anything, anything at all to keep it, and no arrogant little Australian is going to take it away from me."

Petheram sat in silence for a moment. "I can see your point of view," he said. "I suppose if it really came down to a question of losing the firm, I'd look at things the same way." He stood up. "But we'll never get to that point," he said, and moved to the door. "So the option of beating up Barton, or anything else like that, should never arise."

"Let's hope so," replied Trent. "But I'm not holding my breath waiting for Barton to pull back."

"No, that would be a mistake as well," replied Petheram, and walked out of the office.

Back in his own office, Petheram closed the door. Normally he left his office open to the outside world, believing that he should be accessible to anyone who wanted to talk to him. Now, he needed to think.

Petheram was in turmoil. He had always liked Garry Barton, and sympathized with Garry's frustrations over the backward state of business technology in the firm. While he had worried about Garry's arrogance, almost insolence in the criticisms the young consultant had levelled at several partners, Petheram had endorsed the views he expressed. He had refused to sign the letter from the partners demanding the dismissal of Barton, and that had caused some unpleasantness for him.

But now the firm, and with it Stephen's livelihood, was threatened by Garry's actions. Stephen had become accustomed to his life over the last decade. The years of intense work to qualify as an accountant and then as a lawyer had paid off with a rapid rise through the ranks of Porter, Allen & Conway. The sudden promotion when his boss had been killed was exciting and a little frightening, but Stephen knew he had matched the demands made on him. His income was over half-a-million dollars a year, and he enjoyed the wealth.

He had not married, preferring the stimulation of a series of beautiful women who could be attracted by the money, the luxurious apartment in the lake-side hi-rise block and the Mercedes. Every time he drove home from the office and entered within the massive, sculptured, curved walls of the apartment with the beautiful lake views, he felt the delight of his success.

There was nothing else he wanted to do, nothing else he *could* do. The practice of law had never appealed to him. The qualification was a means to an end, but he had never wanted to work in the profession. But now, his whole way of life was at risk. A series of misjudgements by his colleagues, a failure to recognize the dangers when pointed out by Barton, their own arrogance that made them kill the messenger rather than listen to the message, it could bring the golden palace crashing down on his head.

Much as he had once admired Garry Barton, Petheram knew that now he was developing a dislike for him. The need to persuade Barton and his new associates to leave PAC's clients alone was clear in his mind. But it disturbed him that when he had first heard Trent suggest violence, he had felt a twinge of enjoyment at the prospect.

Shaking himself to clear the unpleasant thought from his head, Petheram pulled out his notebook. He had always amused himself with the fact that it really was a little black notebook in which he stored the addresses of the women who entertained him. He perused the list, and felt his pulse speed up at the name of the latest addition. He reached for the phone, and pushed seven numbers.

"Hello, Helen, it's Stephen Petheram," he said.

"Stephen, how lovely!" Her voice was soft, sweet and slightly husky. If it was an affectation, he was prepared to take it that way, he decided.

"Fancy doing something tonight?" he asked.

"Of course, sweetheart," she whispered. "I fancy doing lots of things with you."

He grinned, and felt his breath catch in his throat. "I sort of like the idea of just staying at home. Care to join me?"

"Of course, Stephen. You know how much I like being there."

"Why not get a cab round to my place about nine?" he said.

"I'll be there," she said, her voice full of erotic promise. He hung up, his hands trembling slightly as he remembered the last time she had visited his apartment. He needed more of Helen's extraordinary talents.

To hell with Garry Barton, said Petheram to himself, so forcefully he could almost hear his words. *Nobody was going to be allowed to spoil this existence.*

By seven that evening, Petheram was feeling too tight to work further. The events of the day had disturbed him greatly and he needed to unwind. The anticipation of Helen's visit was too great to let him concentrate.

By nine, he was pacing his lounge restlessly. He had showered, changed into light slacks and cotton shirt and taken a couple of stiff scotches already. He looked out through the picture windows at the darkness over the lake and the edge of the city lights and felt the anticipation build up in him. When the door buzzer sounded, his heart lurched with excitement. He pressed the door release without answering over the intercom, and hovered near the door while he waited for the elevator to bring her up.

When the light tap sounded, he took a deep breath then opened the door. She was standing with a small smile on her lips, her deep red hair falling to her shoulders that were covered by a light wrap. He stood aside and let her walk by him and a tiny whiff of expensive perfume accompanied her warm smile as she deliberately brushed against him, her lips almost touching his as she passed.

In the middle of the lounge she stopped, turned to face him, and slid the wrap off her shoulders. She was wearing a sleeveless black dress, so short it barely covered the tops of her thighs, and scooped low at the neck to display the upper curves of her extraordinary breasts. She was petite, the same height as Petheram, but with her high heels she was an inch or so taller than he was.

"You like?" she asked, her voice low and soft. She turned a full circle for his approval, displaying the backless dress cut down to just below her waist.

"I like," he replied, his voice catching in his throat.

"You mentioned champagne," she said with a laugh.

"Indeed I did," he replied. He walked to her and reached for her hand. She let herself be led to the black leather couch that lined almost the whole wall. An ice bucket containing a bottle of Dom Perignon was already there, and a pair of flute glasses stood on the coffee table.

She sat down, crossed her legs and watched with a smile as he poured champagne into the two glasses. He sat alongside her, passed her one glass, and she snuggled against him as they drank. Her perfume was delicious, he thought, and the warmth of her body was electric. He felt his pulse accelerate rapidly.

"You're very tense tonight, Stephen," she whispered and stroked his arm.

"Business problems," he answered. "I need to forget them this evening."

"I always seem to be able to help you do that, don't I?" she replied with a small laugh and half turned to rest her back against his chest, lifting her legs onto the couch. The deliberate move displayed her cleavage to him and he stared down at her breasts with delight. He finished his drink, replaced the glass on the table, and returned his attention to her. He gently stroked her shoulder with his left hand, and she wriggled against him with pleasure. He slipped one thin strap off her right shoulder and let the top of the dress move down until it barely covered the nipple of her right breast. She sighed happily as he kissed her shoulder lightly.

He pushed the dress down further and covered the bare breast with his hand, breathing deeply at the delicious feel of it. The dress fell completely to her waist and she slipped her arms out of the straps and arched her back against him as he began to stroke both breasts, feeling the nipples rise up in his hands like firm hillocks.

"I think the caviar is going to have to wait a while, isn't it?" she whispered.

"Quite a time," he gasped.

When she left soon after one in the morning, her purse fuller by the twelve hundred dollars he had tactfully left for her in an envelope on the dressing table, Petheram had achieved his night's objectives. He was drained of energy and lay on the silk sheets of his massive bed in a relaxed sprawl. She had been magnificent, he realized, driving him to levels of activity and delight that had exceeded any similar events in his past. Her perfect body had writhed against him and she had screamed in her own orgasms. If they were faked, Stephen had no wish to know about it. She had fooled him beyond any need to question. Helen was definitely worth every cent of the three hundred dollars an hour he paid her.

Later, they had returned to the champagne and the caviar on the coffee table and pigged out happily before she renewed her job, and teased and provoked him until he responded. On the black leather, she sat astride him and screamed again as she jerked and wriggled, her astounding breasts entrancing him as they bounced free above him.

Petheram fell into an exhausted sleep. His last conscious thought was that nobody could have a better life than this one.

Bridget Newman left the office soon after seven and drove her Lexus out of the basement car park. She pushed a compact disk of Bach's third Brandenburg Concerto into the player and carefully drove north on the interstate to the prestigious lakeshore village of Winnetka. A glow of anticipation ran through her. She had a new disc to view tonight.

At fourteen, during her ravaging of the contents of the libraries' shelves in her home town of Evanston, Bridget Newman had discovered the Roman era. Like everything else, she absorbed the literature and the history like a shark in a feeding frenzy. The day she first read about the Roman Circuses was one she remembered. The astounding mass butchery and killing had caused a surge of unfamiliar excitement through her thin body and she had poured over the descriptions with total absorption.

From that point, she searched out everything she could find on the topic until she had exhausted the books of every local library, including the history section at Northwestern University. She went to movies such as *"Quo Vadis"* and *"The Fall of the Roman Empire"* which showed something of the blood-soaked activities in the Roman arenas, and some years later, was able to buy her own copy of *"Caligula,"* which she frequently watched on her parents' player at home when they were out. By the time she was eighteen, she was addicted to death.

Accidentally, she discovered history books that described the public executions of common criminals in England and Europe, and her addiction grew. She studied in tiny detail the descriptions of public hangings and beheadings and read earlier histories of even more bloodthirsty habits of taking human life. Death became the only subject that could excite her. When she visited England in the summer of her twentieth year, she went to see the Chamber of Horrors in the Madame Toussaud's wax works exhibition, and stayed the whole day, enchanted by the gruesome displays despite the obvious tackiness of many of them. She visited the show three more times before she was able to take in some of the more conventional tourist attractions of Britain.

Through a client, she made furtive contact with a

private organization that sold unusual movies. The movies were high-priced, and becoming a client of the distributor was complex, requiring extraordinary qualifications.

By nine o'clock, she was ready. She had taken a luxurious bath and changed into a loose silk gown. She extracted a small block of *paté de fois gras* from her fridge and loaded it onto a tray with a small plate of thin, dry toast. She carried the tray down to her viewing room with its massive television screen. She placed the tray by her armchair before the screen. From the fridge, she pulled out a bottle of white wine and stood it in a silver bucket of ice. She opened the bottle with care and poured some of the wine into a tall glass that she placed on the tray.

Finally, she unwrapped her parcel and extracted the disc. With a slight shortness of breath, she loaded the disc into the player and sat back in her chair. She took the remote control and started the disc then sat back and took her first sip of wine.

The movie began in conventional manner. The camera, evidently placed behind a sheet of glass in the wall, recorded the entry to a bedroom of a young and attractive woman. She took her clothes off in a matter-of-fact manner and lay on the bed. Almost immediately, a man walked in, wearing shorts and a hood that covered his face. The woman showed amusement at the sight and sat up, a broad smile on her face.

She raised her arms at the man in an invitation, and a few minutes of sexual activity took place that left Bridget unmoved. The only sounds so far had been the standard sounds of sexual coupling. The man grunted a lot and the woman emitted patently artificial cries of ecstasy. After a few moments of this, the man collapsed to one side of the girl, breathing heavily.

Two other men entered the room. They wore hoods over their heads as well, but nothing else. The man who had just used the woman's body seized her hands and snapped her wrists into handcuffs that were hidden under the pillow. Each arm was chained to the bedpost. The girl struggled.

"You bastards!" she yelled. "This isn't fair! My guy'll beat the crap out of you!"

Another of the men rolled himself on top of her, forced her legs apart and entered her. But Bridget's attention was sharply taken by the first man, who had reappeared in the camera's vision with a meat knife. Newman's breathing came faster, and she felt her pulse accelerate. The girl on the bed had subsided into acceptance of the extra sexual work and had not seen the developments. The man on top of her raised himself on his straightened arms so that the woman's body was fully visible, and he nodded at the others.

As the woman saw the knife she shrieked.

"NO! Please, don't, oh no, please!" Her voice became a wordless scream as the man on top of her used one hand to take the knife and placed it against her breast. Still thrusting himself into her, he slowly pushed the knife into the woman's ribs.

Bridget was transfixed. She gasped with emotion as she watched the blood flow and the woman lurched with pain, almost throwing the man off her. The camera moved in on the girl's face and lovingly recorded the wide-eyed shock, the pain and the slow death of light from her eyes. The screen faded to black. Bridget gulped down her wine and hurriedly refilled the glass.

Over the next hour, Newman watched two young men and another girl die. One of the men was slowly garrotted by a length of thin rope as he sat at a table where he had been playing cards with two other men whose faces had been blurred beyond recognition. The other was tied to a concrete column and the skin of his chest was sliced into bloody ribbons while he screamed harshly before the final agonised yell was guillotined by the knife in his rib cage. The second woman was killed much like the first, being sexually abused before her throat was cut.

Her heart pounding and her body suffused with warmth, Bridget stopped the disc. She finished her glass of wine and refilled it, taking another small slice of *paté* with the last of the toast. Then she played the disc through again. She had no doubts about the validity of the killings she had watched. It was the best disc she had ever had, she decided, and she was quite sure she had enjoyed the deaths of the young men most of all.

At eleven-thirty, she went to bed and slept soundly till six the following morning.

Chapter 6

Garry needed little persuasion to take up Peter's offer and set up home in the next office. He moved his reference and professional books in and installed them up in the wooden bookcase, hung the aerial picture of Sydney on the wall across from his desk, rigged up his personal computer and laser printer and established a filing system in the desk drawer.

"You look quite at home!" Peter said from the doorway.

"I hate moving," replied Garry. "I get hot and sweaty and crabby."

"Then let's hope it's worth the bother. This office needed someone in it, anyway. Empty spaces scare off the clients."

"I'll do my best to reassure them." Garry straightened the large picture of Sydney and sat behind the desk. "It's the biggest desk I've ever had in my life! What the hell am I supposed to do with it?"

"Fill it with paper, the way the rest of us do," replied Peter. He advanced into the office and sat down across from Garry. "Got something for you," he said, and passed a small box over the desktop.

Garry opened up the box and examined the business cards inside. "Director?" he asked, raising an eyebrow at Peter.

Haywood shrugged. "Seemed like a good title. I had to call you something suitable for this office, after all. And another little goodie." He reached into his pocket and extracted a plastic card. "Parking in the basement," he said, and slid the card to Garry.

Garry picked up the card. "I suppose this means I have to do some work."

"Now and again. When I'm not beating the pants off you at squash."

"Slave driver."

"That's my reputation." Peter rose to his feet. "I called Anne Bertolli and Clive Carter at PAC," he said with a grin.

"You're a fast mover," said Garry, sitting back in the executive chair and rocking back and forth.

"I leap buildings with a single bound, too. They're both joining us in July."

"Bloody ripper!"

"What?" Peter nearly choked.

Garry looked a little embarrassed. "An expression of enthusiastic approval down-under where I come from. You'll have to excuse the odd lapse."

"I thought you people spoke English down there?"

"Sort of."

Peter laughed out loud. "Try and keep it under control, will you? We have sensitive clients in the place quite often." He waved cheerfully, and walked out of the office.

Grinning widely, Garry switched on the computer and tried to concentrate on a report for Cliff Potter's adhesives company. He succeeded for nearly an hour.

"Welcome aboard!"

Garry looked up and swallowed hard. Micky was regarding him with the calm, amused look he found so disturbing.

"Thank you," he said. "It seems I'm a director. Can a director talk to a partner?"

She took the seat recently vacated by Peter. "Providing the odd genuflection is thrown in as a sign of respect."

Garry got a gentle whiff of her perfume. She sat so gracefully in the chair that his stomach churned. "What about directors asking out partners to dinner?"

Her face showed no expression. "Out of protocol," she replied. "It's supposed to say so in your contract."

"I don't have a contract."

"I'm not going to let this happen, Garry."

He tried to control the tremor in his voice. "I don't think I can stop trying, Micky."

She stared down at the floor, and Garry saw the tense lines in her body. "You have to," she said softly. "I don't think I can work with you if you don't."

Garry put his hands on his head with a deep sense of frustration. "I wish I understood."

She stood up and gave him the same calm look with which she had come in. "Understanding isn't necessary, Garry. Only compliance." Her voice held a tone of irritation.

He lifted his hands from his head and held them in a gesture of surrender. "We have to be friends, Micky. This won't work without that, at least."

"Friends, colleagues, business partners, yes," she said and turned to the door. "Nothing else." She walked out, leaving Garry feeling foolish and deeply aware of the loss of colour in the room once she had gone.

Haywood, Levin & Marsh expanded. The client list swelled like a dry sponge absorbing water and Garry found no time to worry about Micky as he worked almost endless hours. Despite the comfort of his new office, he spent most of his time at client sites. He won assignments from other HLM clients, one for another disaster recovery plan for the pharmaceutical firm, and one for an audit review of the computer systems at a metal engineering company. As Spring metamorphosed into a damp Summer, he took an afternoon off to lie on the beach on a rare day of warm sun, and mentally counted up his revenue. With a pleasant shock, he realized he would earn nearly four hundred thousand dollars that year with his departure money from PAC, even if he won no further assignments.

Working at clients' offices generated revenue, and also ensured that he saw little of Micky. She too, was rarely in the office, so their paths crossed only at infrequent intervals. But when they did, Garry felt the same mixture of excitement, frustration and bewilderment as he had from the beginning. She still made his pulse pound and sent flashes of excitement through his body, but she remained cool and unresponsive to his attempts at establishing a closer relationship.

The depressingly cool summer wore on to a chorus of universal complaints in the American Mid-West. Few people used their air-conditioning units, and Commonwealth Edison filed for increased electricity rates to make up for the lost revenue. Garry finished his assignments and was wondering what to do next when the decision was made for him.

"This is Girish Murgabi," said the perfectly-enunciated British accent in Garry's ear.

"Mister Murgabi! What a pleasant surprise." Garry was genuinely pleased. He knew the man's background and held a healthy respect for it. Murgabi was a one-time colonel in the Indian Army and he was now the Corporate Vice-President of Finance at the Sullivan Group, a conglomerate of companies with headquarters near Chicago. Garry had done one large assignment for the group while still at PAC. The Sullivan Group was PAC's biggest client, and Garry took a short, sudden breath at the possibilities that this phone call offered.

"It is a pleasure for me also, Mister Barton," said Murgabi. This surprised Garry. Murgabi had always impressed him with his decisiveness and intellect, but the relationship had been one of mutual professional respect rather than friendship. The ex-colonel was often abrasive and arrogant in his approach to business, and personal warmth had never been part of his character.

"How can I help you, Mister Murgabi?" asked Garry. Anticipating that a meeting was to be arranged, he switched his computer to the electronic calendar system.

"I wish to discuss a number of topics with you," said Murgabi. "They involve both data processing and accounting matters, so you should involve one of your audit partners."

"I can make arrangements for one of the partners to be there," replied Garry. "What time suits you, Mister Murgabi?"

"Shall we say Thursday, at two o'clock?"

Garry scanned his schedule and saw that the time was free. "Thursday at two it is," he said. "I look forward to meeting you again."

"I too, Garry. Thank you."

Garry replaced the phone, aware of the unexpected use of his first name. There were fifteen companies in the Sullivan Group. Garry's mind raced at the thought of the business possibilities. He punched in the appointment on his calendar then stood up and walked into the next office.

Peter was concentrating on his computer screen, but looked up with a grin as Garry entered. "What's up?" he asked.

"I just got a call from the VP of Finance at the Sullivan Group," said Garry, and took a seat across from Peter's desk.

"Sullivan? Ye gods!" Peter sat back in his executive chair and stared at Garry.

"That's what I thought," replied Garry. "I did a job for them a couple of years ago. They're huge, factories and offices all over the place and they want to see us on Thursday."

"Us?"

"Us. Girish Murgabi said quite firmly to bring along an audit partner."

"Holy Cow!" Peter sat up and turned to his computer screen. "I'm not sure but… yes, dammit," he said, as his screen displayed his calendar for the week. "I'm in Waukegan that day. Big property developer is thinking of giving us his audit and tax work. I arranged for Thursday afternoon."

"What about Charlie?"

"He's with me on the same trip."

The two men looked at each other for a few seconds, then Peter turned back to his screen. "Let's have a look at Micky's schedule," he said, pressing a few buttons. "She's free," he said with a grin. "And I've just scheduled her for the afternoon. She's all yours, young man!"

Garry felt a jolt of mixed worry and excitement.

Peter's smile faded. "Problem?" he asked.

Garry shook his head. "Probably not," he replied. "This Murgabi, he's an old school-tie type of person, terribly British and military. I doubt he'd be hostile to a woman partner, so I don't think that's it. No, I suppose I'm nervous about working with Micky."

"It sounds like a perfect opportunity to me," said Peter. "Swing the deal, take her to a bar after to celebrate, maybe dinner. Who knows what could happen after that!"

"You're a crude bastard, Haywood!"

"I know! Ain't it grand?"

Garry chuckled then grimaced. "I just hope I can keep my mind on the task," he said. "She does have a certain distracting influence on me, as you know all too well."

Peter smiled. "Hey! Think I don't understand? Just concentrate on the potential income for all of us if you get a deal, and think what that might do for you in Micky's eyes."

It was an interesting thought, agreed Garry to himself, and cheered up. "Okay," he said, rising from his chair. "Time to go tilting at windmills and all that romantic nonsense."

Hearing a small laugh from Peter, Garry walked round to Micky's office.

She looked up as Garry entered, and her smile made his knees feel weak. He sat down in front of her. "I've claimed your time for Thursday afternoon," he said. "Your calendar is already filled in."

She gave him a suspicious look, and he laughed. "No, dear lady, not a seduction attempt, despite my preferences. All business."

She smiled and brought up her calendar on her computer screen. "The Sullivan Group? We have a meeting with the Sullivan Group?"

"We do indeed. With the VP of Finance, no less. He said quite firmly that I was to bring an audit partner along to talk accounting."

"What about Peter?"

"He was the one who booked your schedule."

"Oh!" She seemed pleased, but also a little unsettled. "So you think there's a chance of some accounting work there?"

"There are fifteen companies in the group. I think Girish will ask me to do some computer work at one of them. I suspect he might be considering passing the audit of one of the subsidiaries to us, maybe as a way of putting some pressure on PAC. Whatever it is, it's too good to miss."

"I agree!" she replied with a growing excitement. "You'd better fill me in on some of the details of the organization."

"Sure," said Garry. He spent fifteen minutes telling her what he knew about PAC's biggest client. As she wrote on her yellow legal pad, he watched her slender hand and fine features. Once, she looked up and the small flush in her cheeks told him she was conscious of the study.

"No point in going in two cars," said Garry, taking a deep breath. "Let's go in mine, and I'll bring you back here afterwards."

"Okay," she said.

Garry walked out of the office, feeling like a teenager who had just made a date with the prettiest girl in the school.

His phone was ringing when he got back to his desk.

"Mister Barton?"

"Yes." Garry was certain he knew the woman's voice, but couldn't place it.

"This is Jenny, Mister Conway's secretary."

"Of course! Jenny, how nice to hear from you." Garry was astonished, but tried to hide it. *Two amazing calls in one morning? Why was the Chairman of PAC calling him?* Nervously, he considered several options. Had he contravened his agreement by allowing HLM to hire two people away from PAC? Or because two companies had switched their audits? He tried to control his nerves. "How are you, Jenny?"

"Very well, thank you." She was being very formal, thought Garry, but understood her reserve. "Mister Conway asks if you would agree to a meeting with him."

Garry sat back in his seat. *A meeting with Jack Conway? What could Conway possibly have to say to him?* He decided to be difficult, sensing the anger in himself at the memories of his departure from PAC, despite the generous settlement.

"Jenny, I'm an old-fashioned man," he said into the phone. "No insult to you, but I believe in people making their own arrangements. If Jack wants to meet with me, tell him to call me himself."

There was silence at the other end of the line, and Garry smiled to himself.

"Yes, Mister Barton," said Jenny. "I'll pass that on."

Garry sat back, aware of his heart beating a little faster. He had only a few moments to wait before the phone rang, and he picked it up.

"This is Garry Barton," he said, formally.

"Hello, Garry. It's Jack Conway."

"Jack, it's nice to hear from you."

"Sorry about the call from my secretary. I agree with you, direct contact is more courteous. I seem to have slipped into the modern way of doing things."

Garry smiled to himself. "Just a thing I believe in, Jack," he said. "Human beings ought to be nice to each other."

He heard the hiss of a suppressed laugh at the other end of the line.

"A good philosophy, Garry, I agree. I wonder if we could get together for a chat sometime soon?"

Garry swiftly pressed buttons on his computer keyboard, and brought up the calendars of Charlie, Peter and Micky, as well as his own, summarized on the screen. "Certainly," he said, his interest rising. "When would you suggest?"

"How would Thursday afternoon suit you?" asked Conway.

Garry stifled a laugh, wondering what Conway's reaction would be to learning of Garry's meeting with PAC's biggest client at that time. "Sorry Jack, I'll be at a client that afternoon. How about Friday morning?" He could see that only Micky was unavailable that Friday. The others were all in the office.

"Hold on a moment please, Garry," said Conway. Garry could hear the rustle of a desk diary being consulted. It occurred to him that Conway had not considered the possibility of Garry being unavailable.

"Friday morning is fine," replied Conway. "About ten?"

"No problem."

"Good," said Conway. I'll look forward to seeing you here, Garry."

"No."

"Pardon?" Conway's voice rose a notch in pitch.

"Jack, I said no," replied Garry, feeling a wild exhilaration at his treatment of his old chairman. "You're the one that asked for the meeting, and you can't assume any longer that I can be summoned to your presence. If you want to talk to me, you can come here."

Garry could almost feel the shock in the silence at the other end, and when Conway spoke, it was hesitant, confused.

"Er... yes. All right Garry. I'll come to your offices for ten."

"Good," said Garry, grinning widely. "I'll look forward to seeing you here, Jack."

He hung up the phone, and sat back, thoughtful. He had no doubt the meeting was to do with the loss of two of PAC's clients, and he suspected Jack would bring some sort of peace offering, but he felt disturbed, nonetheless. He turned to his computer screen and entered the Friday morning meeting with Conway. He entered the appointment to the other partners' calendars then walked back to Peter's office.

"Conway's coming to see me on Friday morning," he said.

Peter raised one eyebrow. "Why?" he asked.

"Dunno. But I want you and Charlie there. Micky's out all day."

Peter drummed his fingers on the table. "Very interesting," he mused. "We've pulled the lion's tail, it seems."

"It seems," replied Garry.

"He'll be trying to stall our business moves on Mid-West and Cambridge, of course. Think he'll bring along a bribe or something?"

"Nothing would surprise me," said Garry.

"Maybe he'll offer us a merger," said Peter with a cynical grin.

"Hah! And you'd accept of course!"

"What, turn down a chance to merge with an advanced, far-sighted firm like PAC? Hell, no!"

Feeling nervous, despite the exchange, Garry returned to his desk.

* * * *

Thursday dawned a beautiful day, a rarity that summer. Garry came in to the office early, conscious of a vast excitement building inside himself, and he found it hard to concentrate on mundane working matters. He read through his file of the work he had done for the Sullivan Group two years ago, and reviewed the financial data on the group to see what changes might have occurred since then. Seeing nothing obvious, he tried to keep calm the rest of the morning, and was able only to drink coffee for lunch. With both Peter and Charlie out for the day, the area seemed quiet.

At twelve-thirty, he walked to Micky's office and stood by the doorway.

"Ready?" he asked, thinking again how beautiful she was. She had on the same grey suit and blue blouse that she had worn the day he had first seen her. She flashed a smile and seemed to radiate the same excitement he was feeling. Telling himself that the smile was more to do with the business possibilities of the afternoon than with travelling in his car with him, he watched her gather her briefcase and walk toward him.

"Let's go," she said, her eyes sparkling.

Trying to control his breathing, Garry walked with her to the elevators. Riding down to the garage with her, he realized that this was the most alone with her that he had ever been. He led the way to his Lincoln Continental and opened the door for her. She smiled as she settled into the luxury of the leather seat, seeming to enjoy the masculine gallantry. He closed the door with an expensive clunk of well-engineered bodywork, and walked around to his own door.

The offices of the Sullivan Group were fairly close to Garry's home, a few miles north of Wilmette in Northbrook. Having looked at the traffic on the Interstate 94 that would be the most direct route, and seeing it almost at a standstill, Garry decided to take the Lake Shore route. They didn't speak at all as he navigated out of the building and along Wacker Drive to the Lake Shore, but as they passed the yacht anchorages by Belmont, Micky gave a longing look at the blue waters of Lake Michigan.

"God, look at that water," she said. "It's beautiful. I haven't been sailing for so long, it hurts."

Garry looked across at her for a moment, then back at the road. The emotion in her voice had been obvious.

"Doesn't Craig sail?" he asked.

"No."

"What does he do?"

"Nothing really. Just works."

Garry felt jolted. There had been so much loneliness in her voice, it bewildered him. "That seems a horrible waste," he said. "You obviously love to get on a boat."

She looked at him for a few moments. "I'm no expert," she said. "And I never want to get like those people who are so hooked on racing and winning that they can't seem to enjoy the sport. I just love being out on the water on days like this."

"Me too," he replied, slowing down as the traffic intensified at the northern end of Lake Shore Drive.

She looked at him again. "You have a boat?" she asked.

He was acutely aware of her look, and turned briefly to meet her eyes. He found it hard to turn back to the road. "Not a sail boat," he replied. "Just a sixteen-foot runabout with a fifty-horsepower Evinrude on the back. Easy to store in the garage and tow behind this thing." He motioned to the back of the car with his thumb. "I like fishing at dawn, and idling up to Wisconsin."

"Gorgeous," she said. He could hear the yearning in her voice.

"This weekend looks like it's warming up nicely," he said in as casual a tone as he could muster. "You can come with me, if you like."

She was silent for a moment. He looked at her, and she seemed tense and sad, her face turned out of the window. "You know I can't, Garry," she said, finally.

"Micky..." he began.

"No! Garry, it's impossible. I'm engaged, you know that."

"When are you getting married?"

She looked hard at him for a second, as if trying to see if his question had any deeper meaning. "We haven't decided yet. Craig wants to get established in his practice, and things are very busy for me right now."

"If we get lucky with the Sullivan Group, things will never get any less busy."

"I know." She turned to look out of the right-hand window and seemed to retreat from him. The silence lasted while they negotiated Sheridan Road past Loyola

University and up to Evanston. As they turned west after passing the soaring beauty of the Bahai Temple, she broke the stillness.

"Are you involved with anyone, Garry?"

"Nobody special," he replied. "It's the usual bachelor existence. I date several women, but nobody sets the senses spinning." He didn't feel like admitting that he was without anyone these days.

Micky gave a small chuckle. "What sort of woman sets the senses spinning for you?"

"Look at yourself," he replied.

"That's not fair."

"It's exactly what you were hoping I'd say."

"Yes, I know," she said after a tiny pause.

He sneaked another look at her. She caught his look and recognized the emotion behind it. She reached out and touched his right hand on the steering wheel, letting her fingers rest lightly between his thumb and forefinger.

"Garry, let it be," she said softly.

He moved his left hand and covered hers for a second. "Okay," he said, and replaced his hand on the wheel as she removed hers.

They said nothing further while he turned onto the freeway and accelerated up to Northbrook. He drove into the car park in front of the glass and steel building that housed the Sullivan Group's head office and stopped. He repeated the courtesy of opening the car door for her, and she looked at him for a few seconds before getting out of the Lincoln.

Once inside in the elevator, Garry spoke again. "Girish is very formal," he said. "Call him Mister Murgabi, he'll address you as Miss Ashley, which is how I'll introduce you. He might call me Mister Barton, though he did call me Garry on the phone the other day. He's very military, a superb executive, very old-fashioned. If he's surprised at seeing a woman partner, he won't show it, but he won't spare you any hard questions because you're a woman either."

She searched his face for a second, but Garry was now thinking business, and she became equally professional. "Okay," she said quietly.

"Let me begin the meeting," continued Garry, "because we've worked together before. Once he gets on to accounting topics though, I'll back away completely."

She nodded, and the elevator stopped, the doors opening onto the luxury of the Sullivan Group lobby. Announcing themselves to the receptionist, they stood silently. Garry was concentrating hard on the coming meeting. He had all but forgotten the conversation in the car.

Girish Murgabi appeared from his office, dressed as Garry had always seen him, in a beautifully-cut three-piece suit, a military striped tie and shoes polished to a bright glow. His black, gleaming hair was short, and a thin moustache was a pencil line on his top lip. He shook Garry's hand then turned to Micky as Garry introduced her as the HLM Audit partner. Only because he was looking for it, did Garry see the tiniest flicker of the other man's eyes when he introduced Micky.

"Miss Ashley, this is a great pleasure," said Murgabi. "Please come to my office."

As Murgabi led them down the corridor, Garry exchanged a brief look with Micky. She gave him the tiniest of smiles. The office was spacious, and Girish showed them to leather armchairs around a coffee table, leaving his desk empty. As Garry knew he would, the Vice-President wasted no time.

"Mister Barton, you made a number of recommendations concerning the operations of the computer facility at the Sullivan Cables plant during your last assignment. Would you be in a position to manage the implementation of those recommendations?"

"Yes," replied Garry.

"They included organizational structure changes in the computer division, a set of job evaluation standards, and then a disaster recovery plan."

"Correct," said Garry, working hard at keeping his tone formal and unemotional. Underneath, his excitement grew.

"I do not expect a fixed price for such a task, but will you quote me an hourly rate and some estimate of the time requirements?" said Murgabi, uncapping a gold fountain pen and opening a small notebook.

"I know the scope of the job," replied Garry, "so I can give a fixed price because I had prepared a quote for you at the time. The entire assignment will cost a hundred and forty thousand. I can complete it in six months." He controlled his breathing, expecting some argument and negotiation. Murgabi merely nodded. "If you will give me a written proposal for that task, I will approve it at once," he said. "How soon can you start?"

"Next week," replied Garry, his head spinning.

"Excellent," said Murgabi. "We need similar assignments at our plants in Milwaukee and St. Louis.

If you can submit quotations for those tasks too, similar approval will be given quite rapidly."

"I'll do that," replied Garry, betraying his emotions with a tremble in his voice.

Girish Murgabi smiled at him, a bright gleam of amusement. "Playing Santa Claus is one of my favourite occupations, you know," he said.

"Mister Murgabi, you do it very well," replied Garry, letting out a deep breath.

"Ah, but we have barely started," said Murgabi. "So, Miss Ashley, shall we turn our attentions to accounting matters?"

Beside him, Garry sensed Micky shift in her seat. He felt a small moment of concern about her ability to stand up to the sometimes overbearing force of Girish Murgabi.

"Miss Ashley," began Murgabi. "The Sullivan Group is reconsidering its present firm of auditors as part of a general organization and structural review of our operations throughout the US."

Garry sat up. This was far more than he had expected. All fifteen companies of the Sullivan Group were on the table, it seemed. The volume of work was far greater than HLM could possibly handle.

"In addition," continued the executive, "I have raised significant questions about the technical expertise in computer audit with our present auditors. Given the drive to more intensive reliance on sophisticated computer usage in the group which Mister Barton will be managing, a change is indicated."

Garry's pulse was pounding. The assignments he had just earned seemed to be merely the beginning. Was he to redirect the entire computer strategies of the group? It sounded that way. He spared a second to wonder how George Elliot and Trent would feel if they could hear this conversation.

"The Sullivan Group has always had a policy of encouraging local organizations," continued Murgabi. "We must, of course, invite other accounting firms to bid on our work, but I can ask you, Miss Ashley, is Haywood, Levin and Marsh interested in and capable of conducting the audits of selected Sullivan Group companies?"

He looked directly at her as he spoke, and Micky stared straight back. "Mister Murgabi," she said firmly. "HLM is certainly interested in taking on Sullivan audits. We have the skills, and I believe we have proved our leadership in computer audit techniques among the smaller firms. We do not as yet have the staff required to service an organization of your size, but we will acquire and train people as needed, provided we can phase in the audits on a company-by-company basis."

Micky, my love, you're magnificent, thought Garry, seeing now why she had been made a partner at HLM.

Girish bowed his head at her. "That would naturally be the way we would manage it," he answered. "We will therefore be sending your firm a formal invitation to bid at a board presentation in the near future. While I repeat, you will not be alone in receiving such bids, I must stress that with our personal knowledge of the quality of Mister Barton's work, and our research into the performance of HLM the last two years, your firm will be considered as the front-runner."

He looked over at Garry again, and the white smile shone through the room. "Some Santa Claus, eh, Garry?"

Garry laughed breathlessly. "That's one almighty sack you have there."

Murgabi's face was straight again. "We do not take decisions lightly," he said. "I am confident we can work together successfully for some years. Now, do you have any questions?"

"Of course," said Micky with a smile.

Murgabi turned to her. "Yes, Miss Ashley?"

For the next thirty minutes, Garry watched as they exchanged questions and answers, and he took pleasure in observing two professionals at work. He made his own notes on the group's structure and proposed changes as they related to the needs of data processing and telecommunications.

"Thank you, Mister Murgabi," said Micky, and closed her notebook. It brought the meeting to an end. All three stood up and walked back into the lobby. Courteous farewells were made, and the elevator door closed between them. They were silent as they descended and made their way to the parking lot, and Garry had driven out onto the road leading to the highway before either of them spoke.

"That really happened, Garry?" said Micky. "I really did just hear us invited to bid on the Sullivan Group and told we were front-runners?"

"If I heard myself win over a quarter-million dollars of consulting work, then it happened."

"Good grief!" she whispered.

"Exactly," he replied with a grin. Silence returned to the car as both of them became lost in their own thoughts. While concentrating on the driving, Garry was thinking that he could hardly handle the work-load without hiring some staff, and wondering how to do that within the structure of the agreement he had with HLM. He looked at Micky and she was concentrating on the passing view. He assumed she was thinking about managing an audit that would have to be worth over a million dollars a year, and grow as HLM gradually took over all fifteen companies of the Sullivan Group.

He turned off the freeway at Wilmette and drove into the car park of a hotel that he knew had a reasonable bar and lounge on the top floor. He had parked and was leading her into the lobby before she seemed to realize something was different.

"What's this?" she said as they entered the elevator, though she didn't seem disturbed by the break in routine.

"Miss Ashley," he said, "you may not need a drink after that, but I most certainly do!"

Her reply came in the form of a small chuckle as she followed him through the almost deserted bar to a table by the window. As the waitress advanced, Garry raised an eyebrow at Micky.

"A rum and coke, please," she said, and he nodded at the waitress. "And a scotch, no ice, no water," he added.

They waited in silence until the drinks arrived, and Garry raised his glass to Micky. "To wealth," he said.

She leaned over and touched her glass to his. "And health and happiness," she replied and they both sipped at their drinks.

"I've never done anything like that before," she

said. "Ever!" She seemed to be radiating excitement, the earlier reverie apparently broken.

"You could have fooled me," said Garry with a laugh. "You seemed totally in command of things, I thought."

"I was just following your lead," she replied.

"Mine? Hell, I was so gob-smacked I could hardly speak!"

She giggled, and that was the most relaxed Garry had ever seen her. Her happiness and excitement were almost an aura. "Garry, do you realize what we've done?"

It was a rhetorical question, and he didn't bother replying. He took another drink and looked at her face with its slight flush and the sparkle in her eyes, and wondered if he could ever love anyone the way he felt about this woman. He decided there and then that there was no way he could leave her to the wimpy Craig.

For a few more minutes they sat in companionable silence. Garry summoned another round of drinks and was content to watch her face and enjoy her presence.

"This has all happened since you joined us, you know," she said, breaking a lengthy pause.

He tilted his glass at her. "You made it all possible," he said. "You provided the name, the office, the clients, the sort of people you are. It worked very well."

"Did it ever!" she laughed. "We're a great combination!"

"Is that a corporate or a personal observation?" he asked.

She looked at him, and with a small stir of surprise, he realized she wasn't quite sober. The mixture of alcohol and excitement had affected her considerably. This would be the worst possible time to talk to her on an emotional level, he knew.

"I really don't know," she said, her words a tiny bit slurred. Ignoring the possible importance of those last words, trying to tell himself she was not in full control, Garry stood up.

"Micky, it's time to take you home," he said. "Leave your car where it is and come in by cab tomorrow."

Obediently, she stood up and followed him to the elevators. As they reached the ground floor, she tucked her arm in his and walked to the car. Garry felt he was walking a couple of inches in the air.

"Where to?" he asked as he buckled himself into his seat. He had no idea where she lived, he realized in some amusement.

"Lake Shore Drive, near Fullerton," she said. He nodded and started the car, heading for the road south. As he drove, she snuggled down in he seat, her eyes closed.

"I don't drink very much," she said suddenly, her voice sounding like a small child's.

Garry laughed. "So I noticed," he said.

She giggled softly, and leaned her head back against the seat. Occasionally, he looked at her as he drove through the traffic towards Lake Shore Drive. As he turned off the Drive at Fullerton, he nudged her gently and asked for her address. He drove into the driveway of her apartment building and stopped, walked round to her side and opened the car door, leading her to the lobby of the building.

"Okay, Miss Ashley," he said in a mixture of amusement and affection, "you're on your own from here."

As the elevator door opened, she suddenly turned to him and put her arms round his neck. "Don't give up," she whispered. She gave him a swift hug then moved into the elevator. The door closed between them, leaving Garry with a tingling memory of her bright eyes and the feel of her slender body pressed for the shortest of moments against him. He walked back to his car, feeling ready to fight dragons. *Craig, you poor bastard,* he said to himself, *you don't stand a chance.*

* * * *

"Garry, Mister Conway is here to see you."

The voice in his telephone shook Garry's concentration. He had come into the office early, intent on finishing the proposal to the Sullivan Group before lunch. What with that and the warm thoughts of the afternoon with Micky, he had totally forgotten about the meeting with Jack Conway. The morning had also been brightened by the reaction of Peter to the news of the meeting with Girish Murgabi the previous day. Garry mentally shook himself and switched his mind away from the text on the computer screen. "Show him into the board room, Monica, and feed him a coffee," he said, suppressing the sharp edge of nervousness he felt at remembering the meeting. He pressed the disconnect button on his phone then dialled Peter. "Conway's here," he said.

"This should be interesting," said Peter. "I'll call Charlie. See you in the boardroom in five minutes."

Garry waited for his partners then walked into the boardroom ahead of them. Jack Conway was sitting at the table, drinking coffee. He smiled as Garry walked in, stood up and extended his hand.

"It's a pleasure to see you again, Garry," he said then froze as Peter and Charlie walked in. He looked at Garry with a question in his eyes.

"You probably know Peter Haywood and Charlie Levin," said Garry.

The other two men walked up and extended their hands to Conway who shook them politely. "Yes, of course," he said. "But I had hoped to have a private meeting with you, Garry."

Peter took a seat at the head of the table, with Charlie sitting at his right, leaving Conway returning to his seat at Peter's left. Garry walked to the foot of the table and sat down.

"Jack, it's obvious why you've asked to talk to Garry," said Peter. "But as of this morning, Garry is a full partner of the firm, so anything you wish to discuss must include us. Micky Ashley can't be with us, but I will brief her fully when she returns."

Garry couldn't look up from the table. He was so stunned by Peter's words he forgot everything, including the reason for the meeting. Under the astonishment, a warm glow of delight began to spread through him. He fought for self-control and concentrated on what Conway was saying.

"I see," said Jack, after a moment of silence. "Then that changes part of what I had come to say."

"You were going to offer me a partnership in PAC?" blurted out Garry. On reflection, he thought, it was an obvious ploy. *Too damn obvious,* he decided.

Conway looked at him. "I certainly had wished to discuss terms under which such an offer might be made, Garry," he said.

"And were all your partners in agreement with this offer?"

Conway smiled briefly. "As you might imagine, one or two expressed some reservations about it."

Garry returned the smile, feeling almost as well disposed to Conway as he had done in the past. "And who would be kicked out first?" he asked. "Trent, Elliot or me?"

Conway looked uncomfortable. "I would hope it would not have to come to that," he said. "We need all the skills we have"

"Indeed you do," said Garry. "Unfortunately, the skills you have aren't adequate."

The temperature in the room dropped and Conway's face took on a rigid expression.

Peter broke the tension. "Jack, I can anticipate your next move," he said. "If Garry can't be brought back into your fold, am I right in supposing that your partners have authorized you to propose a merger between our firms?"

Conway looked frozen in his seat. But he was an aristocrat of the old school and he recovered his composure, sipping his coffee slowly. "You're very perceptive, Peter," he said, replacing his cup in its saucer. "Yes, I have been so authorized, and I have a letter laying out the proposed details."

He bent down over his briefcase, but was interrupted by Peter. "Please don't bother, Jack. I know I can speak for all my partners in telling you that HLM would have no interest in such a merger."

Conway sat upright again, an expression of weariness on his face. Garry began to feel sorry for his former chairman who was witnessing the early stages of the destruction of the firm his grandfather had founded.

"I'm truly sorry to hear that, Peter," said Conway. "In that case, I have to advise you that I shall be lodging a complaint against this firm with the Ethics Committee of the Institute of Accountants, and also instituting legal action against you to prevent further encroachment on our client base."

Peter laughed out loud, and Garry could see the strength in him. "Jack, that's silly," said Haywood. "The clients we have taken from you have all approached us directly. At no time have we made any untoward approach to them, and they will all sign statements to that effect if asked. Your ethics charge has no basis, no more than any legal action has."

"I believe I can get court injunctions to prevent you from approaching any more of our clients." Conway was looking patrician, as if relying on his authority to break Peter's confidence.

"That's bullshit," said Levin, speaking for the first time. "And I'm sure that Stephen told you the same thing."

Conway avoided looking at Levin, and addressed Peter. "The results of legal action may be indeterminate," he said, "but perhaps you should consider the costs of such extended action against you."

Peter was unmoved. "Jack, we stand to earn an additional half-million dollars in revenue this year, a lot of it at your expense." Conway winced. "And I believe we may double that if certain events occur as planned," Peter continued. Garry knew he was referring to the Sullivan Group, but he could not reveal his hand to Conway.

"So any legal costs we may face, we can carry easily," continued Peter. "I therefore recommend that you look toward your own depleted coffers instead, and reconsider your course of action."

Garry sensed it was a complete victory, and Conway knew it. He picked up his briefcase and rose to his feet. "I will bid you all a good day, gentlemen," he said and walked out. Nobody offered to see him to the lobby.

When he had gone, the three men sat back at the table and looked at each other.

"I suppose that means we have to rethink the financial arrangements?" Garry said, struggling for self-control.

"Damn right!" Peter said. "Whatever you earn now is ours. You don't think we could keep paying you those huge sums of money, do you?"

"So you made me a partner to save money, eh?"

"What other possible reason could there be?" commented Charlie.

The room was silent for a few seconds then all three burst out laughing.

Garry decided he had never felt happier.

Chapter 7

The air of tension in the chairman's office was high. Few of the people in the room could meet each other's eyes with any equanimity.

"I told you they wouldn't accept a merger proposal." Trent looked angry. "And I for one am perfectly happy with that. It would never have worked."

"That's open to your judgement and imagination," replied Petheram. "I'm more concerned by the contempt with which they received Jack's approach. Two years ago, that would never have happened. They would probably have leaped at the chance of a merger."

"It was certainly a complete rejection," agreed Newman. "And I got the impression from what you've told us, that they were feeling there was worse to come."

"And you're probably correct," said Conway, looking at the envelope on his desk. He picked it up and pulled a letter from inside. "I received this note this morning from the Sullivan Group."

The room fell silent. All of them recognized the anxiety and sadness radiating from Conway. He unfolded the paper and looked up at his colleagues. "Girish Murgabi has asked us to attend a board meeting next month," he said softly. "We will be required to defend our audits of the Sullivan Group companies and rebid for the business against proposals from three other accounting firms who will be making presentations the same day."

"And I suppose HLM is one of those companies?" asked Trent, taking the letter from Conway's outstretched hand. His complexion had gone pale.

Conway nodded. "Andrew," he said, addressing Whittaker, "have you heard if Barton has done any work for Sullivan since leaving us?"

Whittaker was sitting uncomfortably on a hard chair in one corner. The chairman's ban on smoking during meetings was causing him difficulties. "He's implementing all the proposals for new organizational structures in the computer department, which he made in the job he did with us at one of their companies," said Whittaker. "And then he starts a disaster recovery plan. I gather he'll be doing the same at all the other companies."

"Then we have to assume that HLM will be the front-runners at these presentations," said Newman.

"That's nuts," blared Trent. "They're much too small to handle that size of client."

"Maybe for now," responded Petheram. "But they've already taken our two best managers from us, as well as a couple of seniors. There's nothing to stop them from hiring more of our people."

"And if we lose those accounts, we'd be faced with laying off staff, anyway." The sadness in Conway's face was obvious. "Something we've never done before in sixty years. And anyway, the hand-over would be gradual, one company at a time over two or three years, I imagine."

"Jack, please!" said Petheram. "You're talking as if we've already lost the Sullivan audit. Surely we can defend against this?"

"I wish that was true," replied Conway. "However, I have come to believe that we lack the vital skills for this age of technology."

"This is all Barton's fault!" exploded Trent. "It's time we put a stop to that bastard."

"Barton's fault?" Whittaker looked up at the group, and the anger was plain in his face. "He told you, and I told you that we were at risk. We've been out of date for years, and whose stupid fault is that? Don't try and shift the blame from where it should be sitting firmly and squarely."

"I begin to wonder, Andrew," Newman whispered. "Just where do your sympathies lie? Did we make a mistake inviting you on to this committee?"

"No you didn't," rapped Whittaker, staring firmly in to her black eyes. "Your mistake was not listening to the consultants before this. One thing Garry and I agreed on was that you can't just tell a client what he wants to hear, you have to tell the truth. So pin your ears back, all of you, and listen, because here's the truth. You people have fucked up. Now, if you want to recover from this shit heap, think about *business* ways of doing it, not blaming someone who's out of the picture."

"Out of the picture? Whittaker, have you been asleep these last few weeks?" Trent's face was contorted in anger. "Who the hell do you think is taking our clients away from us? It's your old colleague and friend, Garry Barton."

"I'm well aware who's causing our problems," replied Whittaker with contempt. "But he's doing it in honest, commercial fashion. He's seen our weakness and he's exploiting it. If he's taking clients away from us, it's because they want to leave us. Perhaps you should think of a proper response to that."

"I have," shouted Trent. "We beat the crap out of the bastard and stop him that way."

"That's the reaction I suppose I should expect from you, Bill," said Whittaker. "Ignore the disease and attack the symptom."

"Bullshit!" rasped Trent. "Getting rid of HLM isn't attacking the symptom. Barton's the bloody problem!"

"I've said this before, William," replied Conway. There was weariness and some contempt in his voice. "I want no more of your silly suggestions of violence. This might be the time to tell you of the other small bombshell Peter Haywood dropped on me."

He looked around the silent room, with a small smile that held no amusement. "Even before I could offer them the merger proposal, Haywood advised me that Garry Barton had become a full partner of the firm that morning."

In the silence, Petheram was the only one to find words. "Well, talk about a kick where it hurts, eh?" he said, letting out a long breath. There was a small smile on his face, much like Conway's.

"So somebody else has recognized Garry's true value, even if we couldn't?" Whittaker was laughing, though there was a bitter tone to his amusement. "Looks like we got caught off base again, people."

Before anyone else could utter a word, Newman spoke sharply. "I wish to say something," she said, her eyes fixed firmly on her hands lying flat on her lap. The room went silent. "We've had some conflict in these meetings," she continued, "and I admit to having caused some of it myself. We've reached the point where any differences we have about Garry Barton's views on our state of technology have become irrelevant. Fighting between ourselves must end as of now. It's time we began to combine our abilities and worry about fighting the threat to this firm."

The four men looked at her. Newman's influence on the group had increased in recent weeks.

"What do you have in mind, Bridget?" asked Conway.

"I'm advising all of you that unusual defences may be required against the sudden attack on this firm," she said. "We may find ourselves considering action we might not have considered in the past."

"Bridget, what the hell are you saying?" Petheram demanded in an alarmed tone. "You're surely not endorsing William's crazy idea of some sort of violence?"

"Not at this time," said Newman.

"Nor at any other time!" snapped Conway. "This is getting insane!"

"So is the disaster facing us," replied Newman, not at all rattled by Conway's anger.

"Bridget, I thought better of you," said Whittaker, looking at her with a curious expression. "I thought you had brains. Why the hell don't you apply them to the business problem, the way you did with Mortensen Transport and some of the other people you've kept alive? With your intellect and business skills, not this crap of beating up Garry."

"That's precisely what I am doing, Mister Whittaker," she replied, turning the full force of her stare on him. He shifted in his seat and looked at the table top. "And if you had an ounce of understanding of when limitations have been reached, you'd see that. Now kindly keep your pointless comments to yourself."

"You're off the bloody wall, Newman." Whittaker looked calm, but his voice was icy with contempt. "You're all losing sight of this thing," he continued, looking around the table. "And you can't see what's happening here, either. Can't you see that this woman is leading you by the nose? She's far more concerned about taking over the firm than she is about what's happening to us right now."

"Andrew, that will do!" Conway raised his voice again. "Let's leave personal evaluations out of the discussion," he said more softly. "We've faced difficulties before. We've survived those, and we'll survive this one. There are a lot of business principles we have yet to try. One of them is to stop personal bickering and blame-fixing. The other is to swallow our pride and start investigating genuine improvements to our audit technology." He glared at Trent as he spoke.

Trent folded his arms and sat back in his chair. "I'll do that anyway, Jack," he said quietly. "But there may not be time to get those changes in unless we do something more drastic."

"Then start by getting out to all our clients and assuring them that we're developing and upgrading our business practices," retorted Conway. "And promise them cost reductions in the near future. Whatever you do, make sure we lose no more clients."

"And if that fails?" asked Petheram. "Are we then faced with reconsidering Bill's rather less orthodox tactics?"

"It mustn't fail," replied Conway. "We can't survive much more of this attrition."

"That's exactly what I was saying," said Newman. "Regardless of your hopes, we may not keep some of our remaining clients. And if we start to lose more, then alternative actions will be vital, regardless of what our consulting colleague advises." She stared with distaste at Whittaker who met her eyes and refused to give way.

"We'll talk again if that happens," replied Conway. "But if we work together on this, we can prevent that nonsensical debate."

"It's interesting that we seem suddenly to be regarding Bill's suggestion as a viable possibility," observed Petheram.

"No we're not," retorted Conway sharply.

"On the contrary, I think we are," said Newman with quiet confidence.

"Then this meeting is over," said Conway. He moved behind his desk, opened his calendar and began to make notes.

The others left the office in silence.

As Trent made his way along the corridor, he was surprised to find Newman walking alongside him. Never in his twenty years with the firm, not even in the ten years since he became a partner, had Newman ever shown any tendency to socialize.

"I would appreciate a few moments of your time, William," she said, as he was about to enter his office.

He looked at his watch, as much to cover his confusion as to check the time. "I have a meeting with one of my managers in a few minutes," he said. "Perhaps later on this morning?"

She nodded. "Why don't you come to my office as soon as you're free?" she said, and walked on without waiting for his answer.

He closed the door behind him and sat thinking. The meeting in the boardroom had opened up some appalling possibilities. The Sullivan account had always been the jewel in the PAC crown and Trent had been involved with it since joining the firm twenty years ago. Only the best worked on Sullivan audits, and Trent had been excited by his assignment to the team when he was a newly-hired accountant as a young man of twenty-three. He had worked hundreds of hours in the various factories and offices of the conglomerate, and knew the inner workings of the group better than most of the Sullivan executives. He had grown within the audit team as he had grown within the firm, eventually becoming the manager of the account. Sullivan had been the single largest feature of his business life, and now it was possible that he would lose it. The thought sent icy spikes through his guts. The loss of prestige would be as bad as the loss of income. He could afford neither, not with the house extensions, Margaret's wild spending habits and the constant stream of bills for additional costs that the school kept sending him. He was frightened, he admitted to himself.

Damn that Barton! he thought to himself. *And damn George Elliot to hell!* For five years, Bill had believed Elliot when he had claimed that computer audit packages simply weren't well enough developed for regular use for anything but data sampling and testing. In the last two years, as Trent had talked to other accountants, he had become increasingly aware that Elliot had been lying. Maybe Barton had been right, maybe Elliot was simply protecting his position as the official computer expert by refusing to let anyone else learn anything.

Damn him, damn him, damn him, swore Trent. He had tried to be loyal to his junior partner, tried to discredit Barton to protect Elliot, and finally had swung the forces needed to have Barton removed. Now it had all fallen in on him. And there was little he could do. He couldn't keep protecting Elliot, he had to get some computer skills into the firm. There was no way he could have tolerated the return of Barton, even if that had been a possibility. A man had just too much pride for that. Some of his anger against Barton, he realized with a little shame, was because Garry had somehow learned not to be intimidated by Trent's mass. How Garry had done that, Trent was unsure, but it irritated him that his best weapon had been neutralized.

Trent realized he had painted himself into a corner of horrifying restrictions. His original comments about doing violence to Barton had been made in anger, but not seriously. Now he wondered if there was any other way. He looked at his watch again. Twenty minutes had passed since his exchange with Newman, enough time to make her believe he really had met with a manager. He stood up, walked out of his office and down a floor to the tax department.

He had never been in Newman's office. She had the same location as his, the corner with a view of the city skyline, and he sat for a moment, seeing how even one floor made a difference to the perspective of Chicago's superlative architecture.

"What did you want to see me about, Bridget?" he asked. He felt uncomfortable, sitting on a fragile armchair across the coffee table from Newman. She was very much at her ease as she poured coffee from a black basalt coffee pot into two tiny cups of the same set. She gestured at equally diminutive containers of sugar and cream, and he added sugar, feeling a little silly holding the tiny spoon and trying to shovel enough sugar for his taste.

He looked around the office. The furniture was a delicate white wood with gold inlays. A vase of tulips stood on the desk, and one wall was taken up by a bookcase full of texts. For the moment he was unable to identify what was bothering him about the room until he finally saw it. There was not a single picture of another human being in the place. Nearly everybody had a photo of a wife, husband, kids, siblings, something personal. There was nothing at all of Bridget Newman, the person. A single painting of a cathedral hung on one wall, and that was it for art.

"Firstly, William, I would like to apologize for comments I made at an earlier meeting. I regret to admit that I was feeling the effects of some of the body-blows this firm has taken in recent weeks. I spoke out of turn."

Trent was shaken to the core.   Newman

apologizing for something? This was so out of character and reputation that all Trent's warning reactions went off. *She's after something,* he thought and tensed himself for the moment when she would reveal her intentions.

"Apology accepted, Bridget," he said cautiously. "We've all taken some hits recently."

"I believe we have a problem," said Newman, ignoring Trent's reply and taking a delicate sip from her black basalt cup. She was, as always, dressed in superb fashion, in a black skirt with a cream silk blouse. A single pearl hung from a thin gold chain round her neck.

"A problem? I'll say we have a problem," rasped Trent in irritation. *You silly bitch,* he wanted to add, but contented himself with thinking it. "If we lose Sullivan, we stand to lose about three million a year in audit and tax fees, never mind consulting. I will personally lose over fifty thousand a year. I'm sure your own losses will be high without the tax work."

"I agree, but that is not the problem I had in mind," she said, her composure undisturbed by his tone.

"Oh? I'm surprised, Bridget. Apart from the potential loss of even more business, it's hard to imagine what other problems might be greater than losing our biggest client."

"That's the effect," she replied, looking briefly at him, then concentrating her gaze on the depths of her coffee. "The cause is the increasing weakness of Conway."

Trent felt the breath go out of him. *So this dark witch is planning a palace coup, is she?* Helpless to do more than see out the discussion, he waited. He knew how powerful she was becoming, and didn't wish to make an enemy of her. "How so?" he asked in neutral tones.

"William, I know you may have suggested the idea of physical persuasion against Barton in a moment of anger, but I believe it may be the only way to stop HLM attacking our client base."

He sighed and sensed his own submission to her. "Bridget, I hate the idea, but I agree. It may be the only way. But Jack would never go along with it."

"Then we all have to persuade him, if it comes to it," she replied.

"That may be difficult," he said. "Stephen is dead against the idea, too."

She made a small gesture of irritation. "Stephen I can handle," she said. "I want to be certain that if the situation arises, you'll back me up."

"What can we do?" he asked. "Stephen was right about one thing. How the hell would we organize such a thing? None of us knows anything about that sort of business."

"Not entirely true," she said softly. "I believe I know where I could find such resources."

Jesus, Mary, Mother of God, he said to himself. *What am I getting into? She knows how to organize a hit on someone? If I don't support her, she'll never forgive me. And if we pull out of this, there's no doubt she'll be gunning for Jack's job and probably get it. And that leaves me out in the cold. Even if she doesn't get it, this is the last person in the world to have as an enemy. And anyway, she's right. There's no way to stop HLM now except by taking out Barton.*

"Just what do you plan to do?" he asked. "Getting Jack to agree to this sort of action is most unlikely."

"Difficult, yes," she agreed with a small smile which flickered out of existence as soon as it had appeared. "But not impossible."

"And what then?" he asked, almost holding his breath for her answer.

"Then I believe some new leadership strengths are required within the firm," she said calmly.

Dear God, I was right! Trent struggled for self-control. *The bitch is after Jack's job. And she could well end up with it if she pulls this off and PAC gets over the crisis.* "We certainly will need strength at the helm to recover from all this, I agree," he replied. "Would you foresee any other major changes in the firm?" *Am I safe, you bitch?*

"Not many," she replied with a direct look at him. "You know, Bill, I admire the way you run your department. I can't see anyone approaching your skills there. In fact, I might be concerned that you have nobody obviously in line for eventual succession."

"Thank you, Bridget," he said. *Telling me I'm safe if I support you, eh? Subtle old witch.* "I agree, I should be developing somebody. Have you any suggestions?"

"Not George Elliot, certainly," she said softly. "In your place, I'd be questioning his value to the firm."

So that's it? I have to get some real computer audit skills in here, or you'll be taking on the work that Barton was doing and destroying me? "I've been thinking hard about that, Bridget," he said. "Elliot doesn't seem to have introduced computer technology as rapidly as we'd hoped. I'm sure he has the skills, but perhaps he lacks the personal strengths."

"I agree with that analysis," she replied. "And if I'm in a position to help you later, be certain I will."

Well, that's about as direct as it can be said. "I'm with you all the way, Bridget," he said, and took a deep breath.

"I thought you would be," she replied, and replaced her cup on the table. He realized he hadn't touched his own coffee. When she stood up, he knew he wasn't going to get the chance. The meeting was over. He had been dismissed.

"I have to start work on the Sullivan defence," he said, and moved to the door.

"I too," she replied as she sat at her desk. "Good luck, William."

Trent returned to his office, a mixture of excitement and terror coursing through his body. *God knows what I'm into, but at least it's action. Somebody had a plan, at last.*

Andrew Whittaker walked slowly along the corridor till he reached Petheram's office. Petheram was just sitting down behind his desk when he saw Whittaker at the doorway.

"Andrew!" he said, with some surprise. "Please come in."

"Thanks," said Whittaker, and closed the door behind him. Petheram noted the move with a sense of disturbance. The two men were sociable, if not friends, a twenty-two-year age gap and different professional backgrounds resulting in cultural differences that neither had ever tried to overcome.

"A fairly rough meeting," commented Petheram with a smile.

"Are they always like that?" asked Whittaker. He looked exhausted and irritable.

Petheram smiled slightly. "Not usually," he said. "Only since we got rid of Garry,"

"It's beginning to scare me," said Whittaker. "You guys are going down a path that I can hardly believe."

"Us guys? You're on the committee as well, Andrew."

"I am? Listening to Bridget, I was beginning to wonder about that."

Petheram nodded. "Bridget's starting to have influence, I agree. Is that such a bad thing?"

"It is when she starts to lead this firm along paths of lunacy, yes."

"I'm not so sure she's doing the wrong thing, Andrew."

"She's trying to get us to agree to violence against Garry Barton. You think that's an okay thing?"

"I thought it was Bill's suggestion?" said Petheram.

"Bill's only partly serious," replied Whittaker with a gesture of dismissal. "That's his style. With reasonable debate he'd come round to seeing how stupid it is. But it's Bridget who seems to be picking up the ball and running with it."

"I suppose so. Either way, it's worth considering."

"Stephen, you must be joking!" Whittaker looked astonished. "You can't believe it's a good idea to beat up Garry?"

"It might just be." Petheram looked firmly at the consulting partner.

"What? Christ alive, Stephen, I thought you were a bright man. Are you telling me you believe in that approach?"

"I'm like you, Andrew. I'm making a lot of money doing the one thing I do well. Do you want to lose it all?"

"Of course not! But who says we're losing it all?"

"If we lose Sullivan, we might as well say we're dead." Petheram spoke loudly. "And then bang goes the income, the status, everything!"

"And you think killing Garry will stop that?"

"Killing?" Petheram was astounded. "Who said anything about killing?"

"You can't see it, can you?" said Whittaker. "You'll start down this path and what if it doesn't work? What then? What will you do when PAC has lost its biggest clients and Haywood's firm is still tearing at the flesh? Give up, pick up your bat and ball and go home?"

"Christ, Andrew! You can't be serious? It'll never get to that point!"

"Yeah, and the Titanic was unsinkable and the Japs would never learn how to build cars like Detroit. Of *course* it will get to that point! And then what do you have? Ten years in the pen, that's what!"

"Andrew, you've lost touch with this," said Petheram. "We'll do what's necessary and we'll keep the firm alive."

"Yeah? Well, if Newman swings you the way she wants, I'm out of here."

"Maybe that would be the best thing, if you feel like that."

Whittaker stood up. "Maybe you're right."

He walked out of the office without looking back.

*   *   *   *

For four weeks, the partners of Haywood, Levin and Marsh worked at a pace that threatened their health and sanity. The presentation to the Sullivan Group was given the highest priority, as they all agreed that winning the accounting work for fifteen companies would be the thing that raised the firm from being a small partnership to a forceful presence in the world of public accountants.

Garry probably worked the longest hours. In addition to his twelve-hour days on his clients' projects, he spent a further two or three hours each day at his desk, his attention fixed on his computer screen, building a sophisticated visual presentation. They had agreed that the key success factor was computer audit, and Peter and Micky designed a pictorial representation of the process of such an exercise, which Garry then developed into a sequential series of slides on his graphics system.

"Could get quite turned on by audit, looking at that," commented Charlie Levin, as the four partners reviewed the show a few days before the meeting with the Sullivan executives.

"I wonder if those words have ever actually been spoken aloud before," Garry pondered, and the room erupted in laughter, the four of them welcoming a chance to break the tension of the last weeks. Micky's chuckle was music to Garry's ears.

"You've prepared an outline of your department's work, Charlie?" asked Peter when the laughter had subsided.

"Just a five-minute chat," replied Charlie. "Mainly a recap of some of the savings we've achieved for other clients. Tax is tax, after all. Don't want to send them to sleep, nor detract from that dog-and-pony show you people have dreamed up. I'll just show them what a charming and gifted person I am."

"Good thinking, if based on misapprehension," said Peter with a nod, suppressing his laugh. "And they already know Garry's work. They're certainly paying him a fortune for it! No, I think this is the way to go: emphasize the biggest thing that differentiates us from PAC, and which we know they want."

Murmurs of agreement ran round the boardroom.

"In that case," said Peter stifling a yawn and looking at his watch. "Seeing as it's only nine o'clock, I suggest we call it an unusually early night and get the flock out of here, as the shepherd was heard to say."

In a companionable silence, the four of them gathered up their possessions and took the elevator down to the parking garage in the basement.

Maybe it was wishful dreaming, thought Garry, but he felt that Micky's farewell had been accompanied by a warmer than usual smile. Feeling a mixture of happiness and frustration, he drove home to Wilmette.

Four days later, they made their presentation to a group of stern-faced executives in the traditionally oak-lined boardroom of the Sullivan Group offices. In complete silence, the listeners heard Charlie Levin's brief but pointed summary of tax benefits gained for clients. There was no reaction to Garry's equally short description of the work he was doing for the Group, and he sat down next to Charlie, feeling a twinge of worry that perhaps they had misread the situation.

The slide presentation on computer audit, however, was like magic. The Sullivan board stirred as the first slide was shown, and Garry watched in growing delight as Peter and Micky clearly stole the show. He doubted that the process of auditing a company's accounts had ever been made to seem so interesting and cerebral.

As the projector was switched off and Peter sat down after a few closing remarks, Girish Murgabi stood up.

"Miss Ashley, gentlemen, that seems to have answered all our questions," he said. "And also greatly entertained us. We will advise you of the results of these presentations in two days."

But the tiny wink he directed at Garry told all, and the four partners left the boardroom, holding their collective breaths.

"Oh Lord, I think we've done it," whispered Charlie as the elevator hummed downward. Small grunts from Peter and Garry reflected suppressed excitement.

"The last time I came out of here," said Micky, staring deliberately at the lights of the floor level indicator, "Garry forcibly hauled me to a bar and terrorized me into drinking something with alcohol in it."

Peter and Charlie gasped in mock horror, and Micky struggled to keep her composure. Garry was entranced by the glow in her eyes and the flush on her cheeks.

"So will somebody please force me to that bar again," she continued, her voice trembling with suppressed laughter. "After that meeting, I need to be terrorized some more."

The laughter lasted to the ground floor.

Like college kids going to a party, the four of them drove their cars to the hotel Garry had visited with Micky after their previous meeting with Girish Murgabi. Joining up again in the lobby, they ascended to the top floor bar. It was more crowded than last time, but they found a corner table and ordered drinks.

"This is setting a dangerous precedent," observed Garry as the waitress departed with the order. "Each time young Ashley has left the Sullivan offices, she's come here and proceeded to get zapped out of her mind."

He dodged a peanut thrown by Micky, but her smile was anything but hostile.

"Seems to be a point worth considering," laughed Charlie. "Maybe you should keep this audit to yourself, Peter? A consistently squiffy Ashley is beyond the bounds of acceptable partner behaviour."

Peter grinned then went serious. "Are you certain we've really done this?" he asked the table in general.

"Girish may be the most ruthless and decisive man I've ever met," said Garry, "but he's also the most ethical. I doubt he'd do anything to lead us on if it wasn't true. That wink says we've got it."

"Then we should have another drink," said Peter, and waved to the waitress.

An hour later, they decided to eat. Several plates of *hors d'oeuvres* were brought, and the four of them attacked the food with gusto. Garry felt that he was as happy as he had ever been before. Even with the barrier between him and Micky, he felt relaxed, part of a family, something new to him.

"This is getting to be like shooting fish in a barrel," said Charlie Levin at one point. "How come you never pulled in this sort of business at PAC, Garry?"

Garry shrugged. "I did okay," he said, "but it was frustrating. Most of the partners wouldn't introduce me to their clients, so I had to get assignments outside of the audit base, and that was damn hard work. I think Trent, and especially the computer audit partner, George Elliot, were scared of me for some reason."

Peter nodded, started to speak through a mouthful of chicken wing, and swallowed. He took a drink of beer, and continued. "I've been talking to a number of people," he said, "because the same thing had occurred to me. Why is Garry making magic with us, but could only be reasonably successful with PAC?"

"And what did you hear?" asked Micky. She seemed interested, thought Garry, watching her carefully.

"Mainly what Garry just said," replied Peter. "The PAC partners had no idea how to use his skills, because they knew so little about computers, or consulting. And he's right about that dimwit, George Elliot. I heard that Elliot pressured his partners to keep Garry away from the clients because he was terrified that Garry would reveal just how weak Elliot's work was. So our new partner here won a good amount of work with firms outside PAC's audit base, but was always competing against the incumbent auditors."

"There's another reason too," said Charlie. "Between us, we know a lot of the partners at PAC. How would you evaluate them?"

"Mainly a bunch of fairly nice but not very forceful people," said Micky. "There's nobody there with any great depth."

"I agree," said Levin. "With the exception of Newman. Her depths hide monsters. She's a walking Loch Ness."

"You're right," agreed Peter. "Bridget apart, they're nice, ineffectual people who made their careers in the easy years. But they have no idea of proactive business development in tighter times."

"But now Garry's got active partners," chimed in Charlie, "who introduce him around. And we're well regarded as auditors, too."

"Explosive combination," agreed Garry, feeling embarrassed by the attention. He took a plateful of spare ribs. "Enough of work, people," he said. "There's too much food here. Get eating!"

At nine, Peter stood up. "I had a Papal dispensation to stay out this evening, but this is pushing the boundaries."

Charlie grinned and also stood up. "That's what His Holiness told me, too. Time to head for home and hearth."

With a wave, the two men walked away from the table, leaving Garry feeling excited but uncertain. It was the first time he had been alone with Micky since the last visit to this bar, and he had no idea what to do. He looked quickly at her, then down at the table. She seemed to be smiling a little.

"I've had too much to drink again," she murmured.

"I do seem to do this to you," he replied. "It isn't my intention to get you helpless, honest."

"I know that," she said softly. "But I think I'll ask you to run me home once more. I know it's horribly out of your way, but I daren't risk it."

"Of course not. I wouldn't let you drive home either."

They stood up together and walked to the elevators. Garry was well aware of a pounding in his head, and knew quite well it had nothing to do with the drinks. He had deliberately switched to mineral water after the first scotch, having seen Micky down her first drink with abandon. This ride home had been a probability from the start.

He opened the passenger-side car door for her, and let her settle in the seat before closing it. A few minutes later, he was heading for Lake Shore Drive. On reaching her apartment building, he repeated the same procedures as the last time, tingling inside himself at the possibility that she might embrace him again. As the elevator door opened in the lobby, she smiled shyly at him.

"I can trust you to come up for a coffee, can't I?" she asked. "You deserve that much before driving back to Wilmette."

"I've probably lost a lot of opportunities by being trustworthy," he replied. "It's one of my more boring characteristics."

She smiled and took his arm, walking into the elevator.

Garry rode up the twelve floors trying not to breathe, certain that he would sound like an asthmatic horse. She opened the door to her apartment to reveal grey carpets, light blue walls, and delicate Swedish furniture. Flowers sat in vases on several surfaces, and three fig trees filled alcoves with delicate fronds of green. A huge picture window looked out over the lake where the early moonlight laid a wavering path to the shore.

"Sit down, I'll make coffee," she said, and moved into the kitchen. He sat on the Swedish sofa, idly picking up a copy of Cosmopolitan and studied the astounding cover girl.

"Not what I would have thought would be your type of reading," said an amused voice behind him. He looked up and over his shoulder. Micky was smiling.

"I just wonder where they find these women," he replied. "I never see anyone like this in the flesh."

She walked around the couch and sat down at the other end of the settee. "Sets your senses spinning, does she?" she asked softly.

He looked at her. She seemed to be studying him with a serious expression. "I suppose so," he admitted. "She's got a fantastic body, and she can bend it in a way that no man can do. I doubt any man in the world with even a minimum testosterone level could be unaffected by her."

She moved nearer to him and looked over his shoulder. He was very conscious of her closeness.

"Certainly in a class above me," she said.

Garry studied her. Her hands were clasped tightly together, and she was looking at the magazine cover.

"You're fishing again, Micky," he said quietly.

She moved back to her original position on the settee. Garry thought her face looked tight.

"Micky, what the hell are we doing to each other?" he asked, feeling his own pain at her obvious distress.

She shook her head without answering, not looking at him. Garry dropped the magazine on the floor and moved nearer to her. Micky didn't react to the move. Garry lightly put one hand over hers. "We have to talk about this," he said softly. "Something's going on and I can't cope with it."

She was silent, but one finger disengaged itself from her clasped hands and moved over his. Garry looked at their entwined hands, holding his breath for a moment.

"You frighten me," she said at last.

"It's the last thing in the world I would want to do," he replied.

"I know. But you do it, anyway."

"Why?"

"Because I can control things the way they are. I know what I'm doing. I know what each day will bring, and nothing gets messed up."

"And I threaten that?"

"Yes, you do." She looked sideways at him for a brief instant.

"I suppose you do the same to me, but I'm not afraid of it," he said. "I look at you, and I want to go off and kill dragons, or run for president, or anything that takes my fancy at the time."

She seemed not to have heard him. "I know exactly what Craig wants to do, and I know that he'll do it. He wants to be a judge before he's forty and then form his own law firm."

"And be rich and boring."

"And safe."

"And with me?"

"With you, life would be crazy, exciting, breathless and completely unpredictable." Garry heard a smile in her voice, and tightened his grip on her hands. He thought he sensed a response, but couldn't be sure.

"Is that such a bad thing?" he asked.

"I was married to a man like you once," she said. "He made life tingle. I didn't know I could ever be so happy. And he died." Her voice tightened up and she closed her eyes. Garry could see a tear in the corner of one of them.

"There's no promise that it couldn't happen again," said Garry. "But is that any reason to close off the chance of being happy again?"

"I'm not unhappy," she retorted. "Just safe."

"The last time I brought you home," he said, "you told me not to give up. Do you still feel that way?"

She leaned against him and turned her face up to his. The tears were rolling freely down her cheeks, and Garry tasted the sweetness of them as he kissed her lightly. He put one arm round her shoulders and felt her tremble.

"I don't know," she whispered when she pulled her lips away. "Give me a little more time, please."

"It's the only thing you'll let me give you," said Garry with a smile, and stood up. "I'd better go before my boring and well-mannered veneer falls apart."

"Yes," she said, looking down at her lap. "I know I'm not being fair."

"Then break up with Craig, and give us a chance," he pleaded.

She stood up and moved away. "I can't do that," she whispered. Her face looked forlorn and Garry ached to take her back in his arms.

"Why not?" he begged. "Don't you think we have something?"

"I don't know. I can't be sure." She turned away from him. "And I'm comfortable with Craig," she whispered. "I'm afraid."

"I'd better go," he said. She nodded, tears bright on her cheeks. He moved toward the door.

"I'm sorry, Garry," she said from a long way away.

"Yes," he said, and walked out of the apartment.

Chapter 8

Nobody was sitting down. The atmosphere in the boardroom was explosive, and all five of the occupants of the room were standing, the tension and anger clear on their tight faces.

"I have to lay off eight people because of the Sullivan loss," said Trent, his voice trembling with suppressed fury. "And let's face it, if three of our managers hadn't already quit and gone to HLM, I'd be laying them off, too."

"And I've had four people working full time on the Sullivan tax account," said Newman. "I'll be releasing them next month."

"Why not call HLM and suggest they hire them direct?" snarled Trent. "At this rate, all our staff will be moving over there."

Conway finally moved over to a chair at the head of the boardroom table and sat down. His movements were those of an old, tired man. "Everybody, please, sit down," he said, and waited while the other four took their places. "In all my life," he continued, "I never dreamed that we'd face this sort of crisis. I've had several partners come and talk to me, worried about their futures, something that should never happen. And we can certainly expect to lose more staff as they see our problems and decide to look elsewhere for careers."

He looked around the room, and the same air of defeat reflected in all the faces except one. Newman had regained her customary composure and might have been listening to a presentation of regular income statements, so unaffected did she seem.

"Jack," she said softly, and all eyes turned to her, as if she was a potential saviour to them all. "We've gone beyond any difficulties we might have considered possible," she continued into the waiting silence. "We're into unknown territory here, and the solutions must therefore be outside of the norm."

"I think I know what you're saying," replied Conway, "and I still say no. Violence can never be the solution." But everyone in the room heard the lack of strength in his words.

Trent jumped into the gap. "Jack, we have to consider this," he said. "I'll admit, even though I was the one to suggest it first, I don't think I really believed we'd actually get to this point. But we have, and I don't see any alternative."

"I must endorse that view," said Newman. "Desperate situations call for unusual solutions. This is a time for unusual solutions."

Conway looked across the table at Petheram. "Do you go along with this lunacy, Stephen?"

Petheram looked at the table top and seemed deep in thought for a few moments. "I'm thirty-five," he said. "I have a great lifestyle, I'm wealthy, and I live in a marvellous condo on the lake front. I like going to the theatre, taking holidays in Europe and driving my very expensive car. I think of myself as a reasonably nice guy. I've never hit a kid and I've never hit anyone else since the last time I got into a fight at school. I was eight years old."

He looked up at the faces watching him with understanding. "But suddenly, I'm seeing all this slipping away from me," he continued. "I could go into law as a profession, but I've never practiced law full time. If PAC folds up, where else could any of us go? What other partnership would take someone who had overseen the collapse of his firm? And if we went into private practice, how long before this story got out and the customers faded away?"

He got up from his seat and stared out of the window at the lake, his back to the table as if unwilling to look at them while he abandoned his lifetime codes of conduct. "We have to do something drastic, Jack. Now is the time."

The silence lasted for a full minute before Newman spoke. "I sympathize with everything Stephen expressed," she said. "We are all reasonable human beings, but we are facing an unreasonable situation. Despite our collective intelligence, we haven't found any alternative to this."

Whittaker stirred in his seat, fumbled for his cigarettes then subsided as he remembered the smoking ban. "Jesus Christ!" he whispered. "Are we serious? We're planning to have somebody beat up Garry Barton?"

"Any damage that Garry takes will be temporary," cut in Newman, "while we are haemorrhaging permanent lifeblood. We have to do it."

"Jack, are you going to allow this?" Whittaker pleaded with the chairman. Conway shifted slightly in his seat, turning his shoulder on Whittaker. The dismissal was obvious.

Whittaker stood up. "This isn't my war," he said. "I disagreed with Garry's approach to warning you people about your backwardness, but I never disputed his claims until the end when I told him he was wrong. I'm ashamed that I did that, because he wasn't wrong. You've brought this on yourselves and I deeply regret ever being part of it. I'm sorry I let myself be corrupted by the offer of a place on this committee. There's been no honour for anyone on it, and I'm removing myself as of now."

He walked to the door and opened it. "Jack," he said, "you'll have my resignation on your desk in twenty minutes. I'll also file a copy with my attorneys making sure that the date and time of my departure from this firm are clear. I want nothing to do with this partnership's proposed activities, and certainly nothing to do with you people."

Whittaker walked out and let the door close behind him with an expensive swoosh of heavy oak. The death's head stare of Newman followed him and fixed on the closed door for some moments after he had gone.

"Oh Jesus!" whispered Petheram. "I hope to God we know what we're doing. Do you think Andrew would talk to anyone about this?"

"I think not," said Conway. "It would implicate him, one way or the other, and he wouldn't want that. He'll find another position and he'll keep quiet."

"I hope to God that's true," said Petheram.

"I believe in the adage," said Newman softly, "that God tells us to take what we want, then pay for it. We know what we have to take. Let's worry about payment when we can afford it."

There was a small sigh round the table, and Petheram returned to his seat. A perceptible shift in authority had taken place. All eyes seemed naturally to turn to Newman as the leader.

"A year ago," said Newman, "we rescued Mortensen Transport from bankruptcy and traded him back to solvency. It was a result of Stephen's excellent business skills and the tax concessions we wrung from the IRS."

Nods of agreement met her words.

"Stan Mortensen owes us his life," continued Newman. "He knows it, we know it, and Stan is not one to deny his debts."

Silence hung over the room. All of them had some idea of where Newman was taking them, but they bowed to her increasing authority and waited for her instructions.

"Anticipating that we were approaching this situation," continued the woman, studying her hands intently, "I talked to Stan last night. Now we all know that Stan operates in a particularly hard, competitive business, where the ethics and practices are not always those taught at Harvard."

Newman had never made a joke before. But nobody smiled.

"Applying mild, though unconventional pressures has been a requirement in the past for Mortensen," said Newman, "and Stan knows how to do it. He said he has two excellent men who have done this sort of work before. They will hurt Barton enough to scare him severely, but without causing permanent damage. Garry will get the message clearly. Stan says this level of pressure is almost always enough."

She raised her head and stared round the room. "I take it I can advise Stan to proceed?" she asked. She looked at each of them in turn, willing them to answer.

"Do it," said Trent, pushing his spectacles back up his nose.

"Agreed," muttered Petheram, and stood up to stare sightlessly out of the window. Newman's stare moved finally to Conway. He had imitated her pose of resting his hands on the table top, something nobody had ever seen him do before. The scar of his twisted thumb lay open to the world, and Conway was staring at it.

"Jack?" prompted Newman with a touch of impatience.

Conway ignored her. "This happened when I was eighteen," he said, talking softly, as if to himself. "I was in my first year at Harvard, walking back from a bar after finishing the first batch of exams. A couple of thugs jumped me and beat me up, slashing this hand with an ordinary bread knife. It needed twenty stitches."

He looked up from the table, and tears were running down his cheeks. "I promised myself then, that I would never resort to that sort of mindless violence which revealed only a complete moral and intellectual bankruptcy. And yet here you are, telling me to do just that - and to a one-time colleague whom I like and respect. What sort of world is this?"

"One that's forty years older," said Newman, a faint echo of contempt revealing itself. "Just as you are, Jack. And when it comes to fighting for survival, it's hardly the same thing as you experienced. And we are most definitely fighting for our lives. Far from being mindless violence, this is more like war, Jack. This is an action carefully and surgically directed at a source of sickness. It is no more like your experience of flesh being cut than a doctor cutting away a tumour."

For several long moments, the three of them watched Conway. He finally put his hand back under the table and looked up. He stared at each of his partners in turn, then rose and moved to the door.

"Do it, then," he said. He opened the door and walked out.

*　*　*　*

"I am truly sorry about this, Andrew."

Whittaker looked up from his desk drawers where he had been extracting papers and stacking them on the shelf behind him. He looked surprised to see Conway standing in front of him.

"Quite possibly, Jack," replied Whittaker. "But you're in a bigger mess than I am, and you know it."

Conway closed the door and sat down in front of the desk. "Yes, I know it," he said with a sigh. "I seem to have been unable to avoid the loss of the backbone of our consulting force at PAC."

"That's not the real problem, Jack," snorted Whittaker and slammed the desk drawer closed. He sat down and looked hard at Conway. "The problem is that you're now intent on taking revenge on somebody who was trying to assist this firm."

"No. Please, Andrew, don't put it that way." Conway shook his head violently in denial. "I'm totally without any other solution to the problem of stemming the loss of business. If Garry will see the dangers to him of continuing this vengeful attack on us, we can all come out of this intact."

"Intact? What the hell are you talking about, Jack? I'm out of a job. PAC's consulting arm is dead. You've lost a hell of a lot of business. And that bitch Newman is trying to take over the place. This is intact?"

"We're hurting, I agree with you, Andrew. As to Bridget, that's her privilege to aim at my job. The problem, I repeat, is to keep this firm alive."

"And you'll do it by beating up Garry?"

"I simply can't see any other approach, Andrew. It's a horrible idea, I know. My main worry is what you intend to do now?"

Whittaker laughed without humour. "Worrying about my welfare, Jack? I have contacts in the business. I'm not concerned about being unemployed. Or I could try HLM perhaps, and go and work for Garry."

Conway waved a hand in irritation. "No, Andrew. What will you do with your knowledge of our possible plans?"

"Worried I might tell the law?"

"Of course I'm worried, Andrew."

Whittaker rose to his feet and turned his back on Conway. He began tidying the documents on the shelf and transferring them into a cardboard box. "Jack, I think you're a fool," he said. "I think you've lost your control of this firm, and PAC is on the way to oblivion, just as Garry told you. But I've got my own worries, and I'll look after them first."

"Thank you, Andrew. I appreciate that."

Whittaker turned and looked at the chairman. "Jack, watch out for Newman. She's the most dangerous, evil bitch it has ever been my bad luck to meet."

"But for now we need her, Andrew."

"You may need her, Jack. I don't. I'm glad to be out of here, out of Newman's reach, and heading elsewhere. My resignation is on your desk, and I'll mail the copy to my attorney as soon as I get out of here. I've already had someone witness the date and time of the resignation."

"I'm sorry things happened this way, Andrew. I truly wish you the best of luck."

Whittaker picked up the box of papers and his briefcase. "I'll make my own luck, Jack. But I think you've lost control of yours."

He opened the door and walked out of the office. He didn't offer to shake hands.

Petheram was on the phone when the thin shape of Newman appeared in his doorway. He was talking to an attorney on the subject of the financial collapse of a manufacturing company in Indiana, and the chances of Petheram's department getting the assignment to handle the receivership were sounding good to him.

He paused for a second as he saw Newman then waved her to a seat. She entered, closed the door and sat down. Feeling disturbed at this first-ever visit by Bridget to his office, Petheram turned away from her to concentrate on the phone call. Her presence was distracting, and the telephone discussion had a lot of money hanging on it.

"I believe our record is the best advertisement I can offer you," he said to the attorney. "We've made our reputation by trading companies out of this sort of mess and returning them to business. That increases the chances of both of us getting a proper fee."

He knew he had hit the right nerve with the attorney. The offer of the assignment was made, and Petheram grinned to himself. The job was worth at least four hundred thousand, he estimated.

"I'll send the contracts over for your signature by messenger," he said. "Talk to you later." He replaced the phone and turned back to Newman.

"The Jensen Chapter Eleven mess," he said. "We've got the job of financial guardian angels."

"Well done," she replied, which startled Petheram. He had never heard Newman commend anyone in the past.

"Thank you," he replied, and sat back. Newman never made social calls either, so he waited for her to initiate whatever business she had with him.

"You and I have worked well in the past, Stephen," she said. She sat upright in the chair, studying her finely manicured nails with deliberation. "I believe we understand each other."

"I believe so," Petheram said, curious about her intentions. True, they had worked together, he thought, but the working relationship had always been distant, even off-hand. They had never had lunch together, even when both were at the client's office, or after some of the intense battles they had fought with the hard-faced staff at the IRS.

"We've reached a critical stage in PAC's survival," she continued. "One that requires more creative efforts than we have used in the past."

Ah, he thought. *She wants moral support for the decision to damage Garry Barton. What's she going to trade for my approval?* "I think this morning's decision reflects that new direction, Bridget," he said.

"Not everybody was comfortable with it, however," she replied.

Asking how I feel, eh? Not a problem. "I supported the decision, Bridget, as you know. I believe it was the right one."

"And I'm grateful for the support, Stephen. Do you think Jack was entirely in favour?"

"I think Jack hates the concept, but recognizes the necessity of what we're doing."

"Do you think he'll stay in support? Particularly if we have to escalate the process of pressuring Barton?"

That's interesting. So you think we'll have to do more? I wonder why? And you're wondering if Jack will go the distance. Which means you'll need all the support you can get. So here's where the horse-trading starts. "I can't be certain about Jack," he said. "He may not tolerate anything more extreme than we've already initiated."

"That's my worry, too," she replied, and looked up at him. "So will I have your support if any more persuasion is needed?"

His telephone shattered the tense silence, and he waited for two rings until his secretary picked up the call. The pause was a godsend to him, and he thought fast.

"I sometimes worry, Bridget," he said, "that many of the partners are concerned that I may be too young to be head of my department.   I am, after all, theoretically still only the interim head since Geoffrey died."

He looked at her.   She nodded her head in acknowledgement of the trading gambit.   He continued, knowing she understood what he was asking.   "I've heard," he said, "that one or two partners have raised the possibility of bringing in someone from outside to take up the permanent position."

"My experience of working with you suggests that such a move would be wasteful," she replied.   "You have filled Geoffrey's capacious shoes admirably.   If I were in a position to influence such discussions, I would certainly make that point clear."

"Thank you," he said. *Gunning for Jack's position, are you?* "Of course, confirmation in the role should also result in a more equitable distribution of shares," he continued.   "I still have the equity of the junior partner position."

"Unfair," she said.   "I would also hope to rectify that position and have a larger equity position allocated to you."

"Jack opposed that suggestion at the last partners' meeting."

"I believe that when PAC has recovered from its present crisis, a change of leadership might well be discussed at the general meeting."   Her eyes were firmly fixed on his.

Couldn't be a more obvious trade, he thought. *My support for anything she pushes to neutralize Barton and HLM, plus my vote at the partner meeting when the time is right, and I'm home and clear when she becomes chairman, or chairperson, or whatever. Fair enough.* "That would be highly appropriate," he said. "PAC will be facing new challenges, we need new leadership."

"Do you think Andrew Whittaker can be trusted to keep quiet?" she asked.

The sudden topic change was no surprise. The trading was over, and he knew her well enough to know that she wasted no words.

"At least for a time," he said. "I think Andrew will find another position quickly, and he'll be more concerned about getting established with his new firm. I don't think he has any major separate sources of income."

"But after that?"

Petheram shrugged. "Who can tell? He certainly seemed upset by our decision. He liked Garry Barton, I know that, and of course Garry had helped him a lot in building up the consulting practice."

"That's my concern, too," she replied, and stood up. "Thank you for your advice and support, Stephen," she said, and opened the door. "I won't forget it."

Petheram half rose to his feet as she left. *You'd better not,* he thought. *That was a heavy-duty contract we just made.*

He sat back again, and buzzed for his secretary. He had to get a contract out to those legal hyenas on Michigan Avenue if he wanted that lovely four hundred grand to go into the depleted coffers of PAC.

Chapter 9

Finding a new position had not been difficult for Andrew Whittaker. His success at PAC was known, his work record was excellent, and within two days, he had met with friends and one-time colleagues at a similar-sized partnership in Chicago. The same day, he accepted an offer as Director of Consulting to replace a man who had been promoted to a larger city within the same partnership network. Being divorced, his children already adult and on their own, Whittaker worked long hours to establish himself at his new job, getting home after ten o'clock most nights. Still, Whittaker was a worried man. He had stormed out of the meeting with the PAC senior partners, which now seemed like years ago, horrified at the direction being taken. He had watched as Conway's leadership was corroded and usurped by Newman, and his long-time distaste and nervousness about her had risen to the surface. He wanted no more contact with her or anyone at PAC.

The ethics of his situation terrified him, and even worse, he feared for Garry. But he felt trapped. Who could he tell that the PAC partners were intending to have harm done to Garry? He saw difficulties even raising the issue. He could provide no evidence of PAC's intentions. And even if his words were given some credence, and the police investigated PAC, Andrew would then be expected to testify at some sort of inquiry. His new employers might not regard that with great affection.   The Accountants' Old Boy network was as strong as any. He worried, dithered, and did nothing as he tried to sort out his plans.

This night, the middle of his third week after leaving PAC, was much like the others. He turned into the driveway of his house in Evanston, weary from a fourteen-hour day of client meetings and project reviews. He undid his safety belt, pulled his briefcase from the passenger seat and climbed slowly out of the car.

"You're getting too old for this crap," he muttered to himself, feeling the fatigue in every muscle and bone of his fifty-seven-year-old body. They were the last words he ever spoke.

He never heard the small, wheezy pop from the shadows of his house where the bushes rose to head height by the lounge windows. The flicker of flame from the silenced automatic hand gun sharply outlined the leaves and twigs, and reflected off the windows, but Andrew Whittaker didn't see that either. The nine-millimetre slug entered his head just above his right eye, expanded through his brain, and tore a hole the size of a fist out of the back of his skull. Whittaker fell back against his Cadillac and slumped to the floor like a marionette with its strings cut. Blood and brains marked his progress down the side of the white car. Two men moved silently away, unseen in the tree-lined road. A whiff of body odour and stale cigarette smoke was left behind, but Whittaker was unable to note any of that.

* * * *

The high beam in his mirror had been there for the whole way up the freeway from the city, and Garry had become irritated. He was tired enough from working non-stop from seven that morning till well after ten at night, and this sort of nonsense was unwelcome.

"Pass me then, you stupid bastard," he swore as he pulled over to the right lane and slowed down to fifty. At eleven o'clock at night, the freeway was sparsely travelled, and the driver behind him could have passed at any time since Garry had first seen the beam. The car had appeared two miles after Garry had pulled onto the Interstate, and had stayed stolidly behind him. Garry had taken his speed to over seventy, then down to fifty-five and the glaring headlights had stayed in the same position as if flying in formation.

Even with the reduction down to fifty, a speed that no self-respecting driver in Chicago would maintain on empty roads, the glare had tucked in behind him. The two lanes to his left were completely vacant.

"Must be pissed out of his tiny mind and needs me to direct him," growled Garry. To his relief, the turn-off at Lake Avenue was only a mile ahead and he could leave the freeway. He maintained the fifty miles an hour speed then pulled over into the exit lane as soon as he could. To his fury, the following car did the same, and tucked in even closer to him.

For the first time, Garry considered the possibility that the other car was actually following him.

"This is nuts!" he exclaimed, and accelerated sharply across Skokie Boulevard. The other car did the same. Garry took his speed up to fifty along Lake Avenue, for the first time hoping to see a police car waiting for speeders. He knew that Wilmette Police considered Lake Avenue their best source of speeding ticket citations, but this time, not a patrol car was to be seen.

"Right, you bastard!" said Garry. "Let's see you stay with me, Yank! If you haven't driven sports cars on British roads, mate, you're gone." Even with a Lincoln Continental, he was confident he could shake his pursuer in what looked like a large sedan.

Approaching traffic lights, Garry slowed down, then abruptly accelerated. He flung his car round the right corner and used the full force of his V-8 engine to race up to eighty for half a mile, slammed on the brakes and did another screaming right-hand turn into a side street, switching off his lights as he straightened. Fifty yards further, he turned left into another street, stopped, and took his foot off the brake to ensure the rear lights were not on. For ten minutes, he waited, breathing hard from his tension. The streets of Wilmette stayed silent and unoccupied. He was about to move on, when headlights appeared in his mirror again. Sliding down in his seat, he watched as a car moved slowly along the dark street. But it was a compact BMW that passed him and turned into the driveway a few yards ahead of him. It stopped, and a couple got out, gently closed the car doors and walked into the house, talking quietly.

Garry put the Lincoln in gear and drove carefully down the road, turned back onto the main road and navigated his way to his house. No cars were parked anywhere that he could see, and he relaxed, drove into his driveway and stopped, switching off the engine with a sigh of relief.

"Idiot," he muttered to himself. "You're getting paranoid in your old age!" He decided his first idea must have been correct: the other driver had merely needed a leader, perhaps because of drink, and had then made his own way home once in Wilmette.

Fumbling for his door key, he became aware of the odour of stale cigarette smoke and body sweat. Turning, he saw the shadow by his garage. With a lurch of panic he tried to make it to his door. But the shadow became a large man who moved with surprising speed. Garry never saw the fist that made contact with his head, but he felt the flash of pain. The world seemed to become muffled around him. His legs turned to sand and he folded to the ground. A huge arm grabbed him and held him up, and the smell of stale smoke and ripe body became overwhelming. As if through a muffled drainpipe, Garry heard a car drive up and he was half carried, half dragged to the kerb, then thrown into the back of the car. The huge man slid in after him.

Garry's head cleared a little. He was lying on the wide bench seat, his feet toward his captor as the big man slid in. Garry drew up his knees then kicked out furiously, both feet thumping into the chest of his captor. The man gave a muffled "oof!" but didn't move. It had felt to Garry like kicking a heavy sandbag. A massive hand reached out and seized his shoulder. Feeling like a small child, Garry was pushed down to the floor of the car and enormous feet landed on his back. His face was on the floor, and his nose was assailed by odours of dust, old vinyl and oil. The car was obviously large and old, and the rumble of the transmission and the crackle of the muffler said it was also in a poor state of repair.

Garry's heart was pounding with fear. The speed and ferocity of the attack had astounded him, and the terror of his situation was overwhelming. He tried to control his panic and identify the turns the car was making, but after a few wild swings, he was lost.

The ride lasted only a few minutes. It ended with a slow downhill grind through low gears, then the old car stopped with a jerk. The heavy feet lifted away from Garry's shoulders, and the man above him opened the door and slid out.

For the first time he spoke. "Okay, buddy," he said. "You're with me." It was an incongruously light speaking voice. A hand grabbed Garry's shoulder again and he was hauled helplessly out of the car, pulled to his feet. A pair of massive arms wrapped themselves round his chest, holding him motionless.

But Garry knew where he was. The sound of waves came gently from a few yards away, and in the dim moonlight he could see the shadowy bulk of a building across from a car park. He was on Wilmette Beach, near the trees.

A second man got out of the car, smaller than the one holding Garry, but still a big man. Garry was pulled further into the trees then released. He tried to breath, to control the panic. Despite the fear, he was relieved to be away from the unpleasant mix of smells exuded by the large man. But the relief didn't last.

The big man spoke again in his strangely high-pitched voice. "Now listen, buddy," he said. "I've got a message for you. I have to tell you to stop doing what you're doing. Now, believe me, I've no idea what that is, I just deliver the message, right?"

Garry didn't speak.

The man in front of him moved again with frightening speed. His fist took Garry on the side of his head, and he collapsed, dazed and nauseous. The shadow loomed over him, blocking the moonlight. Garry was hauled sharply to his feet and held there.

"I said, right? Did you understand me?" The man might have been discussing the way to the main road. Garry tried to mumble something, but he had no control of his tongue. The fist rammed hard into his gut and Garry doubled over with a grunt of pain. He was allowed to fall to his knees, but another open-handed slap hammered into his face and he fell sideways on the grass.

"Now we'll give you the rest of the message," said the man. "But I want you to understand that if we have to come for you again, this will only be the beginning."

A boot the size of a small boat thundered into Garry's ribs and the pain lit a galaxy of burning suns in his body. He shouted with the agony but the shout was cut off by another kick to his head. He stayed barely conscious as a battery of blows struck him from all directions. He felt blood pouring over his face and he knew that his legs were so bruised that he might not be able to stand up.

"For Christ's sake, Rich, that'll do!" It was the other man speaking for the first time. "I've got a run to St. Louis tomorrow, early. Let's get out of here."

"Shut up, you idiot!" shouted the big man.

"Christ, he can't hear anything," replied the other. "Let's go!"

Garry heard the vehicle start up again and pull away. He started to offer his thanks that he would live through this night, but the pain exploded all through his body and he blacked out.

* * * *

All the world was pain. Grinding shrieks of agony roamed eagerly up and down his body, occasionally dancing a reel with the sickness that curled patiently in his gut. Only one eye would open, and that only partially. When it did, he could see stones, some grass, and a single ant that walked randomly in the tiny space that was his universe.

Garry concentrated on moving, and despite the dreadful protests of every muscle, he stirred, raised his head and looked around him with one eye. He was in the shade of the trees by the car park at Wilmette Beach. The sun was a tiny red arc over the water and the reflection was painful, even through the thunderous pounding in his head. He was shivering with cold.

He knew he had to get help. In his confusion and pain, only one person's face came to him. Clinging grimly to the image of that face, he forced himself to his knees and crawled the endless concrete desert of the parking lot toward the building that he knew housed a water fountain and a telephone. The traverse seemed to take hours and the sun was distinctly higher by the time he had climbed the cliff edge of the sidewalk and reached the water fountain. Resting for a few moments, he forced himself to his feet, and was at last able to wash the blood from his right eye. Somehow remaining upright, feeling the agony of what seemed to be a broken rib, he tried walking across to the pay phone on one wall. His knees objected strongly to the movement, dull pain roaring around his kneecaps, to his hips and down to his ankles.

He leaned against the wall and picked up the telephone. He fumbled in his pockets and found nothing, no change, no wallet. But he remembered his telephone card number. Slowly, peering carefully at each button as he pushed it, he first dialled a number then entered his own number and the credit card number. He slid slowly down the wall to a crouch as he heard the telephone ringing.

When the sleepy voice answered, he knew he was near collapse again. "Micky," he mumbled. "Please come and help me. I'm on Wilmette Beach."

The phone dropped from his hands and he let his head fall to rest on his knees. The morning faded from his consciousness.

Some immeasurable time later, he returned to the world. He was lying on a stretcher, a blanket over him, and his face was clean, still damp from where the blood had been washed away. Confused he looked around, saw several people, two uniforms, a police car and an ambulance.

She wasn't there.

"Back with us?" A man's voice broke through the confusion, and a peaked hat filled the sky above his head.

"What's going on?" whispered Garry. She wasn't there, and it hurt.

"Wish I knew," replied the policeman. "I was hoping you could tell us. We got a call a few minutes ago from a woman saying there was an injured man on Wilmette Beach. She gave her name as Ashley."

Garry smiled weakly.

"Anyone you know?" asked the peaked hat.

"Yes," he said and faded again.

When Garry woke up, he was in a bed. The room smelled of hospital, and Micky was sitting next to him.

"Thanks," he said.

Micky's face was dreadfully serious. She wore no makeup and wore a blue warm-up suit. She was beautiful, he thought.

"What happened?" she asked.

"Two men," he mumbled. "They picked me up outside my house, took me to the beach and beat the shit out of me."

"Good god!" Her face went white, and she touched his hand lying on the bed cover. "Why on earth did you call me?" she asked. "You should have called 911 immediately, it would have been far quicker. You must have collapsed before you hung up the phone, because I couldn't dial out. I had to get up and go down to my car and use the cellular phone."

"Didn't think. Couldn't think," he slurred. "Just wanted you."

"Oh, Garry," she exclaimed. "You don't give up, do you?"

"Your instructions, Miss." He tried to smile, but fell asleep instead.

* * * *

"You really think PAC was behind it?" Peter's expression was horrified.

Garry nodded, and looked down at his scotch. He was sitting in Peter's office at the end of the day and Charlie Levin was with them. Micky had spent the day at the Sullivan Group offices and hadn't come back to HLM.

"The message I was given so forcibly," said Garry, "was to stop doing what I was doing. I think we've pulled the lion's tail a bit too much, and the lion's bitten back."

"Very hard to believe," said Charlie. He sipped thoughtfully at his glass of beer. "I know all those people at PAC. Conway's just too much of a gentleman to resort to this sort of thing, and I've known Stephen since law school. It's not in him."

"I agree," said Garry. "But we've been pulling so much business away from them, and the Sullivan thing must have blown them apart. Maybe they've just lost it."

"Still a stretch," said Peter. "Mind you, Bill Trent's a violent sort of guy. He scares me a bit from what I've seen of him. This is more his line, I suppose."

"I think so," agreed Garry. "But could he swing the others behind him, or do you think he organized this on his own?"

Peter shook his head. "He'd never do anything like this alone. Trent's not a solo player. He needs group support."

"What about your old boss, Andrew Whittaker?" asked Charles. "I don't know him at all. Is he capable of this?"

Garry thought about it. Andrew had a temper, certainly, but he was far too intelligent to resort to violence. And yet there had been a certain planning and organization behind the assault. "Could be, I suppose," said Garry. "This wasn't just a random blow up, the sort of thing Trent would do. It was planned, prepared. Those thugs knew where I worked, where I lived."

"I have awful trouble believing this was planned by PAC," persisted Charlie. "They may be incompetents but none of them would resort to this."

"What about Bridget Newman?" asked Garry. There was a silence round the room.

"Ah!" said Peter.

"Now there's a complete unknown quantity," agreed Charlie. "I have no idea at all if she's capable of such a thing."

Garry thought about the impenetrable black eyes of Bridget Newman, the coldness that seemed to suck the life out of the room and the absence of any friendliness in her dealings with staff and colleagues.

"Garry?"

He looked up and realised the other two were looking at him, waiting for his opinion.

"I think she is," said Garry.

"So do I," said Peter after a moment's thought. "That woman hasn't got a trace of human warmth anywhere in her skinny body."

"What did you tell the cops, Garry?" asked Charlie. "Did you indicate any suspicion of PAC?"

"Hardly!" snorted Garry. "Can you imagine their reaction if I told them? 'Really sir, an old-established firm of certified public accountants has taken out a contract on you, have they sir? How very interesting, sir. Would you mind waiting in this room, sir while somebody comes and talks to you? Yes sir, this room, the one with padded walls and floor?' Very likely that is, what?"

Despite the laughter, the other two wore expressions of worry.

"The trouble is," said Charlie, putting down his beer glass. "We have no way of knowing. But the question still remains. If we assume that PAC did organize that little activity, what are we going to do? Will we accept another PAC client if we're approached?"

The two of them looked at Garry.

"Damn right we do," he said firmly, trying to hide the wave of panic he felt. "No bunch of thugs is going to stop me getting rich, even if they *are* professionally qualified gentlemen."

"Hell, we can't take on any more even if we wanted," protested Peter. "We're stretched enough as it is, trying to handle the first two Sullivan companies this year."

"Oh yeah?" replied Charlie. "Have you seen the pile of letters from auditors and tax people at all levels asking us if we're hiring? Half of them are from PAC, but the word is getting around. People want to come and work for us."

"We have to make a couple of partners in Audit," said Peter. "The work load is getting too high for Micky and me alone."

"That's easy," replied Charlie. "The two who came over from PAC, Anne Bertolli and Clive Carter - outstanding pair."

"Agreed," said Peter with a wide grin. "Isn't this power wonderful? I think we advise them tomorrow morning, and it's time we had a party."

"Splendid thought!" agreed Charlie with enthusiasm. "Where would you suggest?"

"Well, I think we need to get young Ashley zapped again," said Peter with a wide grin at Garry. "It has a wonderful effect on her. So why don't we keep the tradition going and rent that entire bar where we met after the Sullivan presentation?"

"Sounds good to me," said Charlie. "We have a lot of new business, new staff and three new partners to celebrate. After all, we never really marked Garry's ascension to godhood."

Garry pondered the problems of having a major party while still not fully healed, and of probably seeing Micky come with Craig the Wimp. He decided he could handle both.

"Let's have a party," he said, and drained his scotch.

* * * *

"Mister Whittaker was found dead outside his house two weeks ago, Mister Barton. He had been shot in the head by a handgun."

"Oh dear God!" Garry's exclamation interrupted the question the detective was about to ask.

Detective Sergeant Burroughs of the Homicide Squad was a medium-sized man with thinning fair hair. His clothing sense was neat, displayed by a light grey suit, a dark green tie and a white handkerchief folded in his breast pocket. His arrival at the reception desk and request for a meeting with Garry had caused a stir, and Monica the receptionist had almost squeaked when she called Garry.

"The connection between you and Mister Whittaker, could you clarify it for me please, Mister Barton?" Burroughs was polite, but his eyes were sharp and fixed firmly on Garry's face. Garry felt his every twitch would be registered by those clear eyes, despite the air of fatigue that the detective wore. The shock of Burroughs' words was running through Garry's body like a jagged edge of electricity.

"Andrew had been my boss when I worked at Porter, Allen & Conway," said Garry. He felt his hands trembling and saw that Burroughs was studying the tremble with interest.

"And when did you leave that company?" asked Burroughs.

"July of last year."

"And why did Mister Whittaker leave them?"

"Andrew left PAC?" This jolt on top of the news of Whittaker's death left Garry feeling short of breath. It frightened him to see the detective watching every reaction, and he began to feel a terrible sense of wrongness about the situation. "I didn't know. When did that happen?"

Burroughs looked hard at him. "You didn't know? Mister Whittaker had resigned just over two weeks before his death. He had left the premises within an hour of the resignation being handed to the chairman."

"That sounds like something messy happened at PAC," said Garry thoughtfully.

"That's how I see it," agreed Burroughs. "Have you been in touch with Mister Whittaker since leaving your old employers?"

"No."

"That's a decisive answer, Mister Barton. Did you leave Porter, Allen & Conway on bad terms?"

"Yes, I resigned after some stress," replied Garry.

"Between you and Mister Whittaker?"

"Only indirectly. The main stress was between myself and the senior partners there."

"And yet you received a large sum on parting."

Garry looked hard at the detective, and received a weary smile in return.

"We've been checking, Mister Barton," said Burroughs.

"So it seems," replied Garry. "You think I might have reasons for killing Andrew?" The idea that he was a murder suspect was numbing to Garry. It was a first, and not an experience to be repeated. On top of the news Burroughs had delivered, Garry was feeling queasy.

"It's a possibility," replied Burroughs. "I'm not high on it, myself."

"I'm relieved to hear it," replied Garry with sincerity. His answer received another smile.

"I'm more interested in a possible connection between two people, recently employees of the same organization, one gets killed, the other one gets assaulted, both in the space of twenty-four hours," said Burroughs.

Garry stared across the desk. "You know about the assault on me?"

"Naturally." The detective smiled briefly. "And you're still showing the signs of contact with something hostile. We learn about those things at the Academy in Detecting 101. So tell me, Mister Barton, what's the common factor?"

"Coincidence," replied Garry. "Hard to think of a connection. You said it happened the night before I was beaten up?"

"Yes," agreed Burroughs. "What was Mister Whittaker's relationship with the other partners? Stressed, like yours?"

"Hardly," said Garry. "He had just been appointed to the firm's top management committee. He was the partner in charge of management consulting, and he'd been very successful."

"Then why did he leave?"

"I've no idea. I only heard about it when you told me."

Burroughs looked at Garry for a long moment. "You're not telling me everything, are you Mister Barton?" he said.

Garry returned the stare as calmly as he could. "I've told you everything I know," he answered.

"Possibly. But have you told me everything you *think*?"

The man was sharp, decided Garry. "Anything I might think about this could hardly be evidence," he replied. The trembles through his body were slowly fading but the queasiness remained. Garry felt he needed a cold drink badly.

"True enough," admitted Burroughs. "But it might give an overworked homicide detective some idea of what's going on."

Garry thought for a few seconds, and decided to test the waters, remembering the conversation of a few days earlier when he had joked with Charlie and Peter about just this situation. "Alright then," he said. "I think that the senior partners at PAC took out a contract on me. And maybe they did the same to Andrew Whittaker, though I can't think of a reason why they should."

Burroughs stared at him, then laughed out loud. "Yeah, right!" he said derisively.

"You asked," said Garry with a shrug. He was uncertain how he felt to find his suspicions confirmed on how such an idea would be received. The reaction produced a wave of doubt within himself about PAC's responsibility for his beating. *It was a damn silly idea,* he thought.

The detective seemed enormously cheerful, as if the idea had provided a ray of cheer in an otherwise dull existence. "Lawyers I could understand," Burroughs said with a wide grin. "But accountants? Jesus, man! *Accountants!* So tell me, Mister Barton, why would a firm of respectable public accountants take out a contract on two people who had left them recently? Had you stolen corporate secrets from them? Were you blackmailing them about the executive orgies they were having in the boardroom?" His expression was one of delight, as if he had just had the best laugh of the day.

"I can't speak for Andrew Whittaker," replied Garry, working to retain his calm. "But I have certainly taken some business from them, a lot of business in fact, since leaving that partnership."

"And that's enough for them to want to have you roughed up or even killed?" Burroughs was having trouble keeping a straight face. He stood up and straightened his well-cut suit jacket. "Let me know if you get any more rational ideas," he said, and handed Garry a business card.

"I'll do that," replied Garry and led the way to the lobby. He waited until Burroughs had entered the elevator, and he returned to his office, the memory of the detective's wide grin fresh in his mind.

When Garry sat down, the trembles hit him again. The news he had just heard and the implications he had raised himself were too awful to believe. He felt a trickle of sweat run down his back and his collar felt tight. This simply wasn't possible, he thought. He stood up, feeling the dampness of his trousers in his thighs and at his knees where sweat had broken out as well. He walked into the corridor and took a deep gulp of cold water from the cooler in the reception area. The woman at the desk looked at him with a worried expression.

"Are you okay, Mister Barton? You look quite ill."

"I'm fine, Monica," he replied, trying to regain his self-control. "That cop brought some rather bad news about an old friend of mine."

"Oh, I'm sorry. Is he okay now?"

Garry shook his head. Rather than answer more questions, he walked round the reception area to Micky's office. He badly needed to talk, but Micky was out at a client's office. Peter's room was empty also, and feeling a touch of desperation, Garry walked down a floor to the tax department to look for Charlie.

Luckily, the tax partner was in. Charlie looked up from a thick, legal manual and smiled, then looked shocked. "Good grief, Garry, what's happened? You look terrible!"

"I've just had a homicide cop visit me," replied Garry and took the seat across from Charlie's desk.

"Homicide?" Charlie stood up and moved round his desk to the coffee table in the middle of the office. He sat down on the side next to Garry as if not wishing to leave any barrier between them.

"Andrew Whittaker's dead," said Garry. His throat felt tight. "He was shot outside his house the night before I was beaten up."

"Oh my God!" Charlie slumped in his seat. "Have the cops any idea of who did it?"

"Not that they told me. For a time, I think they believed I might have been behind it."

"Do they still?"

Garry shook his head. "Doesn't seem like it."

"I'm relieved to hear it," said Charlie in a dry tone. He sat up with a jerk. "Was Andrew still with PAC?"

"No, that's a curious point. Andrew apparently left PAC only a couple of weeks before. The cop said he walked out very suddenly, within an hour of his resignation going to Conway."

Charlie stared at him. "There could be two reasons he did that. Either he knew of potential legal troubles hitting the partnership and wanted to be out before the shit hit the fan, or..."

"Or he had a problem with the board's decision to have me roughed up?"

"Exactly."

Garry laughed, a thin, un-amused sound. "Nice to think that Andrew had some semblance of ethics left in him."

"Possibly." Charlie's face showed dismay. "But if that's the case, maybe Andrew was killed because somebody at PAC was worried about him talking to the law."

"That would confirm that it was PAC behind my little skirmish, then?"

"As your attorney, I could make pretty strong circumstantial evidence for that conclusion," agreed Charlie.

"Oh Charlie, this is bad stuff," muttered Garry. "What the hell have I brought to this partnership?"

"A hell of a lot of money, Garry. It's not your fault if Conway and his gang have gone totally off their heads."

"We'd all better take a lot of care," said Garry, and stood up.

"Especially of Micky. I'd worry about her, Garry. She's a way of getting at you."

"Jesus Christ," said Garry. He walked out, badly needing to talk to his lady.

* * * *

"Why did Mister Whittaker leave this company?"

Burroughs was sitting comfortably in Conway's office, across from the Chairman's desk.

Conway smiled. "Firm," he said.

"What?"

"Firm. Professional organizations like this are known as firms."

Burroughs shrugged. "Okay. Why did Mister Whittaker leave this *firm?*" He delicately stressed the last word.

"Differences arose in our respective philosophies of business ethics," replied Conway. His patrician air and the slight note of contempt in his voice were clearly getting to Burroughs, who was having trouble maintaining the air of an investigating cop and the control of the discussion that went with it.

"Such as?" Burroughs demanded.

"We couldn't agree on the relative importance of management consulting within the firm's range of services."

"But you'd just appointed him to the management committee, hadn't you? Isn't that your top group, the people who run this place?"

Conway looked at him. "Yes it is. How did you know that?"

"Sources."

"Yes, we had just appointed Andrew," agreed Conway after a tiny pause. "But it didn't work out. In fact, it made things worse by bringing out the differences more obviously."

"Was the parting amicable?"

"I think so," replied Conway. "He received excellent references from us, and he was snapped up by another firm immediately."

"And yet I understand that Mister Whittaker left these offices within an hour of resigning. He even went to the point of having the precise date and time of his resignation documented and witnessed."

"That is not uncommon, Detective Burroughs," replied Conway. "You must understand that professional partnerships are unusual organizations. If a law suit is filed against us, and such things happen quite frequently, all partners are equally liable to any possible court-enforced damages. Ensuring the precise departure details are known would be a safe thing to do for any partner to protect himself against future possible court actions."

"You're expecting a law suit, Mister Conway?"

Conway smiled. "No sir, I am not. But surely you have seen how frequently such litigation against auditors is launched when companies fail. It's as much a fact of our lives as malpractice suits are for the medical profession."

Burroughs grunted, and changed tack. "Could there be any connection between Mister Whittaker's murder and the assault the following night, on another ex-employee of yours, Garry Barton?"

Conway's eyes opened wide, and his jaw sagged a moment before he regained control. Burroughs saw the signs of shock and felt his spirits and confidence rise a little at this moral victory of the working stiff over the aristocracy.

"A connection?" stammered Conway. "How could there be any connection?" His astonishment appeared genuine to Burroughs.

"I'm asking you. It's just a thought."

"I can't possibly imagine any connection between..." For a fraction of a second, Conway hesitated. "Between the two incidents," he finished.

"Doesn't seem like you're quite certain of that, Mister Conway. Something occurred to you?"

Conway was back to his patrician self again. "No," he said. "I'm certain the two incidents are unrelated and coincidental."

"Then can you think of any reason why Mister Whittaker was murdered?"

"Detective Sergeant Burroughs," said Conway firmly, "we have over a thousand homicides a year in the Chicago region, according to the figures published in the newspapers. Andrew was probably killed by a mugger, or just for the fun of it, like most of them."

"That's probably correct," agreed Burroughs, the weariness in his face seeming greater than when he had come in. After a few more questions, he left.

Conway sat still at his desk, the shock of the detective's question racing round his brain.

A connection? How in God's name could there be any connection? he kept asking himself. He couldn't remember what it was that had entered his mind so briefly and which had caused his small hesitation when answering the detective's question. But the fact that something had caused it disturbed him greatly. He was certain that it had interested the detective too, and that thought left a crawling sense of uneasiness in his gut.

Chapter 10

The atmosphere in the boardroom was pleasantly relaxed and the chairman seemed more interested in the flotilla of sailboats on the Lake on this beautiful, sunny, July morning.

"We may have stemmed the flood," said Newman. "No clients have expressed any sign of moving to another firm, and the reductions in fees have been well received."

"It seems Barton got the message," agreed Trent. "That was a good move on your part, Bridget."

"I think so," she agreed. "Stan Mortensen tells me his men left Barton on Wilmette Beach with no permanent damage."

"Just what did they do?" asked Petheram. His interest seemed academic, without personal involvement, almost the question of an attorney in court.

"The worst damage was a broken rib as far as I have been able to find out," replied Newman. "The rest was just bruises. He was back at work in a day or two."

"And HLM certainly seems to have gone quiet," agreed Trent.

"I think that may be because they are fully occupied servicing some of our old clients," said Conway, turning his eyes back from the water. "I believe you are all forgetting the damage done to us so far."

"We haven't forgotten, Jack," replied Newman. The power in the room definitely rested with her now. "I was about to suggest we discuss some of the recovery solutions we should adopt. Bill, I believe you had some ideas?"

Trent looked a little uncomfortable, his eyes moving between Newman and Conway for a few seconds then he spoke. "I've told all our clients we'll be introducing more advanced computer audit systems to most of them by their next financial year ends," he began. "I've had a couple of preliminary talks with well-qualified people who could join us to assist with that process. I think a couple of them will agree to come aboard."

"And where does that leave George Elliot?" asked Petheram. "Does he agree to this new policy?"

Trent looked embarrassed. "Elliot may have nothing to contribute. I think he'll be looking elsewhere fairly soon."

"And do you think this will be enough?" asked Petheram. "We have a lot of training in these new systems to get through. What if HLM approaches other clients in the meantime?"

"It's most unlikely that will happen," said Newman. "I believe Mortensen's men have given HLM very good reasons to stay away from us."

"And if they try it, we'll just have them give Garry another visit, eh?" said Trent with a smile, pushing his spectacles back up his nose.

"Only with a little more action, I suppose?" Petheram seemed amused at the idea.

"As you say," said Newman sardonically. "But that's highly unlikely."

"Let us all hope so," broke in Conway. "Our business lives depend on it."

"You have nothing to worry about, Jack," said Newman with one of her rare smiles. "The crisis is over."

"And there's no risk of anyone connecting us to Barton's accident?" Trent looked directly at Newman who continued to study her hands on the table.

"None at all," she whispered. "The only risk came from Andrew Whittaker."

"That was terrible," said Petheram. "Shot outside his own home! Ghastly!"

"True," replied Newman. Her face held no expression. "But a fortunate stroke of luck for us all. Gentlemen, take it as an omen. Our problems are over."

* * * *

Garry had debated internally at length on the question of taking a date to the HLM party. Eventually, he decided it was necessary, if only to protect himself against the emotional damage of seeing Micky arrive with Craig.

Since she had seen him in hospital, Micky had been cool toward him. After the evening at her apartment she had kept her distance even more, which

Garry had put down to her embarrassment at her own behaviour.

To lessen the pain of seeing her, Garry called an Australian girl with whom he had once had a tempestuous affair lasting only a few weeks. The affair had cooled into friendship, though they had rarely seen each other in recent months, mainly because of Garry's work-load.

"Garry, my favourite ex-lover!" she exclaimed with a laugh when he called her. "It's been a while."

"Totally my fault, Rosemary," he said. "Life has been a complete zoo for some months!"

"And which wild, uncontrollable woman is keeping your cage warm for you?" Garry could almost see the smile on her generous mouth.

"It's a bachelor cage, I'm afraid," he said. "Not through lack of ambition, however."

"But the lack of a woman who can replace me in your libidinous fantasies, huh?"

"As if anybody could ever do that, Ro!" Garry remembered the storm of some of their passionate moments and grinned to himself. They had been good for each other for the time it had lasted. "I need a favour of you, if Mark could understand."

Mark was a Canadian businessman who had replaced Garry in Rosemary's life some weeks after their affair had ended. Garry had met him, and they had got on well.

"Mark's in Singapore on business for a couple of weeks," she replied. "How can I help?"

"Will you come to a company party with me?" he asked. "As a partner, I should really appear to be all conventional and attached, even if only temporarily. I can offer you free grog all night and a limousine ride there and back."

"How could a wild colonial girl like me refuse an offer like that?" she said with a laugh. "Now tell me the real reason for the invitation. Apart from unrequited lust for my gorgeous body."

"How well you know me, dear lady. While I can still lust for you, I bow to Mark's prior claim. But my true love has been passed to a lady called Micky Ashley. She's a partner at my place."

"And she'll be there with somebody else?"

"Sometimes, young Rosemary, you're too bright for your own good. Or mine. Yes, the lovely Micky will be there with some poof called Craig. She's pretending to be engaged."

"Pretending?"

"Honestly Ro, I know Micky and I have something special. But she won't let go of the safety blanket."

"In this day and age, who can blame her? So do you want me to tell her what a raging stud you are in bed?"

"No!" he said with a chuckle. "I doubt you'll get the chance for that. Just be there to protect my fragile ego, please."

"That I can do. I'll be interested to see just what sort of woman has got your knickers in a knot again."

"A special one," he replied seriously. "A lot like you."

"Heaven help us," she said. "Two sex-goddesses at the same party? Can the country stand it?"

"We'll try hard." He hung up, feeling a lot more confident about his ability to see Micky with another man.

A week later, Garry picked up Rosemary in the limousine he had rented. Feeling expensively decadent sitting in the back, while a driver handled Chicago's traffic, he called her on his mobile phone as they reached her apartment block, and then waited for her on the sidewalk. When she came out of the door he remembered why he had been so obsessed with her. She was quite lovely, with a body that caused heads to turn. He grinned with pleasure and took her arm, appreciating the look of admiration the limo driver gave her.

"Miss Swanson, you are a delight to behold," he said as the vehicle moved off. She was wearing a close fitting, burgundy gown and a dangerously distracting neckline. "You do scrub up well, I have to admit."

"Enough to cause the Princess to get jealous?" she said with a small laugh.

He echoed it, and took her hand. "I wish I had Mark's intelligence," he said. "I'll have to write him a letter of thanks for your company tonight."

"He'll appreciate it," she said, and settled into the luxurious seat of the limo. They sat in a companionable silence the rest of the way to the hotel.

The atmosphere of excitement hit them as they entered the top floor bar. The staff of Haywood, Levin and Marsh had experienced a remarkable year and the party had clearly begun. For a few moments, Garry and Rosemary stood by the doorway and looked over the room. In one group by the bar Garry saw Charlie Levin with a dark, elegant lady he assumed was Rebecca, his wife whom Garry had yet to meet. He pointed them out to Rosemary.

"Can't you just see the intelligence in that man?" she said with an exaggerated sigh. "I've always loved men like that."

"Which is why you adored me so much," agreed Garry, prompting a small dig in his ribs. He winced from the pain, despite the strapping round the broken bone, but managed to hide the movement from Rosemary. He looked further and saw Peter Haywood and Pauline in another group.

"That's Peter," said Garry, with a small wave. "My mentor and the man to whom I owe all this."

"Nice buns," she said.

Garry snorted with laughter. "Lady, you are uncontrollable," he said, and began to lead her into the room.

"Where's the Princess?" she asked. Garry shook his head, feeling a small knot of tension inside.

"Can't have arrived yet," he muttered, and walked up to the group with Peter and introduced Rosemary around. Later, he moved to a small group where Anne Bertolli and Clive Carter stood. Both were glowing with the excitement of having recently been invited into the partnership, and their welcome for Garry was bright and glowing.

"Garry, how lovely!" said Anne and introduced him to a stocky young man named Stuart who was her fiancé. The four of them split off and formed their own circle, and conversation flowed cheerfully for several minutes until Garry suddenly saw the new arrivals at the door. Rosemary sensed the tension in him and looked away from her discussion with Stuart on the subject of Australia's topless beaches.

"Oh-oh, the Princess has arrived?" she said softly to Garry. He nodded, unable to look away.

Micky was wearing a long blue dress that left her shoulders bare. Her hair was upswept in a style Garry had never seen her wear before, and he found the whole effect stunning.

"She's lovely, Garry," murmured Rosemary. "I can see the reasons for this confusion. The bloke with her is a bit wet, though. Can't imagine why she's with him."

Garry dragged his eyes away from Micky and studied Craig. He was a tall, slender man with light brown hair and a face that seemed pleasant but showed no great personality. As he studied them, Micky saw him, just as Rosemary deliberately moved closer to Garry and placed her arm in his. Micky seemed to stare for a few seconds then led Craig into the room.

"Thought I'd give her something to worry about," chuckled Rosemary into his ear, and Garry had to laugh with her.

"I think you and Mark had better get married before you get yourself into trouble," he said, smiling down at her.

"We are," she said cheerfully. "Next spring."

"That's wonderful!" he exclaimed and kissed her, looked up and saw Micky had brought Craig into the group just at that moment. Her face seemed tight, he thought.

"Hello, Micky," he said, as controlled as he could. "Can I introduce Rosemary Swanson, a countrywoman of mine?"

He watched, fascinated as the two women exchanged smiles, Rosemary radiating warmth and friendliness, while Micky seemed uncertain and reserved. Then Micky introduced Craig.

Garry shook hands with him. "Hello, Craig," he said. "I've heard a lot about you. You're a lawyer, I understand."

"Yes, I am," agreed Craig, showing some relief at being given an opportunity to talk. Anne Bertolli jumped in with a question to him, which gave Craig a chance to tell her about a case he was involved in. Garry smiled at Anne's sensitivity then felt a pressure on his arm as Rosemary nudged him.

"The Princess is in a right tizzy," whispered Ro. "This is the night, mate."

He looked at her beautiful profile with a small smile on her lips. "I'll invite you to my wedding if you'll invite me to yours," he said.

"It's a deal, though you're already on the invitation list," she replied and grinned widely. It made the confidence flow through him like a spring tide.

"I think we need a round of drinks," he said loudly to the group of six and was immediately applauded by Stuart and Anne. "What'll you all have?" Garry asked.

Receiving a list of requests, he raised his eyebrow at Micky. "This needs two," he said. "Micky, will you help me get them?"

She seemed confused for a second then nodded and moved with him to the bar. They stood together for a few seconds in silence, tension radiating from Micky until Garry spoke.

"She's an ex-girlfriend," he said. "Once, she made my senses spin like crazy. In the spring, she's getting married to a man I like enormously, and I intend to go to the wedding, hopefully with you."

She looked seriously at him for a moment then smiled. "I was over-reacting, wasn't I?" she said.

He nodded. "Not if it mattered to you," he said, his breath catching in his throat.

"It matters more than I could have known," she said in a small voice. "Garry, what are we going to do?"

"Are we going to do something?" he asked, uncertain just where the conversation was going.

She nodded. "It was always going to happen," she said. "I knew it when you first came to my office. I've fought it all the way because I was safe and secure where I was."

"And bored out of your skull, too," he added.

She smiled and shook her head. "Not really," she said. "Just not disturbed or excited. Safe. Nobody making demands on me."

"And so now we're here - wherever here is."

She smiled at him, and he felt his insides almost turn over. "Here is where you and I start a crazy, disturbing and undoubtedly exciting existence," she said. "With lots of demands on both of us."

"Together, I assume?"

She chuckled and nodded. "Not much point, otherwise."

They looked at each other for another moment, until he was interrupted by the barman asking for their order. Garry tended to that matter for a few minutes while six drinks were poured. Then he turned back to her.

"What we do is this," he said, looking into her eyes. "You spend the evening with Craig, and at the end he takes you home and leaves you there. I do the same with Rosemary, and you and I both play at being very proper partners of this very proper accounting firm. Tomorrow, I call you, and we go for lunch somewhere outrageously expensive and romantic. Then I can tell you how much I love you without being shot down. Sometime after that, if the idea still is okay with you, you'll have to tell Craig he's on his own.   Within minutes, I hope."

Her eyes sparkled. "The idea's okay with me now," she said. "I'll tell him tonight. I don't think he'll really mind. He's determined to be a judge by the time he's forty and I'd only get in his way. A career woman is a scary concept to Craig."

"Then let's get started," he said, and picked up the tray of drinks.

"We could change a small item on that schedule," she said, touching his sleeve lightly. He raised an eyebrow at her. "You could call me tonight when you get home," she said. "I have no doubt I'll be home before you are."

"I'll get a complex if you keep having brilliant ideas like that, woman! I shall call you indeed."

Only a small laugh greeted him and he carried the tray of drinks back to the waiting group. Craig looked uncertainly at Micky's radiance, but he took his glass of beer without comment. As Garry gave Rosemary her drink, she grinned at him.

"Two weddings?" she asked.

"Two weddings," he agreed. "But yours first."

"It's a deal," she said and waved a hand at Micky who smiled happily at her.

* * * *

"Garry, get your ass in here!"   The voice was

Peter's, loudly reverberating through the wall between their two offices. Garry grinned to himself, and walked round to the next room.

Peter still had his hand on the telephone where he had replaced it and he was scribbling notes on a pad. He looked up as Garry walked in and took a seat across the desk from him.

"You bellowed, sir?" said Garry solemnly, like an English butler asking if his master had rung.

Peter grinned at him.   "That was Carswell's president on the phone," he said. "He wants to talk to us."

"Carswell's? Do I know them?" Garry was unsure, though the company name seemed familiar.

"Big firm of earthmoving equipment suppliers in Barrington," replied Peter. "You should. They're a client of PAC's."

Garry felt as if a fist had rammed into his guts. All the forgotten fears surfaced again, and he stared at Peter. "Oh," he said helplessly.

Peter didn't recognize the fear in him. "Oh? Is that all you can say? This is a big...." He stopped and looked confused for a moment. "Oh shit," he said. "I'd forgotten."

"Actually, so had I," admitted Garry. "And we're still not sure it was PAC the first time, either."

"No, but the possibility has to be there. The fact that Andrew Whittaker left PAC so suddenly just a few days before you were attacked, and then got killed makes me suspicious."

Garry had expressed the same crawling worry to Charlie Levin after Burroughs' visit. "Do you think it possible that Andrew left because of the decision to go after me? And that PAC had him killed to keep him quiet?" The idea had haunted Garry ever since that moment

Peter stared back, a look of distaste on his face. "Was Whittaker capable of endorsing the hit on you?"

"He never struck me as somebody who would go along with that sort of lunacy," said Garry. "But there again, I didn't think Petheram or Conway were, either."

"Conway and Petheram have nowhere else to go," said Peter. "Andrew had a good reputation in consulting. He found another home easily enough."

"I suppose so," muttered Garry, lost in the appalling possibilities that these thoughts had been raising for some weeks. "This is a bitch, Peter."

"I'll tell Carswell's we can't take their business," said Peter.

Garry was horrified. "Like hell you will! I said it before, no bunch of thugs is going to stop me from doing what I want to do."

"We'd better have a partners' meeting then," said Peter, looking doubtful. "We should all talk about this one. It's nasty."

"Call it, by all means," replied Garry. "But set up that meeting with Carswell's."

"But what if was really PAC behind it?" objected Peter. "You know what that goon said. They'll be coming for you again. And if it's the same people who shot Andrew, we need to watch out."

"I can't say the idea thrills the hell out of me," agreed Garry. "Maybe I should go and talk to Conway myself. Tell him if he tries any such silliness I'll sell his balls as cat food."

"He'll just deny it and throw you out of the office," objected Peter.

Garry nodded. "But his reaction might be interesting," he said. "I could tell him I'd spoken to Andrew Whittaker just before he was killed. That should scare the bejesus out of him."

"You could also get a lawsuit for defamation," said Peter. "No, forget that course of action. For the moment, at least."

"You're the boss," agreed Garry, and stood up. "Now, check our calendars and make that appointment. I'm nowhere as rich as I want to be."

The two friends smiled at each other, but their smiles faded as they each returned to work.

Chapter 11

"The bastard! Oh Jesus, the stupid bastard!"

Trent's voice bellowed through the boardroom, as he waved the letter with the Carswell logo. Conway, who had just passed the letter to his partner, winced, as if in pain.

"Who, Bill? The president of Carswell's?"

"No, Barton! I thought you said he'd been warned off!" Trent glared furiously at Newman, something he could never have done in the past. She stared back and Trent's rage wilted under the black gaze.

"We don't know how this approach from Carswell's resulted," said Newman. "We don't know yet if HLM will refuse to consider the business, either. However, this simply means that a more emphatic message must be sent to Barton."

"I agree with that," said Petheram. "There's every chance that the other partners at HLM decided to respond to the Carswell approach, and they may not have realized yet that we had initiated the previous message to Barton." A look of anticipation crossed his face.

Conway looked curiously at his colleague. "Only a few weeks ago, Stephen, you were showing enormous distress at the idea of violence on Barton," he said, softly. "Now I get the impression you're rather looking forward to some more."

Petheram looked embarrassed. "I don't know if that's it, Jack. But I have to admit that this is a different kind of business approach. There's some excitement in using these sorts of tactics."

"That's how I see it," added Trent. "Maybe this appeals to the hunter in us, but there is definitely an added dimension to directing this sort of defensive measure."

Conway looked away in distaste.

Newman smiled at him in almost a friendly manner. "I think you see it too, Jack, but you're too well-mannered to show it," she said.

Conway shook his head. "I may have agreed to this, and I may have seen the necessity in the absence of anything else. But as for liking it? There's something sick going on here."

She looked at him for a long moment. "We're agreed then, that we instruct Mortensen to step up the attack on Barton?"

"How far will they go this time?" asked Petheram with a look of excitement on his face.

She shrugged. "I leave that judgment to the experts," she said, folded up her papers, and rose to her feet. "I'll call Mortensen this afternoon."

"Tell him we want results thus time," said Trent. He too, looked interested. "I'm not impressed by their performance so far."

Newman looked down on the two of them with contempt. "This is just a business necessity," she said coldly. "Don't get to like it too much."

Trent and Petheram looked down at the table like chastised children and Newman walked out quietly. Trent and Petheram gathered up their files and stood up, when Conway spoke.

"Stay a moment, gentlemen," he said. They looked briefly at each other then resumed their seats. The discomfort in both of them was evident. "I would like your honest opinion," continued Conway. "Without the influence of Bridget on your speech."

There was a moment of silence at the table.

"In your views, is this the way to tackle the problem?" asked Conway. "You first, Bill, as it was your idea originally. Is violence the best approach?"

Trent looked embarrassed. "Jack, I'll admit that when I first raised the subject, it was more in anger than serious. But the more I think of it, the more it makes sense."

"Why?"

Trent looked more and more like a small boy caught in a lie. He looked around the room as if seeking moral support, pushed his glasses back in place and turned to Conway.

"We don't have time to repair the damage unless HLM stops attacking us," he replied. "I'll admit it to you as I have to Stephen..."

"And also to Bridget?" broke in Conway.

"Er... yes, I've spoken to Bridget," said Trent, his distress showing even more. "I'll admit that Barton was right about a number of things, especially on computer audit. I'm taking steps to correct that, despite what George Elliot says. But I can't do anything if we keep losing clients. Barton has to be stopped!"

"And how much of that is your genuine opinion, and how much of it is Bridget's pressure?" Conway's tone was icy with contempt.

"Jack, I think we can make our own decisions," said Petheram.

"Oh really?" Conway turned to the other partner. "And are those decision based on the welfare of the firm, or on your own individual futures?"

"Pardon?" Petheram looked blank.

"Don't treat me like some over-the-hill old fool," snapped Conway. "I know that Bridget has talked to each of you. It's obvious she's looking to replace me fairly soon.   What has she offered you both? Guaranteed support if you go along with her now?"

"My discussions with Bridget must remain my own business, Jack," said Petheram firmly.

Conway stared at the smaller man for a few seconds then swung his eyes to Trent. "How about you, Bill?"

Trent flushed and wouldn't meet the chairman's eyes. "We've talked, yes," he said. "But not about replacing you."

For a few more moments, Conway studied both his partners. "Let's get back to this war against HLM," he said, his tones more relaxed. "I'll ask you again. Is this the way to defeat HLM? Stephen?"

"Jack, I was completely against the idea at first," replied Petheram. "But I agree with Bill. We don't have time to repair the damage if HLM keeps up this guerrilla action against us. Somehow, we have to slow them down."

"What's wrong with competing on the basis of professional competence?" Conway's tone was calm. "We've done that well for the last sixty years."

"Because we've fallen too far behind," protested Trent. "I'll admit a lot of that is my fault, I listened to Elliot too much. But I can't catch up that fast, Jack."

"So we surrender the firm to the modern management tactics of Newman, is that it?" Conway's expression was bitter.

"Jack, if we come out of this, you're still the chairman," said Petheram. "You'll have led the firm out of the depths and recovered. Not Bridget, not anyone else."

"So you're both convinced that doing physical harm to an ex-colleague who did the firm a great deal of good, that's the way to do this?" Conway's tone was neutral, but his words were acidic.

"I'm sorry, Jack, but I am," replied Trent. Petheram nodded his agreement.

Conway stood up and walked out of the boardroom without another word.

"Christ!" said Trent, letting out a long breath.

"He won't help us," rasped Petheram, and followed the chairman from the room.

Petheram walked hurriedly to his office and closed the door to let himself think. Things had taken on a momentum of their own, he decided. Instead of being in control, as he normally was, he felt at the mercy of the influences working on the firm. Conway's words had been painful, because Petheram knew that inside of himself, he really was looking for strong leadership which Jack was failing to provide and which Newman was demonstrating.

But at the same time, he was remembering Andrew Whittaker's words in his office some time ago. Bridget was certainly demonstrating leadership and influence, but was it for the good of the firm or of Newman? Petheram was horribly mixed as to his opinion. He was also unhappy at his own realization that he wanted physical damage applied to Garry Barton. Whether that was because he sincerely felt that such a course of action would achieve the objective of dissuading HLM from further encroachment on PAC's clients, or because he wanted revenge for his own failings, he could not say. And that bothered him just as much. He pressed the coded buttons on his telephone for a rapid dial of a number.

Her voice was a lushness of erotic promise. "This is Helen."

He took a deep breath. "It's Stephen. I hope you're free this evening."

Her throaty laugh gave him goose bumps. "Of course, darling," she said. "You're very special to me, Stephen."

"About nine then? I have champagne on ice and lots of that caviar stuff you like so much."

"Nine it will be, darling."

He disconnected the phone call and took a deep breath. He really needed the special talents of Helen this evening.

Nobody was going to take that away from him. Nobody. Despite the heavy eyelids and the lassitude that held Petheram on the edge of sleep, that fact was clear to him. After experiencing another evening of stratospheric heights of sexual frenzy with Helen, Petheram could not wave goodbye to them. Nothing would stand in the way of having more of the same. *Even if they had to kill Barton...* For a second, he woke up fully as the shock of what he had just thought reached his fuzzy mind. To hell with it, he decided, falling back again on the silk pillow. If they had to kill Barton then Bridget's contacts would take of it. Nothing could come back on him, he was certain. *Hell, let's just decide to kill him anyway*, he mused. *The little bastard deserves it. God, those fantastic breasts...*

Petheram fell asleep as happy as he could ever remember being in his life before.

* * * *

Conway was having painful thoughts and was unable to sleep. After three hours of restlessness that was causing Madeleine obvious difficulties, he got up, put on a light dressing gown and went down to his study at the rear of his house. He took the armchair by the window and sat heavily in it, feeling strength draining from him. Much as his authority within PAC was doing, he mused in some pain.

"Christ," he muttered. "How the hell did I let it get to this point?" The dark window declined to respond. He stared at his distorted reflection in the glass and felt his pain. "Dad, I never intended this to happen," he said softly. He had spent many hours this way in the past, seeking advice or discussing business concerns with the imaginary ghost of his dead father. Conway had always found the sessions useful. They made him think about how his father would have tackled the problem, and he usually found an answer.

"Jack?"

The voice from the doorway made Conway jerk with surprise. He hadn't heard Madeleine coming.

"What's happened, Jack?" she asked, moving into the room.

Conway struggled to lift the depression enough to be able to reply. "More than I can tell you," he said. "I'm really afraid that it's gone beyond recovery."

She came and sat in the armchair next to his. "The firm?" she asked.

He nodded. "The firm," he said. "The firm my grandfather founded together with yours. The firm my father and your father built up even more. I think I've lost it."

She stayed silent. They had been married over thirty years and childhood friends for twenty years before that, and she could follow his mood. She knew he would tell her.

"I let them throw out Garry Barton about a year ago," he said after a few minutes of silence. "I was out of town, it was that week you and I were in New York. When I got back, Bridget had almost taken control of the place."

A small indrawn breath met his words. Madeleine had expressed her detestation of Bridget Newman many times over the years, but had never said more, knowing Newman's value to the firm.

"I met Garry at the Christmas party a couple of years ago," she said. "I liked him."

"So did I," said Conway. "And he was good. Built up a useful consulting practice for Andrew. But he was just too quick to tell the firm about our shortcomings."

"And Bridget didn't like being told," replied Madeleine. It was a flat statement. "So she killed the messenger."

Her words made Jack shiver. He couldn't tell his wife just how true her words were. "Pretty well," he replied. Silence returned to the room.

"I'm sick of it," Conway said abruptly. "Bridget can have the damn place if she wants it."

"And what will she do with it?" Madeleine's voice was cold.

"Probably kill it, like she kills everything else," snapped Conway. His words sent a streak of ice through him. He recognized his own sudden insight. Newman was a killer. In her black, shrouded soul, Newman attracted death. Conway looked at his wife for the first time since she had come in.

"The time for a Conway or a Porter to be involved in the place is over, Madeleine," he said. "It's not our world any more."

"You're hiding your head in the sand," she replied coldly. "What you mean is that you've screwed up. Our families built the firm up and you've destroyed it in less than a year."

Conway hunched his shoulders as if defending himself against a blow.

"You never were the man your father or your grandfather were, I've always known that, Jack," she continued. "My father told me that, and he was right. I don't plan on living with a failure."

She got up from her seat and walked out. Conway stared at the wall for a long time, his insides feeling cold at his failure and his recognition of the truth of

Madeleine's words. He knew her well enough to know that she would be gone by the next day.

"Damn you, Barton," muttered Conway. His career was over, Conway could see that, and so was his marriage. He had salted away enough money over the years to retire in extreme wealth, but that was insufficient comfort. He had presided over the death of old Harrison Conway's firm, and nothing could ease that pain.

"I hope they kill you," muttered Conway, and sensed the flood of fury that ran through him. He had made much of opposing the idea of violence against Barton, but he knew that inside himself, he wanted it to take place. Somebody had to pay for the death of his firm. Frightened as he was by the evil within Newman, he knew he would wait and see how she would persuade them to agree to the death of Barton. And persuade them she would, Conway had few doubts. Newman had caused the murder of Andrew Whittaker, he knew that, and another death would be simple for her.

He would announce his retirement as soon as this crisis was over, he decided. And if Newman wanted his office, so be it. He wanted nothing more to do with the place.

* * * *

Walking out of the Regency Hotel, Garry felt good. He had finished a successful business dinner with three vice-presidents of a hardware distribution company in Atlanta. Within an hour, they had agreed on a sizeable consulting project and had then forgotten business and talked freely about a range of topics. As always, Garry's Australian heritage had provoked interest, and he had entertained them all with stories of the extraordinary land down under. "Crocodile Dundee, I owe you one," he muttered to himself, and set off on the short walk to the multi-story car park block or two from the hotel.

Reaching the building, he took the elevator up to the fifth floor and began to walk toward his Lincoln. He saw a small movement out of one eye, turned his head, and was just able to see a large, bulky man move out of the shadow of a small pick-up truck. The figure was frighteningly familiar. Garry turned back to the elevator and the stairway next to it, flung open the door to the stairs and began racing down the steps, a pounding fear in his stomach. He heard the door slam open again behind him, and the thunder of heavy boots on the concrete stairs. The man called Rich was in pursuit. Garry reached the second floor as a party of young people dressed in formal tuxedos and ball gowns walked up towards him. They were chattering loudly. Garry ran straight at them, dived into the middle of the group, and forced his way through. Loud yells and a few screams accompanied the effort but he ignored them and ran on. A few seconds later, the noise intensified as Rich hit the same group. In the confusion, Garry reached the ground level, flung open the door and was on the street. He looked around him in a panic. There was nobody near. He turned to his right, heading towards Michigan Avenue, lights and safety, breaking into a run after only a few steps.

Across the road, in the shadow of a doorway, he saw the second man move into the open and begin to follow. Another wave of fear ran through Garry and he accelerated. He found himself reacting like a hunted animal. He turned, let the man reach him and swung his foot heavily straight into the man's groin. The man screamed and fell to the ground. Feeling no pity, Garry kicked hard at the man's head, and ran for the lights of the city.

But the delay had given Rich a chance to catch up. Racing at full tilt, Garry emerged into the lights of Michigan Avenue. He saw Rich race out of the darker side-street and stop, looking for Garry. Despite the heavy late-evening traffic, Garry ran straight onto the road, dodging cars, narrowly missing being hit by a Red Camaro accelerating sharply down the south-bound lane. Ignoring the flash of terror, Garry darted across to the north-bound lane, reaching the safety of the sidewalk.

Behind him, he heard a screech of tires and a small shout. He risked looking back and saw Rich sprawled on the centre strip, clutching his leg. Deciding not to risk losing time, Garry ran on, blessing the minor accident. Turning off the Avenue, he walked along another side street and came to an open car park. It was one of those where the attendant moved the cars to maximize space utilization, which meant the keys were normally left with the vehicle. It had always seemed a risky procedure to Garry, but it gave him an idea.

Controlling his breathing, he walked into the parking lot. The attendant was hunched over a magazine and ignored him. Garry walked to the end of the lines of cars, looking for one that could be moved without assistance. A small Toyota Corolla looked promising. He opened the door, crouched down and felt around the floor under the seat. Sure enough, the small lump under the mat indicated the keys. Sliding in, he started the car, looked for the parking ticket and found it on the passenger seat. He took out his wallet, kept it in one hand and began to move slowly toward the exit. At the attendant's stall he silently handed the ticket to the man who reluctantly turned from his reading to examine the ticket.

"Nine bucks," he said. Garry silently handed over a ten dollar bill, waved the change away and drove thankfully out on to the road. His head began to clear and he needed to think. But first he drove, uncertain of his direction, more interested in placing distance between himself and the site of the attack. He realized he had little time. The car's owner might already have returned to the parking lot and put out a stolen vehicle call to the police.

Reaching a decision, Garry headed north through the city streets, finding an all-night supermarket near Fullerton Road. He walked in, searched out the aisles he wanted and rapidly bought a small overnight bag, toothpaste, brush, comb and some cheap underwear and cotton shirts. Paying by cash, he walked out of the supermarket, left the Toyota where it was with a muttered prayer for its well being, and walked to the busy intersection. It took ten minutes to find a vacant cab, but finally, he waved one down.

"Airport Hilton," he said to the driver and settled down in the scruffy, torn leather seat.

Some twenty minutes later, the cab pulled into the luxurious forecourt of the Airport Hilton, and Garry climbed out after paying the fare. He walked into the lobby, looked around then walked out again, by which time the cab had left. Feeling a little exposed in the open, despite the certainty that Rich could hardly have followed him here, he set off for a fairly lengthy walk away from the luxury hotels in the immediate area.

Nearly half an hour later, he found a small motel. Registering, he took a small second-floor room and locked the door behind him. He went straight to the phone.

"Micky, I'm in a tatty motel on Mannheim, near the airport," he said when she answered. "I'm okay, but there's been another attack." Her gasp of worry down the line was loud. "Micky, I'm okay," he repeated firmly. "I got away before they could do any damage."

"You're sure?" Her voice was sharp, panicky.

"I'm certain," he said. "And I love you to pieces."

"Well, that's alright then," she said, her smile obvious to him.

"I'm worried about what they might do next, though," he said. "And I'm terrified about you. So can I lay down some orders?"

"Ooh, an authoritarian man," she chuckled. "I do love being overpowered!"

"Micky, hush!" he said, aware of his smile at her humour, but frightened about how much time they might have. "Is the door properly locked?"

"It is," she replied. "And I'm twelve floors up. You can't be serious, Garry, surely? They'd attack me?"

"I doubt it," he said, not as certain as he tried to sound. "But before you go out tomorrow, I'm going to make sure you have company."

"Okay," she said, a serious tone in her voice. "I suppose that's the best thing to do."

"I'll call you early tomorrow," he said. "And let you know then what the arrangements are. Please, Micky, don't go out until you're certain the right people have arrived."

"I won't. Garry, I love you. Take just as much care yourself, please."

"I promise," he said. "I'd better make a start on those arrangements. I'll call you tomorrow, early."

"Yes," she said. "Any time you want to. I'll be ready."

"Sweet dreams, Princess," he said with a smile, and hung up. Immediately, he phoned Peter. "The PAC goons are at it again," he said when Peter answered.

"What? Are you alright?" The alarm in Peter's voice was acute.

"I'm fine," replied Garry. "I got away, and one of them can now sing in a girl's choir. I'm holed up in a motel near the airport."

"Want me to come and get you?"

"Not a good idea. They might be watching you and could follow you here."

"Jesus Christ!" exploded Peter. "It's time we called the cops in."

"Not yet," said Garry. "There's no proof of any connection. I'm more worried about Micky."

"My God, yes," said Peter. "Have you spoken to her?"

"Yes, and she's keeping every door locked until we send someone over there. Any suggestions about that for tomorrow morning?"

Peter was silent for a few moments. "We have a couple of oversized young men working for us. Paul

Sentry is about six-four and two-forty pounds. Played tight end for the Illini. And he's got friends of similar size. How about I have them escort Micky to the office tomorrow?"

"Sounds good. She'll know them?"

"Oh, for sure. Paul at least. He's in her new team for the Sullivan audits. And it's hard not to know these guys. They cause an eclipse when they come in to the office."

"That should do it. Tell them to meet her at her apartment at seven-thirty. I'll call Micky and let her know to expect them."

"Garry, this is insane!" Peter finally blew his temper. "If we find that PAC is really behind this, I'll kill every one of those bastards on the board!"

"Take a number and get in line," replied Garry. "And if they hurt Micky, or even try and hurt her, they'll regret it till hell becomes a theme park."

"I'll call the boys," said Peter, and hung up.

*   *   *   *

The atmosphere in the HLM boardroom was subdued. Micky had arrived as Garry was walking out of his office, and she looked tiny next to the three mountainous young men who were escorting her. She and Garry embraced without words then she smiled her thanks at her protectors.

"We'll see you for the ride home, Micky," said the largest of the three, a dark-haired man of classic athlete's build, wide, sloping shoulders and slim hips. He looked down at Garry and grinned. "Don't worry, Mister Barton," he said. "They called us the

Mini-Monsters of the Midway when we were at school. Nobody would want to mess with us."

"Nobody with sense, that's for sure," laughed Garry, and extended his hand. "Thanks, Paul, all of you. I'll come along too, and perhaps we can go to the place I left my car last night. I'd like backup for that."

"You bet, Mister Barton," replied the young man and followed the other two out of the lobby.

The moment of humour passed as the partners met in the boardroom.

"It's not at all funny," said Charlie Levin. "And we have no more idea of who's behind it than we had before. You're quite sure it was the same two guys, Garry?"

"Dead certain."

"You'd never go to court with this evidence," said Charlie.

"I'm not sure about that," mused Peter. "We get the first attack as a warning after we take the Sullivan Group. The second attempt comes soon after we talk to Carswell's."

Levin shook his head. "Inadequate. If I were opposing counsel, I'd eat you alive."

"There's no question of court," broke in Garry. "We have to put a stop to this mess ourselves. If it's PAC, you can bet your life they're covering any connection."

"And how do we stop it?" asked Micky. Her face was pale.

"One of two ways," replied Peter. "We bow to the pressure and take no more PAC business, or we fight back."

"And how do we fight back?" asked Charlie.

"I've no idea," replied Peter, his open face deadly serious.

"There's absolutely no point in bowing to pressure," said Garry. All eyes turned to him. He smiled slightly. "It won't save PAC," he said. "I think the rot has set in too far, already. Other clients of theirs have already moved to different auditors, not just to us. Even if we sat back, PAC will collapse soon. So why not go for our share of the booty?"

A murmur of agreement ran around the table.

"So I suggest some extreme measures," continued Garry. "And I really hate to think that I've been instrumental in causing this to happen to you."

"Hardly your fault that your old employers are turning into a pack of loonies," murmured Peter. "So, let's hear the suggestions."

"Okay. First, beef up the security on all your homes. Solid locks, internal alarms, all that sort of thing."

"Jesus Christ, you think they'd attack us in our homes?" Peter looked horrified, but Garry was firm.

"I don't know," he said. "But they went for me, they may go after you. Second, Peter and Charlie, hire guards to take your kids to school and bring them back, and to stay with your wives any time they go out."

"Good God!" Charlie was astounded.

"He only helps those who help themselves," said Garry with a small smile.

"And what about you and Micky?" asked Peter. "Armed guards for you?"

Garry shook his head and smiled at Micky. "If we can arrange for young Paul Sentry's crew of monsters to escort Micky to the office and back each day, we'll make our own arrangements," he said.

"This is all fine and dandy," objected Charlie. "But when does it come to an end?"

"When PAC's people come to their senses, or they've gone to the great accounting school in the sky," replied Peter. "Neither of which should take too long."

"Let's hope so," replied Charlie, looking doubtful.

"For everybody's sake," finished Peter, and stood up to leave. Garry and the others did the same and Garry walked back to Micky's office with her.

"The arrangements I mentioned," he said as they closed the door behind them.

She looked at him with a cool smile. "I was wondering about those," she said. "Do I get a chance to review them?"

"Very much so," he said. "They can't happen without your approval."

"Yes?" Her gaze was almost as calm and cool as the first time they had sat like this. Her composure pleased him.

"It seems to make sense," he began. "Though I don't want you to think I'm using this for the wrong reasons..."

"You want to move into my apartment?" she asked.

Unable to say anything clearly, he nodded.

"Then why didn't you just ask?" she said, and opened up a writing pad. "This evening would be a good time, don't you think?"

Trying to imitate her coolness, he stood up. "I think I could just about manage that," he said. He walked to the door and opened it, just in time to hear her muted chuckle.

*   *   *   *

"Garry Barton to see Mister Conway," said Garry to the receptionist. She was new, thought Garry, or at least she had joined after Garry's departure from the firm.

She showed no recognition of Garry. "Do you have an appointment, Mister Barton?" The woman's tone was chilly.

"Mister Conway will see me. Just tell him I'm here."

The receptionist gave him a doubtful look tinged with contempt, but dialled Conway's office. Something in the reaction at the other end made her look up at Garry with startled reappraisal.

"Would you take a seat, Mister Barton?" she said, her voice considerable more polite than before. "Mister Conway's secretary will be out shortly."

"I thought she might be," replied Garry, and took a seat in the lobby. He picked up a copy of *Time* and idly perused it, trying to still his nerves. The wait was drawn out. Garry wondered just what was going on in Conway's office. At one point, Garry looked up as the door into the lobby opened, but it was another of the audit partners. He stared at Garry with shock in his face.

"What the hell are you doing here, Barton?" he demanded.

"Good morning, Patrick," said Garry, pleasantly. "How nice to see you, too."

The other man turned to the receptionist. "What's he doing here?" he repeated.

The woman looked astonished. "He has an appointment with Mister Conway," she said, her voice up a notch in pitch.

"Jesus Christ!" muttered the man, and stamped out of the lobby to the elevators, anger showing in every rigid line of his body.

"I'm very well, thank you, Patrick," said Garry. "I trust you're in good health, too?" The other man glared at the elevator doors until they opened and gave him an escape from Garry's verbal dagger. Garry smiled at the receptionist who had stared at the interchange with dismay, and he returned to his magazine. He fought to keep himself calm at the prospect of the coming meeting, but several times, the rage he was feeling at the brutality of the attacks on him threatened to overwhelm him. Twice, he stood up and walked around the lobby to regain self-control, conscious of the receptionist's curious stare.

Another ten minutes passed before Conway's secretary appeared. She looked hostile, and glared at Garry, saying nothing.

"Good morning, Jennifer," said Garry, determined to maintain his own standards of social conduct. He replaced the magazine, stood up and walked into the office area. Jennifer merely returned to her own annex office, leaving Garry to walk unannounced into Conway's.

"Good morning, Jack," he said politely.

Conway stood up from behind his desk and briefly shook hands. "Take a seat, Garry," he said, and walked to the door to close it.

Newman was sitting in one of the armchairs. Though an unpleasant reality, Garry had been expecting it. "Hello, Bridget," he said, not offering to shake hands. "I trust you are well?" In the silence, he took a seat opposite her. Conway sat on his Queen Anne couch against the wall.

"This is an unexpected visit, Garry," said Conway. He looked nervous. Garry studied both the partners for a few seconds. The woman was looking calmly at him and Garry sensed that the authority in the room was with her, not the firm's chairman.

"It's an unexpected situation that demands it, Jack," said Garry. "And this will be a difficult meeting. I bring you both some news and a message."

"Then let us proceed." Conway's arms were folded across his chest, the scarred hand hidden under one arm. He was clearly not comfortable.

"Some weeks ago," began Garry, looking at Conway, "I was attacked outside my house. I was taken in an old and smelly car to Wilmette Beach, and beaten up rather seriously."

Conway said nothing, but the sudden movement of his throat indicated a touch of nervousness. Garry shifted his eyes to Newman. She was studying him with equal attention and Garry thought he saw a tiny smile on her face.

"That, of course, is regrettable," said the woman in a sibilant tone. "But neither Jack nor I can possibly understand why you should bring this to our attention."

"Of course you can't," said Garry, with a pleasant smile. "We'll come to that."

"Are you okay now, Garry?" Conway's question seemed sincerely concerned, and Garry looked at him.

What hell is Conway going through? he

wondered. *Is this use of violence endorsed by him? If not, is Newman truly in control of the firm now?*

"Just some bruises, Jack," he replied and returned to watching the woman. "A couple of things about the attack made me think," he continued. He saw Newman become perfectly still, almost like a lizard on a rock watching a fly, and he knew his suspicions were confirmed.

"The man who did the beating, whose name is Rich, by the way..." He paused and saw the flicker in Newman's eyes. The news of some small piece of information in Garry's hands had clearly disturbed her. "He told me I had to stop doing whatever I was doing, or the next time would be worse."

"Mister Barton," interrupted Newman. "This is a sad and terrible tale. But I fail entirely to understand why you are wasting our time telling it to us."

Garry smiled at her. His confidence had risen with the confirmation that PAC was the guilty party in this affair. "Because you see, Bridget," he said, "try as I might, the only people I can identify who are being hurt by anything I'm doing, are you lot."

"Which only shows that your intellect is extremely limited," she said, coldly. "Jack, this man is wasting our time."

"I agree, Garry," said Conway. "If that was your news, we can't see the relevance. You said you had a message. I hope it's of more importance."

"Oh, it's crucial, Jack. But I have to add something to the irrelevant news first. The same two thugs had another go at me two nights ago. They failed. What's more, one of them had the misfortune to be slightly hurt in the proceedings. He may not contribute any more of value to your cause."

This time Garry saw the evidence clearly. Both partners looked at each other, and the small shock of anger was quite evident in Newman's face. The tension in the room had clicked up several degrees.

"So, now that I have your attention," continued Garry into the silence, "I'll give you the message."

Neither of them spoke. Conway was looking out of the window, but his distress was evident to Garry. Newman was studying her hands on her lap.

"Terrorist campaigns against us won't work," said Garry. "None of the partners at HLM will let your actions interfere with our business plans...."

"*Our* actions, Mister Barton?" The woman glared up at Garry and he could see the rage in her face. It was the most extreme emotion he had ever seen in her. "Just what do you mean, *our* actions?"

Garry was not disturbed by the outburst. "I mean the actions of desperate people using any means they can to survive their own stupidity," he said calmly. "That means hiring thugs to deter me, or anything else you may consider."

"Your words are defamatory," snapped Newman. "A legal action may result from this."

"Then I hope you've been recording the conversation," said Garry and watched them. It was clear that the idea had not occurred to them. "You weren't?" he asked, and shrugged his shoulders. "Too bad."

"Is that all?" demanded Newman. Garry could see the tension in every line of her body.

"Not quite," he replied. "I'd like to ask you both a question."

"Ask it then, and let's get this nonsense over," said the woman sharply.

Garry looked at both of them to watch for reactions. "Did you have Andrew killed?" he asked. He felt his words fly into a world of ice. Conway looked shocked and frightened.

Newman smiled back with contempt. "If I hadn't known you to be a fool already, that question would have confirmed my opinion."

She did, said Garry to himself. *She had Andrew killed. I wonder if any of the others know it?* "As you seem to have confirmed mine," he replied. The woman's eyes blinked and her face went cold.

"Garry, it's time you left," said Conway. There was a pleading note in his voice.

"Almost, Jack," replied Garry. "I just want to complete the message."

"Complete this nonsense then, and get out," said Newman. She had regained her composure.

"Certainly," said Garry. "This is it. I intend to find out who Rich is. I'll find out who employs him, and then I'll know how it came to be that PAC used his services. Meanwhile, I'd like to suggest that all the effort is useless. Whether or not we end the seduction of your clients, PAC's dead and in far less time than I had forecast to you only a few months ago. Whether HLM feeds further on the carcass, or we leave it to the rest of the jungle, your time is done."

"Garry, go!" said Conway.

Garry stood up. "I'm sorry you had to let it end this way," he said, and walked to the door. "I'm getting wealthy on your death, but I wish it could have been done differently."

He opened the door and walked out. He returned to the lobby and stood silently, sharply conscious of the receptionist's stare. Sweat was running down his back and his armpits were soaked. The reaction to the meeting had set in.

Dear God, she killed Andrew, he thought, again and again. *If she's capable of that, what else will she do? From the way she looked at me, she would have killed me there and then. And she's taken over from Jack, that's obvious. Thank God I've suggested we step up the protection. And Micky, by God, if they try and harm Micky, I'll kill each of those bastards slowly until they scream for mercy.*

Garry didn't go back to the office. He knew he could never put his mind to work after that meeting. He needed a shower to wash away the sweat and the blood-lust that talking with Bridget Newman had caused.

* * * *

Behind him, Garry left an office broiling with tension.

"That is a very dangerous and unpleasant young man," said Newman as she stood up in preparation to leave.

"He is dangerous, certainly," replied Conway, remaining seated. "As would anyone be who is determined to attack us where we are so obviously undefended. The rest is your personal judgment, and I'm beginning to question that."

"I beg your pardon?" Newman was startled by Conway's words.

Conway was looking out of the window at the lake, and didn't see her deadly glare. "You heard me, Bridget," he said. "I'm beginning to have serious concerns about the direction this committee is taking to solve our problems."

"Well you're the chairman of this committee, Jack. Any direction we're taking is with your authority." The derision in her voice was noticeable and Conway looked up at her.

"Bridget," he said. "We both know that your influence is shaping the committee's policy. That's appropriate, it's how top management should work. But when the directions become as tainted as ours are becoming, I must begin to take action."

"Action?   You, Jack?"   Her contempt was blistering, but Conway was undisturbed.

"I know that I don't take the sort of action you would like Bridget, I agree. It seems that's a good thing, if Garry's question is anything to go by."

"What question was that?"

"Did you have Andrew Whittaker killed?"

For a second, the room was as still and silent as a morgue.

Newman slowly moved back to her seat and sat down. "Don't be silly, Jack."

"I try not to be, Bridget. What worries me is not my silliness, but perhaps my stupidity in letting you go on so far. Did you have Andrew killed?"

"I had nothing to do with Whittaker's death. Your question is offensive."

"That's a subjective assessment also, Bridget.

What are your intentions regarding these current difficulties? Apart from taking my job, that is."

Again there was silence as the two stared at each other.

"I have no aims at your position, Jack."

"Then you disappoint me. You should have aims at my job. Every partner should."

Newman shrugged. "Long-term, perhaps."

"Okay, let's accept that, Bridget. What are your short-term goals?"

"To get this firm back on its feet. What else could they be?"

"That's precisely what worries me. I want to be certain that the firm's recovery is the primary goal, not taking revenge on Garry Barton for doing exactly what he should be doing."

"Our actions against Barton are aimed at the firm's recovery, surely you understand that?"

"I'm less certain, Bridget."

"Then veto our proposals. You're still the chairman."

"I think we both know that things have gone too far for that. The rest of you are sold on this approach and having no other immediate course of action that I can propose, and, to be honest, being uncertain that the approach might even work, I have to let it go on."

"Good. Then let's stop wasting time and get on with it."

"We haven't settled the matter of Andrew Whittaker."

"Yes we have. I told you I had nothing to do with his death."

"I know you told me. But Whittaker took direct aim at you before he left, and I know you considered the possibility of Andrew talking to the authorities."

"We all did, Jack. It was an obvious concern."

"Yes, it was. But you're the only person I would believe to have the will to carry out the action."

"Now you're being subjective."

Conway nodded. "Yes, I am. And if I'm right, I have to worry about similar results if any of us stands up to you, Bridget."

"Not only subjective, but paranoid. Jack, is this getting too much for you?"

"It's only paranoia if there is no justification for the fear. That judgment is open."

"Nonsense. Andrew was obviously killed by some mugger. Jack, I assure you, I had nothing to do with it and I regret the incident deeply."

Conway stared out of the window for a few more moments then stood up. "I'll call the committee together again this afternoon. We have to discuss Barton's approach to us."

"I agree. And let's focus our attentions on that problem, not imaginary worries. We have enough to concern us."

Conway nodded, but he did not look at her as she left the office.

Chapter 12

"Barton called on us this morning," said Conway. He sat at the head of the boardroom table, Newman on his left, Trent across from him and Petheram on his right.

"That bastard's been here?" demanded Trent. "If I'd seen him, I'd have beaten him to a pulp."

"We leave that to the professionals remember, William?" said Newman in a bored tone. "There's no need for anyone to over-react."

"But it means he knows we're behind this!" shouted Trent, rising to his feet. His face was red.

"No, it means he *thinks* we're behind it," responded Petheram more calmly. "We all know Garry's bright, and it doesn't need rocket science skills to work out we're probably the cause of his recent difficulties."

"Exactly," said Newman. "There's no possible way he could ever prove any connection with the men doing the work."

"What about that work?" Petheram demanded. "Haven't they completed the next stage against Barton yet?"

Newman looked intently at her hands. She seemed a little tense as she spoke. "They tried last night, it seemed. But Barton was able to evade them."

"Evade them?" Petheram was irritated. "He gave them the slip? Bridget, I'm beginning to wonder about the so-called expertise of these men you have working for you."

"Working for *us,* Stephen, working for *us,*" said Newman, gently. "It was nothing serious. Barton was able to find a crowd to hide in." She said nothing about the damage inflicted on one of the hunters.

Petheram seemed to accept the argument. "Just what did Barton say when he came in, Bridget?" he asked.

"He told us that HLM would not be deterred by such action," she began. She made no mention of Garry's statement that PAC was already dead, nor of the fact that he knew the first name of one of his attackers. "I suggest the fact that he was worried enough to visit us is, in fact, an indication that the reverse is true."

"I'd agree with that," said Petheram, nodding. "No point in coming otherwise."

"Maybe not," objected Conway. "It could easily be that Garry has enough civility in him to try and tell us to stop now before we hurt ourselves any more."

"I doubt that," said Newman abruptly, cutting off Conway before the idea could take root. "I think we simply have to try a slightly different path."

The three other faces looked at her. She glanced round the room and looked back at her hands again. "I suspect that one of the problems at PAC," she said, "is that the other partners still see Barton as being an outsider. The attacks on him are somehow perceived as Barton's problems, not truly their own."

"And you think that's preventing them taking this more seriously?" asked Petheram, nodding his head in understanding.

"I do," she agreed. "Which means we have to bring it home to them quite firmly."

"What, attack Peter Haywood or Charles Levin, too?" asked Bill Trent. He was looking nervously between Newman and Conway, as if hoping Jack would assert himself and perhaps end the discussion.

"Not Levin," said Newman, shaking her head. "We don't want to have an attack misinterpreted as simply another case of anti-Semitic hooliganism."

"So Peter Haywood then?" said Petheram. He seemed to be displaying no air of doubt at all.

Newman shook her head again. "My people tell me that Barton has established a relationship with Michelle Ashley, another partner at HLM," she said. "I believe that makes him highly vulnerable, and is the real reason behind his pathetic plea to us earlier today. Action against her would be the key."

There was a stir around the table.

"Bridget, you can't be serious!" blurted out Conway.

Newman didn't look at him. "I'm completely serious," she retorted. "I'm not talking physical damage," she continued in a slightly more conciliatory tone. "Merely that our men should remove her and hold her for a time. I doubt that Barton would be expecting such a move, so any abduction will be simple."

"At least that would send the message to the whole partnership," said Petheram.

"Christ, I'm a little worried about hurting a woman," demurred Trent. "I don't mind Barton getting banged up, but a woman? Bridget, this is getting a bit heavy."

"Nonsense!" For the first time, Newman showed irritation. "Forget this silly gallantry, William. We have no intention of hurting her, I just said that. We'll hold her for a few days and use her to get Barton and his crew to promise to behave."

"And if they won't?" asked Conway coolly. "Will we kill her, Bridget?"

"Of course not, Jack," she snapped. "We mustn't get melodramatic on this. The men will simply hold her a few days, Barton will agree to behave, and we let her go. They'll make sure she has no idea of where she was, and nothing can tie the incident to us."

"You'd better pray so," replied Conway. "Because if the truth ever came out, we're looking at prison - all of us."

"Impossible," said Newman. "Jack, if this is getting too much for you, maybe you should do the same as Andrew Whittaker, and resign from the partnership."

The two stared at each other in the tight silence.

"My name has been on this firm's shingle from the beginning," said Conway, ice in his tones. "Far longer than you have been around, Bridget. And maybe I'm still more capable of sound judgment than you are.

You are beginning to lead this firm down paths with no return. Do you wish to try and see whether I can have you removed from the partnership? I'm beginning to think that may the best course for us, not this war against HLM."

In the silence, Trent spoke with hesitation. "Jack, nobody's thinking of getting anyone to leave. We all need each other."

Newman backed down, recognizing the edge of the precipice. "I agree, Jack. We need to remember we still have to overcome this problem."

Conway ignored her. "Stephen, do you think this new direction may achieve the results we need?"

Petheram blinked. "I do, Jack," he said. "I think it would send the right message to an expanded audience. After all, Levin and Haywood recruited Ashley, developed and promoted her. They'll have a lot more emotional connection to her than they do to Barton."

"That's a good thought," added Trent. "And I support Stephen on this one, Jack. Provided no harm comes to this woman, that is."

Conway seemed lost in thought for several moments. Then he rose to his feet and walked to the door.

"Do it," he said.

The other three stayed seated for several minutes of silence. Then they too, left.

Newman walked back to her office feeling a warm sense of accomplishment. She could begin to taste the sensation of seeing her plan culminate in success within a few months. What had begun as merely a plan to strengthen her own position within the firm had developed to the point where she knew that the chairmanship itself was attainable. Conway's time was severely limited, she could see that now.

It was so clear to her. Garry Barton was a problem, the problem could be removed. Why there was so much fuss attached to the idea that an irritating, stupid man like Barton should be killed was beyond her. If only she could be in charge! She would have had Barton removed by now, just as she had made her own decision to remove Andrew Whittaker. The man had been a fool, overly emotional, and therefore a risk to her. She knew she would have had a long, hard path getting agreement to neutralize Whittaker, and she also knew that they didn't have the time for such foolishness. She doubted any of them would have the intelligence to link her to the killing. It would be seen as just another murder in the Chicago region.

God, they're all so stupid, she thought to herself. So wrapped up in their silly little lives of families, money and status. And Conway was the worst. He was chairman just because of the name. Well, that wouldn't last. She knew she was intellectually superior to every one of the other partners. Being a woman was a slight problem. The other three woman partners were all so dedicated to being *women,* she sneered. So determined to cause no problems, to let the men run things, to offer no threats to those fragile little egos. Well, she wasn't like that. She would demolish Conway during this emergency, she would lead the firm back to prosperity, and she would stand for election as chairman.

She thought back with a mixture of pleasure and frustration to the phone conversation with Stan Mortensen when she had told him how the operation was to work.

"I don't follow you, Bridget," said Mortensen, when she had first told him what she wanted. "Why are you asking me to have them attack the little jerk if you want him to escape?"

She took a deep breath and controlled her irritation. *Why were people so slow?* "Because I want them to realize that Barton needs the full treatment. He's not going to stop what he's doing just because he gets beaten up. The other partners will keep going, anyway. It will only work when he gets killed."

"Then why don't I just have my men kill him, anyway?" The puzzlement in Mortensen's voice almost made her want to scream.

"Because my people have to be prepared for it," she replied. "If we do it right away, they'll run like startled rabbits and back away from the whole thing. They have to be brought to the point where they're desperate and it's their decision. Then they'll stay with it."

"I see," said the voice in her ear, but Bridget knew that he didn't see at all. She took another slow breath and kept her voice in its usual cool pitch.

"Just bear with me, Stan," she said. "Have them pretend to attack Barton again and let him get away. Then we'll have them make an attempt to kidnap that woman of his, and they'll fail again. After that, we'll have my partners fully primed. I know what I'm doing."

"You always do," replied Mortensen. "I've got good reason for believing that. Okay Bridget, I'll tell them what to do."

"Good," she said, and hung up.

"And they thought I was embarrassed by the failure to get Barton this time," she murmured aloud in the privacy of her office. She smiled a cold twitch of her lips, remembering her internal amusement as she sensed the feeling of superiority in Trent and Petheram as they thought they could criticize her. Had they but known it, she was on the exact path she wanted.

All it needed was a little more time to persuade them that killing Barton was the only route open to them. She had led them by the nose, step by step, and the time would soon be right. If the present activities by those fools that Mortensen had set on to Barton had the right effect then well and good. She knew that they wouldn't, and she was able to enjoy the anticipation that the men would fail. The prospect of Barton's death gave her an astonishing sense of pleasure, much like the anticipation of receiving a new video from her supplier. But it also aroused a sense of *dejà vu* that puzzled her for a few moments. When she solved the puzzle, she felt a mixture of amusement and annoyance at herself. The sensation of pleasure at the anticipation of Barton's death was the nearest thing to the mild excitement she had felt lying under the grunting, thrusting Phillip Wareham, twenty-five years ago. Suppressing the mix of emotions, she returned to work.

Conway was disturbed by the meeting and he entered his office with a nagging worry. His distaste at the prospect of carrying the hostilities further and against a woman at that, were coloured by something else, a sense of satisfaction. It disturbed him greatly and he was unable to identify the cause of the unease.

He called Jennifer, his secretary, and asked her for a fresh pot of the British Earl Grey tea for which he had long had an affection, and took a seat in his armchair looking out over the lake.

What could be causing these strange emotions? he asked himself. It was not the departure of Madeleine from the house, he was certain. That had been merely the conclusion of years of growing tension and distance between them, and he felt grateful for his solitude. Nor did he have doubts about the already distasteful measures being taken against Garry Barton and his partners at HLM. But he was deeply disturbed that he was unable to think of any more useful measures to be taken. Costs were being cut to permit reductions in fees, though the reductions were eating into the firm's cash reserves. Grudgingly, there now seemed to be some acceptance of the statements by Barton that had caused this grief, that the firm was backward in its technology. Trent was embarrassed by the fact, but appeared to be moving towards doing something positive at last about George Elliot. Conway was also embarrassed, because as chairman he knew he should have seen this problem and acted on it earlier.

"Dammit," he mumbled. "I heard all these guys talking about computer audit at accounting seminars and business meetings, and I never thought to question what that dimwit Elliot was really doing. We've probably paid the man a million in salary the last five years, and all he's done is keep us in the dark."

Maybe that was one of the causes of the sense of satisfaction, he thought to himself, the recognition that something had to be done about Elliot.

His musings were broken by the door opening and Jennifer bringing in his tray of tea. Gratefully, he smiled at her, and resumed his thoughts as he poured the tea into the china cup.

Definitely start with Elliot, he decided. Have a chat with Trent soon and start laying down the groundwork for removing a partner. Not an easy thing to do, and likely to get expensive as they paid out his equity share in the firm, but worth it, Conway was certain. But that wasn't it. There was something else teasing his memories.

Finally, it came to him. Conway almost laughed when he saw the solution. With the disasters that were hitting them, had come the need to do something different from the prosaic management of an accounting firm. Conway was now leading a military action against another organization, with literally physical operations being conducted. Just like he had once dreamed of doing as a seven-year-old boy determined to follow his father into the US Navy.

He liked Garry Barton, he knew. But Barton was definitely threatening Conway's lifelong commitment, the firm his grandfather had built. Conway was doing something real, something exciting, something dangerous. There was risk here. But there was likely to be real damage, possibly even blood, or worse.

Conway felt a shiver run through him. If all the threats failed, he began to see that maybe even the unthinkable would have to be faced. Barton might even have to be killed.

"Christ!" he said aloud. "I hope we don't get to that point." He shivered at the realization of the boundary he had just crossed. But the trace of excitement at the prospect wouldn't go away.

Conway's tea was cold. He emptied the cup into his waste basket and poured another one. This time he added some milk and drank it.

It should never come to anything drastic, he thought. *I hope to God it doesn't, anyway.*

Goddam! I'm the one that got them here! Trent was also lost in a brown study sitting behind his desk. He remembered with a mix of shame and pleasure, his initial outburst about doing physical harm to Garry Barton. He knew that he had been only semi-serious at the time, the words resulting from a mix of simple frustration at what was happening to his firm and its partners, and his own anger at Barton for no longer being susceptible to Trent's overwhelming size and personality.

But now he felt a flood of pleasure at the thought that he had influenced the committee to accepting his recommendation.

I may only be a poor kid from downstate, he thought with a smile on his round face. *But I sure as hell brought this bunch of rich aristocrats round to my way of thinking.*

He wondered what would happen if this new dimension of attacks failed to achieve the objectives. With a small shiver of anticipation, he suspected that it wouldn't.

Actually, I hope it fails, he thought. *I don't like the idea of involving the woman, even if she is Barton's girl friend. That was Bridget's idea. God, she's a hard woman! The way she looked at Andrew Whittaker when he walked out on us, I thought she'd kill him... Jesus Christ!*

Trent's smile faded and an icy current ran through his veins. The thought had not occurred to him before. Somebody, Petheram he thought, had expressed a worry that Andrew might tell the authorities about the activities of PAC's management committee. Trent hadn't thought much about it at the time. But Whittaker had been killed within a few days of that moment.

Good God Almighty! Did Bridget get the same thugs who were assigned to Barton to kill Andrew? Trent felt more frightened then than he had done since his childhood, faced with a beating from his father. He had no doubts in his mind at all that he was right. Newman was prepared to kill to achieve her objectives.

And maybe that's what we have to do, he thought, the situation taking a clear shape in his mind. *Maybe that's the only way to be certain that Barton and his partners would be stopped. Maybe I should suggest to Bridget that she instruct Mortensen to have his men mess up the attack on Barton's woman? Then we'd have no alternative but to go all out and kill him. That would certainly finish this thing off and we could get down to recovering the business.*

He thought further down this path, and rejected the idea. He wanted to have no part in a decision to kill Barton, unless it was a joint agreement. Just for a second or two, he thought about how far he had strayed from his old standards. He was coldly planning on having a man killed and a minute trace of worry shivered through his mind at the idea.

And Jesus! I'd better make sure Bridget knows I'm totally with her! Any signs of fading and she might think I need removing as well. The idea left a cold feeling in his bowels, and he forgot about the worries over his own humanity.

* * * *

"They're in the lobby," said Garry, replacing the telephone. It was the third day of living with Micky, and however happy he had felt before, it faded by comparison with how he felt now. He watched with enjoyment as Micky gathered up her bag and put the final touches to her hair at the mirror in the hallway. She smiled at Garry's study of her.

"Ready for inspection, sir!" she snapped in military fashion.

He grinned back. "I believe you'll do," he said. "The youthful admirers in the lobby will agree with me, I'm certain." Garry had watched with amusement the way the three young men had taken on their guardianship duties with Micky. Their frank admiration had been a pleasure to see. Garry felt he'd rather face a pack of Dobermans than these three man-mountains if somebody tried to hurt Micky.

"Let's go," he said, and opened the door. They moved to the elevators, and waited a few moments. This early in the day, there were few people leaving, and they had the elevator to themselves. Without a pause, they reached the lobby, and held the doors open as Paul Sentry and only one of his friends entered.

"Good morning guys. Only two of you?" Garry felt nervous.

"Sorry, Mister Barton," replied Paul. "Wayne had a dentist's appointment this morning."

Garry considered this for a second then relaxed. "Should be enough of us," he said. The elevator car creaked ominously as the two men entered, and they descended the final stage to the garage.

As the door opened, Garry stepped out first and checked around. Despite two days of peace and tranquillity in the morning, he felt worried about Micky's safety, but also a little foolish. Would they really consider something so outrageous as an attack on her? He doubted it, but the events already were far enough removed from civilized standards. He looked around the silent rows of cars, sniffed the warm air with its permanent odour of oil and garbage, saw nothing ominous.

"Okay," he called, and the other three moved out, advancing to Micky's pride and joy, her red Porsche. Only then did he see the tiny flicker of movement behind the large Buick Roadmaster.

"Micky," Garry shouted. "Get in the car, quick! Paul, stay with her. We've got company!"

Ignoring the gasp of pain from Micky as Paul seized her arm and hurried her to the Porsche, Garry turned to face the movement. "There's probably a second one," he said. "Don, watch out."

"You bet," replied the second young man.

Feeling a wave of panic, Garry saw the man called Rich stand upright and leap at him. He had time to see the face - a broad, chubby face, with a child's innocent expression on it, marred by a couple of day's stubble - then the avalanche hit him.

Garry fell before the onslaught, and stumbled against a Toyota Corolla. Out of the corner of his eye, he saw the second man move on Don. The younger man was far more effective. He stood up to the attack and landed a thumping fist to the head of the second man.

Garry saw Rich move towards Micky's car, and despite a wave of sickness, got to his feet. But Paul was there first, standing with his back to Micky's car and a face like thunderclouds. Rich swung hard at Paul, landed a partial blow, but Paul moved fast, and drove a hard right fist at the bigger man. Rich staggered backwards, straight at Garry, who exploded with rage. He flung his arm round Rich's throat and hauled tight, despite the fact that Rich was several inches taller and many pounds heavier. Rich swayed back, unable to get his body upright, and Garry pulled the huge head, forcing Rich off his balance completely. Red-eyed with fury, Garry slammed the head against the side of the car nearest to him.

"You bastard!" he yelled, and drove the man's skull into the metal again, enjoying the grunt of pain that Rich let out. A few feet away, he saw Don hit the floor, and Paul jumped over to attack the second intruder. The momentary loss of concentration was all Rich needed. He drove his legs upright, forcing Garry to lose his grip, and slammed a heavy fist into Garry's ribs. Garry collapsed, winded.

"Go!" yelled Rich, and raced for the exit doors, kicking Paul's legs as he passed. It was enough to let the second man get free, and the two of them banged through the door and into the open.

Climbing slowly to his feet, Garry moved to the Porsche. Micky flung her door open and jumped out. She was weeping, and she clung to Garry. He wrapped his arms around her and held tight.

"Sorry, Mister Barton," mumbled Paul. His mouth was badly cut, and a massive bruise on his forehead was already erupting in colourful pain.

"God, they were hard men," said Don. He was holding his ribs with care, and blood was dripping from his nose.

"I'm just glad you were both here," said Garry, feeling a mix of fear and rage at the events of the last few moments. Micky was gaining control, and she lifted her head. "Thank you, all of you," she said, her voice shaky. "Is everybody alright?"

"No worse than after the first quarter of a game," said Don with a wheezy laugh. "Nothing that a hot tub won't fix."

"Okay, those bastards have gone," said Garry. "You guys get your car and go and get checked up before you come near the office. Call in when you've been seen to."

Dabbing at blood on their faces, the two men left, and Micky opened her handbag and began to comb her hair. She seemed to be recovering her composure as she repaired her appearance.

"Why don't I drive while you do that?" asked Garry.

She stopped pulling at her hair and looked at him. "So that's why you wanted to move in," she said. "Just to get your hands on my Porsche?"

"What other reason could there be?" he asked innocently.

She grinned. "Well, it failed. I'm driving," she said, and firmly opened her car door. "A Princess has to have her life saved at least twice before any Prince Charming gets to drive the Porsche."

"It's a tough life," he complained, and walked round to the passenger side. "But at least this way, I get to see your legs while you drive."

"It will have to do," she said, her smile almost hidden, and started the engine.

*   *   *   *

"It proves it's PAC," said Peter Haywood. The distress on his face was acute.

"We already knew that," replied Garry. The nausea from Rich's blows had faded, but the memory of the terrifying power of the man lay like a disease on his mind.

"But we still haven't told the cops that," said Charlie Levin. "Maybe we should have, this time. They're highly suspicious after your last episode."

"As we said before, who'd believe a firm like PAC has taken out a contract on us?" objected Peter. "They'd think we're nuts."

"Of course, it could always be Craig Hampton, Micky's old boyfriend causing this," suggested Charlie with a smile. "Jealous ex-lover, a classic case."

"I think not," replied Micky, responding to the smile. "If it doesn't help Craig become a judge, it's unimportant. And I didn't help that way."

"No, it's PAC alright," said Garry. "That last meeting made it plain enough. Newman was enjoying the fact that I knew but couldn't do anything about it. And I did suggest to the cops that PAC was behind it all."

"You did? Jeez, what did they say to that?" Peter looked astounded.

"Exactly what we thought they'd say," replied Garry. "I told that detective who came to see me that I thought PAC had taken a contract out on both Andrew Whittaker and me, and he laughed himself silly."

"With justification," replied Charlie. "However true it may be, it sounds crazy."

"On which subject, what do we propose to do?" asked Peter. "Any constructive ideas?"

"I think it's time we took the initiative," said Garry.

All eyes turned to him.

Peter laughed. "Take it?" he said. "We've had the initiative by the short and curlies ever since you got here! Just what are you suggesting?"

"We agreed before," said Garry, "that the way to stop this nonsense is either to give in, or wait until PAC goes to meet the Great Auditor in the Sky."

"That's true," agreed Charlie. "And we're not giving in, so we wait? That's it?"

"Not at all," replied Garry. "We hasten the demise."

"Ah!" said Peter with a smile of comprehension, and stood up, walking out of the boardroom. A moment later, he returned, carrying a reference volume of American companies and their auditors. "We go for their last major clients, eh? Nasty, evil thinking, Barton. I love it."

"Unethical, but a humane killing," agreed Charlie.

"To hell with ethics," said Micky loudly. "Let's get them!"

The other three looked at her in astonishment.

"What she said," murmured Garry, taking Micky's hand for a moment.

She grinned in embarrassment at her unusual show of temper. "Let's get them," she repeated, more softly, but still angry.

"Let's get them," echoed Peter, and opened the reference volume. For several moments, he poured over the pages while the others waited undisguised impatience.

"Mid-West Dynamos," said Peter with a smile. "We got them, courtesy of young Garry here. And Cambridge Modelling, the same thing. Carswell Enterprises and ESR Chemicals both went to Hopman and Darman."

Another few moments passed in silence, before Peter broke it again. "Illinois Metals has just moved over to Price Waterhouse, and Blackman Engineering is wobbling, planning to move to Deloitte's, I believe. My God, PAC's really bleeding to death! Maybe we don't need to do anything, they'll be folding up within six months."

"In six months, they could do a lot of damage," objected Garry. "To Micky, to me, or to any of us. No, kill them now."

"Kill them now, it is," murmured Peter and returned to studying the reference text. A few more minutes passed before he broke the silence.

"Mortensen Transport is pretty big," he said. "But they'd stay loyal as long as possible after the rescue job Newman and Petheram did on them last year."

"Agreed," said Garry. "And not a client I'd want, anyway. Nasty bunch, a reputation for questionable business practices."

"Hmm..." said Peter, drifting into study again. "The Sullivan Group, we know they've lost them." He grinned widely at the listeners, and returned to the book. "Then it's probably Chesterman Carter we should be going for."

Garry thought about the name. Chesterman's was a client to whom he had asked Trent for an introduction, knowing of the company's obsolete computer systems. Trent had consistently refused. There was an elegant justice in this selection.

"A good choice," Garry said. "Anne Bertolli was the audit manager there when she was with PAC."

"Splendid!" said Peter Haywood. "Call her in, and let's get this show on the road."

"Something we should think about, first," said Charlie Levin. His face was serious. "It's clear that the major targets of violence are Micky and Garry. I don't think that'll change. I'd be happier if Micky was away clear before we launch the final assault."

"I can take my chances with the rest of you," protested Micky. But the reaction in the room was against her.

"It's causing havoc trying to protect you here," said Peter. "And using our employees as bodyguards is against every rule in the book."

Micky glared at him, and then turned to Garry. "Are you in this conspiracy, too?" she demanded.

He took her hand. "Dead right I am," he said. "Micky, worrying about you will paralyze us, and PAC knows that. I'd be a lot more comfortable if you were safely elsewhere."

She looked around the table then subsided. "I suppose I can see that," she said. "What would you suggest?"

"Remember last year when you proposed we establish an affiliation with British accounting firms to give us a European link?" asked Peter. Micky nodded, her eyes opening wider as she saw the point of the question.

"This seems like a good time to check out Britain," continued Peter. "And it's a genuine trip too, no holiday. You were right then, and we need the connection even more now that we've grown so much."

"Okay," she said.

"Good," said Peter. "Now call Anne Bertolli."

* * * *

"It's a follow-up call, Mister Barton."

Detective Sergeant Burroughs lounged at ease in the chair across from the coffee table in Garry's office. The policeman's visit, coming as it did only a day after Garry had seen Micky off on her flight to London, was unwelcome. Garry had not told the police about the attack in the apartment building parking lot, and the appearance of the law worried him.

"Follow-up to what, Detective Sergeant?

"To my confusion, my ignorance and general discombobulation, Mister Barton."

Despite his unease, Garry grinned at the other man. "I doubt all those things, detective. How can I help you?"

"I'm still investigating the death of Andrew Whittaker," replied Burroughs. "I have to tell you, there's something not kosher about that incident."

"I told you my concerns. You crapped all over me."

"Let's say I had no reason to believe such an extreme piece of imagination," replied Burroughs.

"And now you think that perhaps I'm not such a crackpot as you first thought?"

"Mmm." Burroughs was noncommittal.

"Why?"

"I had a fascinating little chat with Jack Conway soon after I talked to you."

"You did?" Garry was astonished. "And what did Jack have to say?"

"He said that Andrew Whittaker had left PAC on the best of terms, and with excellent references."

Garry shrugged. "I can believe the excellent references."

"But not the best of terms?"

"No, but that's only my view. I can't give you anything more concrete."

"I raised the question of why two recently-departed members of PAC would be attacked within a day of each other," continued Burroughs. "Mister Conway seemed a tad upset at the thought. I think the idea surprised him."

Garry was silent. *So, Jack hadn't been part of Andrew's murder*, he thought. *That meant Bridget Newman had probably organized it herself. Who the hell did she know who could arrange a killing?*

"So have you revised your opinion of what happened?" Garry was becoming irritated by the detective's attitude. He seemed to be revisiting old ground and had not asked any new questions.

"I hadn't, until your episode in the Ohio Street parking lot the other night."

"What?" The detective's words hit Garry like a fist.

"You're not the only people with a computer network, Mister Barton," said Burroughs with a weary smile. "I saw a little item about some goon chasing a man in a tuxedo and crashing into a group of young people in the process. One of those youngsters gave a description somewhat similar to the one you gave of your attacker to the Wilmette police."

Garry said nothing, but his nerves tightened a notch.

"And the description of the man being chased could have fitted you, too," continued Burroughs. "And it also fitted the description given by a clerk at a deli on Fullerton, of a man in a tuxedo buying over-night stuff at twenty minutes after midnight. The same store where a Toyota Corolla was found after being reported stolen a couple of hours earlier."

Garry felt a light sweat on his back.

"Am I making you nervous, Mister Barton?" The detective's tones were hard and clear, the air of fatigue gone.

"Who stays calm, being interrogated by the Homicide Squad?" asked Garry, trying to hide his worry.

"Innocent people," replied the detective coolly. "But I can see that somebody who steals a car after being attacked, and stays in a seedy motel near the airport could be less than completely at ease. Especially when that person earns enough to stay in the

Presidential Suite at the Hilton if he had wanted to, and that's where the cab dropped that person."

"You're a good detective, aren't you?" Garry took a deep breath and tried to calm his nerves.

"I don't think I have enough to charge you with grand theft auto," replied Burroughs. "Especially as the owner isn't making charges. He says thanks for taking care of it, by the way."

"I'm relieved to hear it," said Garry.

Burroughs grunted. "So what I'm left with is this," he continued. "I have a man dead in Evanston, shot by a nine-millimetre hand-gun. I have an ex-colleague of his assaulted the following night. The same ex-colleague narrowly escapes another assault, apparently by the same man, a few weeks later. And then, if that don't beat all, you get another incident in your girlfriend's parking lot a few nights ago."

The two men stared at each other. Garry felt his heart pounding, and the sweat on his back felt clammy.

"Another resident came down in the elevator as it was all going on," explained Burroughs. "She gave us a good description of one of the men who attacked you."

"I see," said Garry. He was at a complete loss for anything more intelligent.

"I said grand theft auto was out," continued Burroughs. "But obstruction of the law is not. Now, Mister Barton, what the hell is going on?"

"I told you what I thought, the first time we spoke," replied Garry. "I think PAC is trying to stop my firm from expanding our business at their expense."

"But Andrew Whittaker wasn't involved in that," retorted Burroughs.

"I can't explain Andrew's murder," said Garry. "But if he'd left PAC just a few days before, maybe it was because he knew what they were going to do."

"Then why didn't he tell the police?" Burroughs looked angry.

"Would you have believed him?" Garry's own anger broke through. "Look how you reacted when I told you the same thing. You thought I was a lunatic!"

Burroughs looked shamefaced. "Yeah, I suppose so," he said. "But the time for that is over. Mister Barton, do you have a mobile phone?"

"Yes."

"Then, if you see either of the two men who attacked you, I want you to call the police immediately. Got that?"

"I've got it."

"And don't go near PAC."

"Why should I?"

"You've done it already, Mister Barton. Don't do it again."

"You keep astonishing me, Detective Sergeant Burroughs. Okay, no more visits to PAC."

"Good. Now, is there anything, anything at all, you can tell me that you've left out so far?"

"I don't think so."

"I hope that's true. Obstruction of a police investigation is still on the cards."

"Yes, Detective Sergeant Burroughs."

Chapter 13

"I think we received a very clear signal from HLM," said Conway. "They have not been intimidated at all. It leaves us in a perilous situation."

"Chesterman's are definitely moving their account?" asked Petheram. The silence from the others around the table answered him. He leaned back in his seat and looked out of the window.

"Six partners have written to me with their resignations," continued Conway. His face was without expression. "Fourteen other people have resigned this week. Many of them have taken positions with HLM and continued their work with the same clients."

"I have to ask now," said Trent, "is there any hope for this firm?"

"Of course there is," hissed Newman. "Being defeatist is the worst possible thing right now, William."

"Really?" Trent was unmoved. "We've been defeated all the way down the line," he said. "And your men have not been as effective as you promised."

"No, I agree Mortensen has not been up to standard," replied Newman, her voice icy. "I've expressed my displeasure."

"They failed again when they tried to take Ashley?" asked Petheram. "Seems to me they've failed just about too often. What happened?"

Newman locked her fingers together. For the first time any of the men at the table could recall, she looked uncomfortable. "Barton had anticipated our action," she said. "He had two very large escorts and they fought off Mortensen's men."

"Jesus Christ!" said Petheram in disgust. "They'd better improve on that sort of performance!"

"Regardless of that," said Conway, "we are now desperate. We really do face extinction, and I'm ready to consider any suggestion."

"Then we have to look at the whole cause of this crisis and take the final measures," said Newman. "I'm still certain that if we remove the basic cause of this problem we can recover."

Conway stirred in his chair. His face was a little paler than usual, though he appeared otherwise composed. "Is this what happened to Andrew Whittaker?" he asked quietly, his eyes directly on Newman. "Have you already taken such action to remove a problem?"

The room was silent. Trent and Petheram were holding their breaths.

Newman recovered from her momentary discomfort. "Andrew was a threat," she said, softly. "None of you would believe it, but I knew. It was too early for you to face up to the need for direct action. So I took it on your behalf. It was necessary."

"Oh God," whispered Petheram. "You had Andrew shot?"

"It was necessary," she repeated calmly. "Just as this next stage is necessary."

The silence lasted over a minute, and none of the four would meet anyone else's eyes.

Finally, Conway broke the stillness. "Which brings us to the question of Garry Barton," he said, tapping his gold pen on the cover of his desk diary. "I suspect we have all been waiting for this moment to arrive."

"It is certainly time we settled that question, once and for all," agreed Newman.

Conway looked at her. "Had you intended to reach this point since the beginning, Bridget?"

She didn't return his glance. "That question is meaningless, Jack. The point has been reached, and that's the only matter for discussion now."

"Nonetheless, I'd like an answer to it, as well," broke in Trent. He stared hard at Newman, looking more self-controlled than in recent weeks.

"Then I'm afraid you'll have to be disappointed, William," she replied coldly. "This is wasting time. We must make a decision and make it immediately. We have our firm to rescue."

"Will it make any difference what we decide, Bridget?" asked Petheram, a grim smile on his lips. "Or will you take unilateral action the way you did with Andrew?"

All three men were looking at Newman with fascination. She stared at each of them for a few seconds in turn, and one by one, their eyes dropped.

"And if I did," she replied, "just what exactly would any of you do about it?"

The room was silent, until Conway shifted in his chair and cleared his throat. "As Bridget says, the matter of Garry Barton is now on the table," said Conway. "Does anyone wish to make any suggestions, or add a comment?"

He looked at each of them in turn, tapping his gold pen against his lips. For the first time since the meeting had started, four faces looked at each other openly, without tension, and a decision was reached without words being needed. Newman spoke for them all.

"We have him killed, of course," she said quietly.

* * * *

Newman closed the door to her office and took her seat at her desk with a small smile on her face. *It had worked!* She sat back in her luxurious seat and almost wriggled with delight. They had all come around and almost begged for Barton to be killed. Now they'd all know it was *her* leadership that had achieved it. *Her* courage when Conway had been too cowardly to do it. *Her* knowledge of how to get such unorthodox actions put into operation. She had them now, she knew. Give it six months for the business to start recovering, and she'd move a vote of no confidence in Conway's chairmanship at the next full partners' meeting. She'd brief Trent to second the motion and to propose her as the next chairperson. He'd go along with it, she knew. He was too scared of her to resist, and he was equally certain that she'd succeed. Trent was just cattle to be led where she wanted.

She took a deep breath. Not only was the chair within her grasp, but so was the special prize, the one she had been driving toward for months. She waited a few moments, breathing carefully to aid her self-control, trying to ignore the excitement in the pit of her stomach. She picked up the phone and dialled the direct line for Mortensen's office.

"It's time to finish it," she said when he answered.

"I'll see to it at once," he replied.

"And there's one more thing," she added before he could hang up the phone.

"What's that, Bridget?"

Newman took a deep breath. She was about to ask for the most wonderful, glorious and exciting gift she could have ever dreamed of giving herself, and she wanted to savour the moment.

"I want to see it," she said, her voice revealing a tiny tremble of emotion despite her attempt at rigid control.

"What?" Mortensen sounded puzzled.

"I want to see it happen," she said, iron discipline back in her voice. "I want to be there when your men complete the business."

Mortensen was silent for a few seconds. "I wouldn't advise that," he said eventually. "The whole point of this arrangement has been your lack of any connection with the process. You want to keep it that way."

"Stan, if there's no risk to you then there's no risk to me. I want to see this thing completed. Indulge me this small thing. You owe me."

Mortensen was silent again for a few moments. She heard his small sigh of acceptance over the phone and felt a wave of excitement run through her.

"All right, Bridget, I'll make sure you're there when it happens." Mortensen sounded subdued. "I'll have to check with the men, of course."

"Thank you, Stan," she replied. "I'll never forget this."

"I can guarantee that," he said dryly and hung up the phone.

Newman shivered with delight and anticipation. The chair of Porter, Allen & Conway was soon to be hers. She could almost taste the sensation of having the partners unanimously vote for her. And she would see Barton killed! She visualized several scenarios of that event, and felt twinges of pleasure in her belly.

By God, Phillip Wareham, she thought with a sudden rush of emotion. *If you were here now, we'd surely repeat that odd little session on your carpet we had at university.*

Chapter 14

For the next two weeks the partners of HLM sweated out their anxieties. They had walked into the lion's den and stolen its food. Any moment now, the beast in the shape of the management committee at Porter, Allen & Conway was going to snarl and bite. For Garry, the tension was compounded by the absence of Micky, even though it eased his mind to know that she was away from danger. The silence echoed from PAC and the screws tightened each day that nothing happened.

Late in the second week, Peter broached the possibility that perhaps the partners of PAC had recognized the reality of the situation and were concentrating their efforts on survival, rather than revenge. Garry hardly dared let himself believe that.

Late on a Thursday afternoon, Garry left the offices of a client in the north-west suburbs of Chicago. He had been reviewing the work of two of his consultants on a systems development project, and his mind was heavily occupied by the questions that had been raised by the review.

The client had recently moved the offices to a new industrial park outside Barrington and few of the buildings were complete. Garry was driving across a wide expanse of empty fields when a station wagon suddenly accelerated and passed him on his left. Seeing the shape materialize, Garry looked idly to one side and froze as he saw Rich's blank stare at him across the small gap between the two vehicles. Garry slammed on the brakes but he had no time for evasive action. The station wagon stopped almost as abruptly and reversed back to Garry's car. Desperately, Garry shifted into reverse, and accelerated away. But the road was narrow, and there was nowhere to turn. The pursuer continued backward, keeping pace with Garry. When Garry tried one turn of the wheel to throw his car around, he went off the road and his wheels stuck in loose earth.

Rich leaped out of his car, reached Garry's door and flung it open. Garry had barely undone his seat belt.

"You're coming with me, buddy," mumbled the huge shape filling the sky outside the car window, and he grabbed Garry's shoulder. His other hand fastened on Garry's throat and Garry was unable to apply enough pressure to free himself. Choking, fighting for air, he was hauled out of the Continental just in time to see a white cloth descending on his face. The powerful hand on his throat was released, and uncontrollably, Garry took a deep breath. He barely had the time to recognize the smell of ether when the surrounding industrial park faded from his view and he blacked out.

He had travelled through time, back some months to a nightmare. That was his first thought as he struggled through the storm clouds that filled his head with pain. He was face down in the same old car in which he had been taken to the beach at Wilmette. The same crushing feet held him rigid, and the same odours of mildew, oil and stale cigarette smoke assaulted him.

The memories of the attack near Barrington rushed into his clearing mind, and he struggled to move.

"Just stay where you are, pal," said the mild tones of Rich, and the pressure increased sharply in his shoulders. Garry subsided. He could not have shifted that weight any more than he could pull a locomotive. Instead, as the fog in his mind cleared, he concentrated on the car and the sounds from outside, but learned little that was informative.

They were on a highway, that seemed evident. The car had not varied in speed or direction since he had emerged from the clouds of pain, and the speed seemed quite high, judging by the sound of the engine and the whine of the transmission immediately under his chest and face. But he had no idea of how long he had been out, or in which direction they were travelling. Nor did he have any idea of what... The first wave of fear hit him and his throat constricted sharply. He could not be certain of what his captors intended to do with him but he could guess. Rich's warning the last time had been explicit enough. At best, he was going to be badly injured, perhaps permanently. At worst... He had to face up to it, he decided. He might be going to die.

The next hour was as bad a time as he could ever have imagined. The appalling fear that sat like rotten, maggot-ridden meat in his gut was accompanied by dryness of the throat from the ether and a pounding headache. Every muscle in his body was issuing pain signals from his cramped, forced position on the floor of the car, and the smell of dust, oil and mildew combined with the stale tobacco reek so that at one time he gagged painfully and retched, but nothing came out of his dry throat.

Eventually the car slowed, turned off the freeway and travelled for what Garry estimated was another twenty minutes with occasional stops. One more turn was made at very slow speed, and the ancient vehicle lurched and swerved. There was a clanking of a gear shift accompanied by muttered words from the driver then, with a whining of gears the car began to reverse down a steep incline before stopping. The driver got out and Garry heard a sound like a large door being opened. The driver returned, reversed the car a few more yards into darkness, stopped and switched off the engine.

Rich finally lifted his huge feet from Garry's shoulders and slid off to one side, forcing open the car door with a screech of protesting metalwork, and got out.

"Okay, pal, you're with me," he said in his curiously high-pitched voice, and hauled Garry off the floor of the car and out through the door.

Garry stumbled and nearly fell as his legs failed to hold him. But Rich caught him and held him upright, giving Garry yet another unwelcome face full of unwashed clothing, stale cigarettes and bad breath. He was pulled along the floor and lowered to the ground against one wall. To Garry's dismay, the second man approached with a hank of rope. He shoved Garry forward against his knees and seized his wrists. While Rich held Garry's head, the other man bound his wrists then tied them to some part of the building structure before Rich released him to lean backward again.

"That'll hold him," said the man, and stared down at Garry. Garry looked back, trying to fix the details of the man's thin face in his mind, and then screamed in pain and shock as the man swung his boot into Garry's ribs. The man stood back and watched with pleasure as Garry shook with the pain of the blow.

Rich grabbed his partner. "There's no need for that," he said loudly.

"There sure was," snarled the other. "He hurt me real bad the last time."

Garry was gasping for breath and the fact that he couldn't reach the point of the pain to hold it made it that much worse. Luckily, Rich led the other man away back toward the station wagon.

Trying to ignore the fear and pain, Garry looked around him. He was in a boathouse. Two small dinghies lay on trestles at one end of the building, and a long sail mast ran almost the whole length of the building on a series of smaller trestles down the middle. The place smelled of oil, paint and stagnant water.

He looked at the tiny, dirty windows that lined the far wall. They were too high to see through, but it looked like it was still daylight outside, though the light appeared to fading. He tried to work out how long it had been since his capture. He had left the clients' offices about five. Judging by the light, he thought it might be some time around eight. *God,* he thought in desperation, *we could be over a hundred miles away from Chicago.* There were hundreds of lakes around. He could be in Wisconsin, downstate in Illinois near Springfield, or on the lake shore in Michigan. How could he ever know where he was?

Rich and his sidekick pulled a couple of wooden chairs away from one wall and placed them by the station wagon. Rich lit a cigarette then took a newspaper from the car and settled down to read. The other man merely sat down and stared dully at the floor. Garry looked at them for a few moments in dreadful fascination. They were his executioners, he was certain. *How can they sit there undisturbed when they are about to kill a man?* he thought in horror.

The fear filled his body. If he had thought that begging for his life would have worked, he would have done it, he knew, without shame. He thought about the life in Australia he had left twelve years ago with such excitement as he went to England and then came to North America. Life had seemed too narrow in Sydney, too far away from the centres of business action. Now he thought about the beaches, and the superb climate, the seafood and the long, brilliant days floating in his sailboat on the beautiful harbour waters. The pain of longing filled his body, tears rose into his eyes and he sniffed.

Micky. Oh, Micky, he thought, and streaks of pain ran through his mind. *How could I have been so foolish, so full of macho bravado? Why did I not remember the old saying that this too shall pass? Why was I so sure that PAC had folded? They had displayed enough insanity already. Why would they just give in without a fight?*

Garry was certain then that he would die that night, and the only time he had left was until the two men sitting so calmly by the station wagon decided it was dark enough to kill him.

Where the hell was he? Again and again that question rumbled through him, though he was horribly aware that the answer wouldn't save him. Nobody could find him, nobody could come and rescue him. For a few seconds, he let his mind run free, rather than think about his situation. In a movie, Rich would leave the boathouse. Garry would somehow work his way free and escape. Later, he would return and exact dreadful retribution.

He tested his bonds. No escape. He was going to die.

The dark grew more intense and Rich stood up to switch on a light. The miserable gleam at one end of the boathouse somehow made it even worse for Garry. He would not see the light of a day again. Anger, pain, fear and horror squirmed in his insides like a mound of writhing worms, and he struggled to retain control of himself. Somehow, he refused to show fear to his killers, it had become the only important thing in his remaining life.

He was aware that the two men were shifting in their chairs and examining their watches with increasing frequency.

"He's late," he heard the unnamed second man mutter at one point, but Rich's answer was unclear, merely a rumble in the shadows. The second man spoke again.

"Should probably put him under right now," he said, and Garry saw Rich nod and stand up. Blind terror ran through him, churning his insides like the spiked wheels of the old war chariots, and his breathing stopped for a few seconds. He watched as if through a fine mist as Rich walked to the station wagon, extracted a bottle of clear liquid and some loose cloths, and began to walk down the boathouse. Garry began to struggle against his bonds.

"No!" he gasped, as Rich bent over him. "Please, don't!" He fought to keep his face away from Rich's hands, but the huge man grabbed his hair and held him still.

"C'mon, guy," he muttered, and moved the cloth towards Garry's face. "It'll be easier this way."

Despite the pain, Garry jerked his head then raised his feet and kicked out at the bottle, knocking it away from Rich. Clear liquid spilled on the dirty concrete floor.

"Shit!" swore Rich and picked up the bottle again. He poured the last few drops of ether into the cloth and once more took hold of Garry's hair. With a solid thump, the cloth landed on Garry's face. He struggled, holding his breath, broke free for a second then the cloth covered his universe and the miserable scene faded from his view.

Garry felt himself being carried outside. For a blink of time, he saw the moon and smelled the water. In another blink he was lying on a wooden surface, and a vague shape was floating past his eyes. There had been nothing between the blinks, but he had moved, as if some celestial film director had cut between scenes.

A dark face stared at him during one small flicker of the universe. Black eyes sparkled in the row of small lights that lined the jetty. The eyes seemed to suck his soul from him as if feeding on his terror. He knew the face. It had lived in a world he had left behind long ago. Creation blinked again.

He just had time to see another shape before the next flicker. *"Lion,"* said his mind for no reason that he could comprehend. He fell into a dreamless sleep...

... and woke up in a dreadful crash of cold that covered him like an avalanche and tore the breath from him, filled his nose and covered his eyes. Completely without understanding, he concentrated on the single most important thing his mind could hold, to get air into his lungs. Shapeless gleams of light moved before him, burning irons were grinding down in his chest, and his head broke into cold air. He held his head vertical, his mouth toward the bright stars, as if by doing so the air would flow more quickly. He sucked oxygen into his body like the intake of a jet engine, sobbing as he grabbed hold of life.

His mind refused to function. He could only experience breathing, while without thought he moved his hands and feet slowly to keep his head where it was. He was in deep water, that much he could tell himself. A shape darker than the night moved away from him, accompanied by a murmur of engines. Beyond those small things, he knew only that he could breathe, that his hands were free... *his hands were free!* It came back to him with a roll of fear, like slimy water falling on his head.

He had been put to sleep by Rich, that was the last thing he remembered. Somehow, he had woken up when Rich had thrown him off the boat. That was surely wrong, he decided. The outcome for which his captors had been aiming for was that Garry would drown while still unconscious. His bonds had been removed, so that if the body was found, the police might think Garry had fallen off a boat by accident, rather than been murdered.

How could this have happened? he pondered, still not awake enough to consider how he might get out of this situation without creating reality out of Rich's scenario. No answers came to him. *Damn, he was still wearing a business suit!* With difficulty, he shrugged off the soaking jacket, removed his tie and was unable to stop swallowing a mouthful of dank water as he pulled his shoes off. The dizziness began to return to him. He forgot Rich and boathouses and murder attempts... He let himself float on his back, and stared at the stars. *The water was cold for Sydney Harbour in summer,* he mused dreamily. *I should be seeing the lights of the city... got to watch out for sharks... ah look, there's Sydney... funny, can't see the Opera House or the Bridge... should always be able to see the Bridge, what am I doing swimming in the harbour at this time of night?...* A faceful of water slapped him awake again, and he struggled for breath. *My God,* he thought, for the first time realizing the situation. *I'm in the water, miles from anywhere.... no, I just saw lights... where the hell are the lights?* He floated vertical, let his legs drop and turned around. *There! Lights! God knows where I am.* He began to swim.

After a while, he turned on his back again, and kept swimming. The dream-like state returned to him, and he lost contact with reality. *I was always a backstroke swimmer at school, never any good at the Australian crawl, that's why I didn't make it on to the lifesaving squads on Bondi Beach... pity really, the girls really went for the lifesavers... got to watch for those sharks... are those lights getting any nearer? Keep paddling, Garry, and you'll make it... should be seeing the Opera House at some point, at least the Bridge... hope there's no large ships moving out of Woolloomooloo docks...*

He bumped into something and screamed. *A shark!* His whole body exploded with fear. He came fully awake. He'd hit a structure of some sort. Breathlessly, he grabbed for support, groped wildly and took hold of a metal bar. Fatigue and cold were draining the strength from him as if his life was pouring through a tap in his feet. Somehow, he hauled himself up and found he was on a flat surface. His legs were still in the water. He drew on some strength that had been hiding until now, and climbed a little higher. Another flat surface. A staircase of some sort. *Where the hell was he?* But he was out of the water. He just had time to grin at himself for the moment of uncontrollable terror, reminding himself that sharks were not that plentiful in America's lakes, and blacked out, clinging on to a bar of wonderfully secure metal that held him up.

"My God! Are you okay?"

The hand on his shoulder and the insistent female voice dragged Garry from insane dreams of raging thirst, huge faces approaching him with bottles that held terrifying fear, and visions of staring lions that roared as they prepared to kill him with one bite to the neck....

The fearful thirst was the element that remained as he opened his eyes, but for a second he forgot even that. She was about eighteen, and wearing a minuscule bikini. She was standing over him, and the expression of concern on her face dragged his eyes away from the rest of her for a few seconds.

"Yes, I think so," he croaked, and looked around him. A sailing boat of generous proportions was tied up to the structure that was supporting Garry and the nymphet. Half a dozen more faces were staring at Garry from the boat. The sun was fairly low in the east still, but hot and bright, and several other boats were on the water. It was Saturday, realized Garry. The backdrop of scenery pleased him intensely. He had rarely seen Chicago look more beautiful. He knew where he was. The large metal structure was one of the water treatment stations on the Lake. He had sailed past it many times.

"But how did you get here?" demanded the young woman.

Garry managed a smile at her. "Had a boating accident overnight," he rasped. "Could I get a drink?"

"Of course," she said, and put a hand under his arm to help him stand up. He needed the support, as she walked him down the metal ramp to the boat's prow, and he stood still for a moment as the crew pulled the boat into contact with the metal. He was able to clamber aboard, and more hands helped him walk to the back of the vessel. A young man stood by the wheel and studied him.

"Trouble?" he asked economically.

"Fell off a boat last night," repeated Garry. "Can I have a drink?"

The young man smiled widely and pointed at a cooler behind him. Another bikini-clad girl reached in and pulled out a can of beer. The hiss and click as she opened it was one of the most beautiful sounds on earth, thought Garry, and the taste as he poured the beer down his throat almost made him faint with delight.

"Can we take you back?" asked the man at the wheel.

Garry nodded. "Please," he said with feeling.

"Belmont Harbour suit you?"

"Perfect," said Garry.

The man reached into a small locker by the wheel and extracted a mobile phone. "You could probably use this, I think," he said, and laughed at Garry's expression. Garry took the phone and dialled Peter's number. The wait while the phone rang at the other end was psychic torture, but Peter answered after only two rings.

"It's Garry."

"Oh Christ! Garry! Where the hell are you?" The relief in Peter's voice was overwhelming. "We've had a police hunt going since your car was found near Barrington last night."

"I'll tell you later," said Garry. "Can you meet me at the sailing harbour at Belmont in about an hour? I'm being brought in by a good-sized sailing boat."

"Belmont? A sailing boat?" The questions were loud in Peter's voice, but he wasted no time. "I'll be there."

"Good. Call off the police search."

Garry switched off the phone and handed it back. He drained the beer can, and looked at the girl who had given it to him. "Can I trade this in for a full one?" he asked, and watched in thirsty agony as she extracted another can and gave it to him.

The rest of the way in, he sat at the back of the boat and looked at the skyline of Chicago. Fortunately, the others did not pester him with questions, and settled into their own routines of sunbathing. A CD player was set up in the bow and the music of some unnamed rock group caused several of the youngsters to start dancing. Garry idly watched the display, thought how beautiful the kids looked, and realized they didn't have anything to make him forget Micky.

"Must be getting older and wiser," he muttered to himself. For a second, he wondered how he could be so calm under the circumstances then abandoned the thought as the boat entered the harbour area.

He could see Peter's Mercedes parked near the dock as the boat was gently brought alongside. He shook hands with the boat's skipper, and jumped off, leaving the boat to return to the open waters.

Peter was staring at him. "What a bloody mess you look!" he said then surprised Garry by grabbing him and hugging him. "We thought we'd lost you for sure," he said.

"You nearly had," replied Garry and returned the hug. "Get me somewhere where I can change my clothes, for God's sake."

"My place," said Peter, and turned to the Mercedes. He opened the passenger door and Garry collapsed in exhaustion into the seat. He slept some of the way back to Peter's house and came awake as the car turned into the driveway. He followed Peter into the cool of the house, and fell limply on to a couch.

"Food, I think," said Peter, and moved to the kitchen.

Garry struggled back to his feet and followed him. "Some more to drink, too," he added.

In the large, well-equipped kitchen, Garry took a bar stool by the hatch. Peter took a large jug of orange juice from the fridge and passed it to him with a glass. Garry busied himself lowering the level of juice, feeling life flow back into him.

"Bacon and eggs okay?" Peter was unwrapping packages from the fridge, and Garry's stomach rumbled at the sight.

"Magic," he replied and took another long drink of the orange juice. A few minutes of silence reigned.

"There's a tracksuit hanging in my cupboard," said Peter. "Go and grab that, underwear in the drawer. They'll just about fit you."

Garry stumbled into the bedroom, found the change of clothing, left his ruined trousers in the bathroom and came back to the kitchen.

"Pauline's shopping with the kid," said Peter into the silence. "They'll be back about noon."

With a shock, Garry looked at his watch. It was functioning and showed the time to be just before eleven.

"It was the same two thugs again," he said, watching several rashers of bacon being laid out in a pan. "They caught me where you found the car, and knocked me out with ether."

Peter gave him a startled glance then pushed four slices of bread into a king-sized toaster.

Garry recounted what he could remember of the last hours, reliving the fear and pain of the experience. "They tried to kill me," he said at the end.

"Jesus Christ!" Peter broke several eggs into the pan.

"I only survived because I didn't get a full dose of ether," continued Garry.

"Makes sense," said Peter, and placed a huge plate in front of him. Garry forgot everything else and attacked the food.

"The police want to talk to you as soon as you can get there," said Peter. Garry nodded, too occupied with the wonders of fried bacon and eggs to say anything.

It was thirty minutes before anyone spoke again.

"Those loonies at PAC have gone completely out of control," said Peter, removing the plates and stacking them in the dishwasher. "The whole thing was insane. They hadn't stopped us before the attack on you, and the firm is about dead, anyway."

"Revenge, rather than persuasion," nodded Garry. "I think they'd forgotten what the objective was by this time."

"What are you going to tell the cops?"

"Nothing about PAC, that's for sure," replied Garry. "The same problem remains. We know they're crazy, but who'd believe us? I'll just describe Rich and his little pal."

"And then?"

"I have to find out who Rich and his number two

work for," said Garry. "If I can find the house where I was kept last night, we'll have the answer."

"How the hell will you do that?"

"Can't be too difficult. The place is obviously on the shores of Lake Michigan. Judging by the distance I think we drove, it's either north towards Milwaukee, or south and east on the Michigan side."

Peter nodded thoughtfully. "Some biggish houses along the Indiana-Michigan coast," he agreed. "Along the dunes near Michigan City and places like that, going up to Benton Harbour."

"And also north," said Garry. "All that old money with mansions in Wisconsin."

"But how will you know the place?" asked Peter. "You were out cold when you left the boat house."

Garry shook his head. "There's something bugging me about that," he murmured. "Somehow, I'm certain I'll know the place when I see it. But God knows how. It's just an idea in the back of my mind."

"Why did they motor all the way back to Chicago to dump you?" asked Peter. "Why not just drop you off well out in the lake?"

"Strange, that," agreed Garry. "But they'd taken the ropes off my arms. Maybe they wanted me to be found near the city. It would look like a boating accident. But you and the others at HLM would get the message."

"God almighty!" Peter looked thunderstruck. "What a bunch of bastards!"

Garry stood up, stretching with some difficulty. "There I agree with you," he said. "But I need to get home and have a shower and get some decent clothes on. Then I have to get to Barrington, talk to the cops and get my car back."

"Is it safe to go to your place?" Peter looked frightened. "What if they're watching for you?"

Garry shook his head. "They're sure I'm dead," he said. "No need to watch my place any more. Can you give me a ride?"

"Of course. I called Charlie and gave him the news while you were changing, and I'll leave a note for Pauline."

Garry sat down sharply in the couch as if the strings had been cut from his muscles.

"Jesus, Peter!" he choked, his voice almost failing him. "They tried to kill me!" Only then did the fear and the shock strike him so deeply that his control dissipated. He broke into tears and wept with a desperate, explosive pain that lasted twenty minutes while Peter tactfully left him alone. When the weeping, the shivers and the agony faded, he took several deep breaths, stood up and walked into the washroom to throw cold water over his face.

"Sorry," he said with a tiny grin as Peter walked back into the room, a few minutes later. "I lost it for a time."

"Hardly a surprise, Garry. I was wondering how you had stayed so cool."

"It's time to get the bastards, Peter."

"Long overdue."

For safety, despite his certainty that his enemies would believe him dead, Garry stayed at Peter's house that night. The two men and Pauline consumed large steaks, killed a bottle of Californian red wine, and talked at length on every subject they could find. Later, Garry helped put Jennifer to bed with some stories about life in Australia, and by ten, he was dead to the world in the comfort of Peter's guest room.

He spent the Sunday in a mixture of sleeping, and reading, while his mind cleaned out the horrors of the past two days. Twice more, he collapsed in a storm of weeping as the shame of his fear took over again. Peter and Pauline stayed with him, unwilling to leave him alone. Charlie Levin and Rebecca came during the afternoon, displaying the same gladness to see Garry safe and well as had Peter.

When he felt his strength had returned, he went with Peter to the police and signed all the statements and paperwork they asked of him. Not at all to his surprise, the immaculately dressed Detective Sergeant Burroughs appeared as he was completing the last of the papers.

"A word with you, Mr. Barton," he said.

"Of course," said Garry and followed the detective into an interview room.

"I may have under-estimated you," said Burroughs.

"Hardly surprising. I can barely believe this is happening myself."

"You're still of the belief that PAC is behind all this?"

"I am. But I can't prove it."

Burroughs shook his head. "It's still beyond any rational thought. And I can't go back in there and accuse them of it."

"That's the problem," Garry said. "There's no obvious connection."

"But you can describe the two guys who grabbed you?"

"Oh yes. And the place they held me."

"But you don't know where that is?"

"I don't."

For the next thirty minutes, Garry gave the detective a detailed description of his captors and the boathouse that had been his death row for the agonising hours of the previous night. Finally, Burroughs nodded his approval for Garry to leave.

"Don't do anything stupid, will you, Mr. Barton?" he said as Garry was ready to walk out. "No grand heroics, no solo hunting down of the bad guys, guns blazing and all that Rambo crap. That's our job and we're better at it than you."

"I'll keep that in mind."

Burroughs sighed. "Somehow, that answer worries me," he said.

Garry said nothing and walked out to where Peter was waiting.

Another two hours were taken to head out past the airport to the security lockup where the Lincoln had been taken, sign more papers, pay some money, and then Garry followed Peter's Mercedes back to Evanston. Garry slept another three hours when he got back.

But after dinner, Garry stood up. "I'll stay at home tonight," he said. "I've got an early departure."

Pauline looked frightened, but Peter nodded. "The search begins?" he asked.

Garry smiled. "It begins. And I'll find the bastards, one way or another."

They waved him off at the door, and he drove the short distance home. He was asleep early again, and slept sweetly, the horrors falling away before the excitement of pending decisive action. He was taking the war into the enemy's camp.

Chapter 15

Garry was up at four, wide awake. He packed his picnic basket with a mixture of fresh bread, cheese, a jar of olives, and cold cuts from the local delicatessen. Several cans of orange juice went into the cooler with packs of ice and he carried the load into the garage.

Esmerelda Finklestein III sat primly on her trailer. She had barely been outside this wet summer, and she seemed to be chiding him as he loaded the provisions.

"No worries, old girl," said Garry, and patted her side. "This is the best weather of the year. Time we went walk-about again."

She seemed to agree. He checked the fuel tanks and topped them up from the large tank he kept behind the garage. The air outside was lovely, fresh and warm, an Indian Summer in mid-September. After the poor summer, this was a wonderful change. He opened the main door to the front, hauled the boat up to the Continental and connected up the hitch. Soon after four-thirty, he eased out of his driveway and headed for the launch ramp at Evanston.

Several other boats were being put in the water and he waited patiently. But by five-fifteen, Esmerelda Finklestein III slid happily into the waters of Lake Michigan. Garry parked the car and returned to his boat. The Evinrude started without hesitation and he pulled out of the breakwater and headed south-east.

He decided to check the Indiana and Michigan area first, though both areas, that and the Wisconsin and upper Illinois shoreline would have to be examined in detail. He continued south-east after leaving Evanston, and after thirty minutes, took a compass reading on the smoke stacks of Gary, Indiana. The Evinrude purred sweetly as he passed along the Chicago skyline, a little further from the shore than the water treatment plant that had been his refuge two nights before. The city looked splendid in the first gleam of dawn and his spirits lifted from the black horrors of the night. The sun was well up as he passed to the north of the town of Gary. Steam rose in monstrous clouds over the city as the steel works pounded away. He pointed the bow toward Michigan City and poured a mug of coffee from his thermos flask in the picnic hamper. The day was warming up nicely and he extracted his Polaroid sunglasses from the boat's locker and put on a blue and white baseball cap with the HLM logo.

Soon after eight he reached within a mile of the white sands of the Indiana Dunes, a mile or two below Michigan City, pulled in nearer to the shore and began the search for boat jetties. Despite his drugged state the other night, Garry was clear on two things. He had been dropped from a fairly large boat that had required an equivalent-sized jetty at which to park, and he would recognize that jetty when he saw it. How he was certain he could not have explained, but certain he was.

He traversed Michigan City with nothing to jolt his recognition. A few boats were already on the water and some early morning swimmers were playing in the waves by the beautiful white sands of the local dunes. A pair of jet skis passed him with a roar and Esmerelda Finklestein rocked in the wake. He saw not a single boat jetty of a size that would set off the recognition warning in his mind.

He worked his way up the shoreline, past New Buffalo and onward. Twice, he saw large jetties standing out in the water and each time, his breath came a little quicker and he felt his pulse accelerate. But each time he approached he saw that the jetties had no large house nearby, and no steep incline led the way to a boathouse. The unknown trigger in his head that he knew would explode with recognition when the time came sat inert and passive.

Soon after ten, he reached Benton Harbour. It was a pretty spot which he had visited a few times, and it marked the edge of the boundaries he felt limited the distance he could have been taken by Rich. He toured the harbour, examined the breakwaters, looked up at the town and decided this was as far as he went in this direction.

He was sure that this was not where his intended executioners had taken him. He took a compass bearing on Evanston and set the steering to automatic for the forty-mile haul across the lake.

By two-thirty, he was back in home territory. The straight drive had been peaceful, almost entirely without company, and accompanied by a pleasant meal of cheese, fresh bread, and a few slices of roast beef, washed down with more coffee. Twice, he had to take manual control and give way to a sailing vessel cruising in a pleasant westerly breeze, and he had exchanged cheerful greetings with the occupants of the boats. At Evanston, he resumed the search, patrolling a mile off the shoreline and studying the coast through his binoculars. Some of the houses were spectacular, purchased by old aristocratic money, by mob money from Al Capone's heydays in Chicago, and by the new aristocracies of professionals and amoral politicians.

But there was nothing in the stretch from Evanston to Waukegan to shake his calm. The only sizeable marine structure he saw was at the Great Lakes Naval Training Centre, and then the harbour at Waukegan, and by four, he crossed over into Wisconsin waters and continued north.

The jetty stood out like a mountain ridge, defying the waters of Lake Michigan, and Garry's heart did a rapid Barn Dance. He slowed the engine down to a musical trickle of water along the sides of Esmerelda Finklestein, and raised his binoculars. Behind the jetty, a mansion-sized boathouse stood at the foot of the steep hill down from the southern edge of Milwaukee.

His heart racing, Garry extracted a can of mineral water and drank a few mouthfuls to ease his dry throat. Under the pounding of his pulse, trickles of fear added to the hunter's excitement. He sat down at the wheel to hide his face as much as possible behind the windshield, and lowered the peak of his baseball cap.

Pointing straight at the jetty, he crawled at barely enough speed to maintain steering, and a few yards away, stopped the engine and drifted.

The warning sentinel in his head refused to get excited. Whatever the mental observer was looking for, this jetty had not revealed it. Sitting for nearly twenty minutes before he let himself recognize the fact that he had not found his objective, Garry started the engine again and continued north.

The huge structures off the shore at Milwaukee were like a marine town, and the parkland along the coastline looked green and attractive. From only a few hundred yards out, Garry could see the picnickers and sunbathers taking the last of the evening sun, couples strolling along the pathways, and children running around with the incredible energy that could exhaust professional athletes. He checked his map. Again, he was almost at the arbitrary boundaries he had set, and he began to worry. A few more miles only he decided, check out the wealthy coastal areas of Shorewood, Whitefish Bay and Fox Point. If nothing had been found by then, he would reconsider the plan and the boundaries.

Daylight was fading, and Garry was thinking about anchoring for the night somewhere off Whitefish Bay. He decided to cruise for another twenty minutes.

When he saw it, the light had almost gone. He was nearly upon the big jetty before he saw it in the gloom. He raised his binoculars and studied the scenery around the jetty. Just as he had seen before, a generously-proportioned boathouse stood at the inland end of the jetty, and a steep hill behind it reflected the last rays of the setting sun on the trees. Near the top of the hill, a huge house looked over the lake. No lights could be seen in either the boathouse or the main house on the hill, and no boat was moored.

Garry reduced speed to idling and drifted towards the wooden structure. When he was about fifty yards away, he raised his binoculars again and studied the jetty.

This time, the sentinel exploded like a fireworks display, and the hunter's blood began to race. He had found it. On the last posts at the end of the jetty, two large, white carved shapes stared out to the water. The wooden lions stood upright, snarling almost audibly from massive, tooth-lined jaws.

The last time Garry had seen these particular lions, he had been barely awake, being carried out to the deep waters of the lake to be murdered.

He switched off the engine and drifted to a gentle kiss against the jetty. Catching the framework, he reached for the rope under one seat and tied Esmerelda Finklestein securely against the structure beside the ladder that conveniently reached down to him. Taking a deep breath, he climbed the ladder. He walked along the jetty and looked into the boathouse through the small dirty windows. It was the right place, he was already certain, though the sight of the dinghies on their trestles, the long reach of the sail mast and the ropes confirmed it.

He looked up at the house and saw no lights, though by now it was nearly dark. He began to walk up the road from the boathouse and moved into the shadows of the trees as he neared the house. When he reached the nearest wall of the house, he stopped and moved into the trees a little further. For ten minutes he waited silently, but saw no movement. Finally, he walked to the house front and again moved into the trees. Still nothing moved or showed signs of life.

He was about to move out and up to the road, when lights gleamed from further up the hill and moved towards him. A car! Nerves tingling, he moved as far back into the trees as he could, blessing the almost total night that had now fallen. He watched as the beams moved slowly down the hill, and the sounds of the engine reached him. A luxurious car he decided, judging by the discretely muted note of the engine. A few seconds later, the lights at the front of the house came on, triggered by a movement sensor, he assumed, and he froze behind the tree.

The car slid into position by the front door, and stopped, the tiny purr of the engine fading almost without being noticed. A large man climbed out of the driver's side and walked around to the passenger side, opening the door further with a courteous gesture. Garry could not recognize him, or the woman who got out. She was beautiful, dressed in a white suit with a short skirt, blonde hair reaching down to her back.

The two laughed at something, and walked into the house. Two minutes later, the lights at the front went out, leaving only a warm yellow gleam in the hallway and a soft glow in one of the upstairs rooms.

Garry shifted as silently as he could from his shelter and found his way through the dark to the driveway again. He continued his path upward and eventually reached the road. He looked around him. Street lights provided good visibility despite the tiny glow of the new moon. He walked up the road a few yards and came to a crossroad. He read the names of the two roads. The house which had held him captive was on Marigold Avenue. The other road was Dennison Drive. Beyond the fact that he was somewhere north of Milwaukee, Garry had no idea where these roads were. He walked back to the house to note the number, intending to find this location by land once he had got home, but he struck pay-dirt without expecting it.

Above the brass plate that displayed the address of 14 Marigold Avenue was a name. It proudly announced to the world in engraved Gothic characters that Stanley Mortensen was the occupant.

Mortensen! Garry stood upright from bending over the plate. Mortensen Bloody Transport! Only a few weeks before, the name had come into the conversation as the partners at HLM had looked for the last major clients of PAC. Garry remembered how he had rejected the idea of trying to win Mortensen because of the company's unsavoury reputation. *Jesus Christ!* he thought. Somebody, Charlie Levin he thought, no, it was Peter, had even suggested that Mortensen owed PAC considerable debts because of the rescue from bankruptcy that Petheram and Newman had conducted.

"You bet they owe some debts," Gary muttered. "And now we know how they pay them."

Setting off down the path again, he reached the house and worked his way past it by staying in the trees. He moved on down the path to the boathouse and looked back. Sure enough, lights were on at the back of the house and huge picture windows gleamed brightly. Certain that nobody could see him in the dark, he reached the jetty, climbed back to the welcoming cockpit of Esmerelda Finklestein and undid the ropes. Letting himself drift a few hundred yards out into the lake, he started the engine and turned south. After a mile, he dropped anchor, turned on his navigation lights and crawled into the tiny cabin in the bow.

He slept like a log until just before dawn.

"Mortensen," Garry said into the phone.

"Mortensen Transport?" Peter's voice was almost a squeak. "Christ, weren't we thinking of tackling them a while ago?"

"We were," agreed Garry. "But as you so rightly said, they owed PAC big."

"Can you imagine the results if we'd decided to approach them?" Peter was laughing outright, the initial shock fading. Garry felt almost relaxed, now that he knew who was doing these things to him and why.

"So now what?" asked Peter, returning to the matter at hand. "Can we call the cops in?"

"Still not yet," said Garry. It was early afternoon, and he had just returned the boat to the garage after the haul down from Wisconsin, had a shower and a long cold beer. "I still can't prove a link between Mortensen and PAC, not enough to pin an attempted murder charge on them, anyway."

"So what do you have in mind?"

"I really don't know," replied Garry. "I think I'll have more luck tackling the rats than going directly for the Pied Piper."

"Er..? Oh, I see," said Peter then he became alarmed. "Tackle Rich? You're crazy, man! He's twice your size!"

"I know," replied Garry. "But he's got the least to lose by admitting everything. He's just a common goon, and could probably face the idea of a relatively small jail term if I could somehow get him to make a deal with the prosecutors. That way, we could tie in Mortensen. And then we can see a path to PAC."

"Jeez, I dunno." Peter's worry resounded down the telephone line. "How do you propose to do all that?"

"Buggered if I know. I'll call you if I get any ideas. But it has to be done quickly."

"Why so?"

"Because Micky just called. She's fed up being away, she's got a couple of companies interested in forming associations with us, and she's coming home. The poor girl misses me terribly, and who can blame her?"

"Conceited bastard!" Peter laughed. "When?"

"Three days."

"We can't wrap this mess up in three days!"

"We have to, Peter. I can't take it any more than that."

"But what can you do?"

"I'll think of something."

"Let me know when you do, Garry. And take care."

"Take care? You bet your bloody life I'll take care. The best reason in the world gets back in three days."

"That's what I meant. We can get by without taking any action against PAC or Mortensen. At least PAC will be facing the undertakers within weeks."

"I know," said Garry. "But I need to get it cleared up. When somebody tries to have me killed, I tend to get a mite peeved."

"Sure. But didn't somebody or other in the bible say something about revenge being His? Can't remember who it was, but He was a heavy dude, I'm sure. Remember, we want you in the office again. There are invoices to raise and money to collect."

Garry laughed. "I'll watch it," he said, and hung up.

* * * *

All day he worried at the subject like an aggressive puppy. He snarled at it, walked around it, studied it from different directions and mentally pounced when he felt the problem might be looking the other way.

The glorious weather of the last few days had given way to cool and overcast conditions. Garry sat in his lounge all morning and ground away with his thoughts, pushing his mind to drive away the fear of confronting the men who had tried to kill him. Any time he felt the fear return, he dwelt on the amoral attitudes that had corrupted his old employers at PAC and driven them to seek his death. Then the rage burned up in him again like a campfire in the path of a sudden stiff breeze, and the fear vanished behind a thick, impenetrable blanket of lust for revenge.

At lunchtime, not worrying about being seen, he strolled along to the Japanese restaurant where he was well known. Those that mattered believed him dead and would not be looking for him. He enjoyed a meal of sushi and hot sake and returned to his house to fight the problem further.

He thought about the one visit he had paid to Mortensen in company with an audit manager in the first few weeks of his work with PAC. There had been a possibility of designing a new payroll system, but the idea had fallen apart as the company's financial problems had mounted. He remembered climbing into one of the truck cabins just for interest. The trucks were all fitted with small sleeping compartments behind the driver's section and Garry had admired the Playboy centrefolds that adorned the walls.

He shook his head and returned to the problem.

At nine o'clock he had it by the throat.

For this plan to work, a few chances had to be taken, he knew. He was not even certain that Rich still worked at Mortensen, but felt it was probable. Anyone entrusted to commit murder as part of his job description was not to be easily let go by a corrupt employer. But Garry felt like taking those chances, feeling a certain inexorable quality about his action.

The rental company was a little unhappy about delivering the Grand Marquis to Wilmette that late in the evening, but they eventually agreed after a promise of a minimum three-day rental. Garry needed a car that Rich would not recognize.

When the car arrived, he took the keys from the young man who had brought it, watched as he got into the small Toyota that had accompanied him then went back inside, locked the doors and went to bed, not sleeping for a long time until the excitement and nerves finally died away.

Chapter 16

Well before dawn, Garry rose, showered, dressed and packed the picnic basket again. He refilled the thermos and carried the load out to the Grand Marquis. He put one other item into the car. The .22 calibre rifle had never been used for anything but target shooting in the past. At four, he set out through the night for the south side of Chicago. A short call from his cellular phone to Mortensen made him nervous, but he put on his best southern drawl, praying his Australian accent would be hidden by the exaggerated vowels.

"Ah'm looking for Rich," he mumbled when a loud male voice answered the phone. Garry hoped that the first name was right, and that nobody would ask for further identification.

"Not here yet," snapped the voice in irritation.

"You'd be expectin' him, raht?" *Oh God, I hope I can keep this up,* said Garry to himself.

"Yeah, I'd better be. He's got a run today. Who is this?"

Garry replaced the phone without answering. His accent was becoming seriously strained. He had the information he wanted.

By five-thirty, he was sitting in the luxurious leather seat of the Grand Marquis amid the damaged and abandoned buildings lining the street on which he had parked. Across the street and fifty yards away, the sign for Mortensen Transport was new and fresh. At six, cars began to arrive, some driving into the Mortensen gate, others parking on the road near the rental car. Garry studied them all, waiting for one specific arrival. Nobody else existed.

Garry was almost dozing, relaxing back in the leather seat, when he idly looked in the side mirror on the right. He came fully awake in a second as the familiar sight of the battered old Buick station wagon filled the mirror. Garry slid a little lower in his seat and watched. Rich was driving, his partner, the thin-faced, balding man in the passenger seat. Neither looked at Garry's out-of-place vehicle as they ground past in low gear, the rumble of a deteriorating muffler system drowning out the radio in the Grand Marquis.

Rich parked the old Buick by the kerb at the other side of the Mortensen gateway and the two men got out. Garry stared at them, feeling a mixture of hatred, fear and excitement. These men had tried to kill him and very nearly succeeded. Only a miscalculation and perhaps a forced change of plans by somebody who had the boat had saved his life.

The men walked into the truck yard, and Garry settled down again. He had chosen his position well. Any truck leaving would have the driver's side nearest to Garry and he would be able to see the face. Only one face interested him.

At seven, Rich's partner left at the wheel of a semi-trailer, the large red script of "Mortensen Transport" standing out sharply on the pea-green background. He turned left out of the gate and passed within feet of Garry. Fifteen minutes later, a similar rig pulled out. Rich paused at the exit, looked carefully over the lowered window to both sides and turned right. A cigarette dangled from his lips.

Garry started his engine and moved out of his spot, driving slowly behind the Mortensen rig. They drove in convoy for twenty minutes through the mean, ugly streets of Chicago's south side. Rich's machine was obviously heavily laden, judging by the care with which he slowed at stop signs and the painfully slow acceleration away.

The trailer dragged itself up a ramp and entered the east-bound lane of Interstate 94 heading for Detroit. Garry tucked in behind, let the rig accelerate and allowed two more vehicles to slide in between him and the Mortensen machine. The speedometer showed sixty-five miles per hour and Rich appeared to settle at that speed, half a mile ahead. For a time, the two vehicles in between also hovered at that speed, but neither appeared to have cruise control because both of them slowed as a slight hill appeared in the highway, and Garry passed them, still hanging half a mile behind the trailer.

It was a few minutes after seven-fifty. The cloudy day hid the sun, which was a relief, as it would have been straight in Garry's eyes. The highway swung left round the bottom of Lake Michigan and followed the eastern shore, heading north for Benton Harbour. A line of vehicles merged from the Interstate 294 and Garry was happy to let several of them take position between him and Rich. However much Rich believed Garry to be dead, letting him see too much of a car following him could alert the big man's attention. People who killed for an occupation would have finely tuned senses for pursuit, Garry thought, and dropped back another few hundred yards.

The highway cut across the top corner of Indiana past the previous day's marine search areas of Michigan City and New Buffalo, and a large sign proclaimed a welcome to Michigan. Garry saw the Mortensen trailer increase the distance ahead and he accelerated up to seventy, letting his cruise control hold him at that speed. Tucking in again, he had three cars between himself and Rich. He decided that was safe enough.

The convoy reached Benton Harbour and the road swung east again for the straight line to Detroit. Garry began to worry. What if Rich was bound for the Canadian border? He hadn't brought any documentation along that would satisfy an Immigration check, either going into Canada or returning. Without his Green Card to prove his status as a US resident, he was stuck within the borders. Garry shrugged. If he lost Rich, so be it. Another time would do, though it meant the affair would go on over the date of Micky's return in another day.

At a steady seventy miles an hour, they passed the turnoff for Kalamazoo, Battle Creek and then Lansing on Interstate 69. The road signs indicated that in the distance, he could expect to reach Jackson, Ann Arbor, and Ypsilanti. The dashboard clock said ten-thirty.

There was a large sign the other side of Jackson, saying that the police monitored CB radio bands.

"I had no idea that was still in use, but it seems a good idea," muttered Garry, and tuned the car radio to find a new station. The journey was becoming increasingly boring, and he wondered how truckers could survive these endless hours on endless freeways.

'Prison Area - Do Not Pick up Hitch-Hikers,' said the sign approaching Ann Arbor.

"Maybe this is where you'll be in a few days, Rich," said Garry. "And I sure as hell would never give you a ride." He stretched, and wondered if Rich was going to stop for lunch at any time. With the thought, his fatigue dissipated, the cramped muscles eased and his excitement rose. This was the day, he knew, sensing the conclusions just ahead.

Another sign advertised a truck stop at Dexter, fifteen miles ahead. It was close to noon. If Rich was going to take a break, Dexter would be a good spot, decided Garry and decided to close up nearer to the large rig.

His intuition was good. A mile before the Dexter turn off, Rich slowed and signalled a right turn. With only two cars between them, Garry cautiously watched and followed the turn off the Interstate and on to a ramp. The ramp ended at a T-junction and the truck stop and restaurant were directly across the road. The trailer had to wait several moments before Rich could pull across, but eventually he did so and headed for the parking area where a number of similar vehicles lined up like sleeping whales. Garry eased across the road, his attention on the Mortensen trailer.

He drove through the car parking area, staying well away from the trucks and saw the bulky shape of Rich climb down with a folded newspaper under his arm. Garry's eyes followed the big man until he had entered the restaurant then he moved his car into a vacant spot and parked. He put on his baseball hat and dark glasses again, got out and cautiously approached the restaurant. Through the side windows he saw Rich take a seat in an area with a sign advertising it as reserved for professional drivers only. Rich unfolded a menu, studied it for a few seconds then opened his paper. He appeared to be settled for a while. A waitress approached him, held a short discussion then moved away.

Garry left the restaurant and walked to the car, keeping his back to the dining area. Back in the Grand Marquis, he started the engine and carefully drove round to the truck parking area, stopping next to Rich's vehicle. He got out of the car and looked around. There seemed to be nobody in sight. He climbed up the ladder of the Mortensen machine and breathed a sigh of relief when he found the door unlocked. He descended to the ground, returned to his car and drove it over to the edge of the parking area where it would be less conspicuous, not so much a tiddler among the whales.

When he got out again, he was carrying the rifle. Holding it down by his side, he returned to the Mortensen trailer and climbed awkwardly up the ladder again. He opened the door and was assailed by the stench of stale cigarette smoke. Pulling a face, he climbed inside, closed the door and turned to the back of the cabin. As he knew he would from his visit to the company four years ago, he found a sleeping compartment behind a tatty curtain. He crawled in to the compartment, drew the curtain behind him and sat on the hard bunk, his rifle across his knees. He settled down to wait, trying to ignore the heat, the smell of stale smoke and unwashed bodies, and prepared his mind for the coming confrontation.

After twenty minutes, as his guts were starting to tighten up and his confidence began to dissipate, he heard a harsh cough from a few feet away and froze. The truck cabin shook and swayed as a huge body climbed the ladder and the door opened with a welcome surge of fresh air. The cabin seemed to darken as Rich climbed in, sat heavily in the seat and rummaged in a glove compartment, pulling out a packet of cigarettes. He struck a match, drew in a deep breath and launched into a fit of helpless coughs, finally regaining control of his breathing. He swayed around as he found his seat belt, snapped it in place and opened the window to his left. Garry could see the shadow of the massive shape moving through the curtain.

Rich leaned forward, turned the key and started the engine with a bellow. The cabin began to vibrate. Garry pushed the curtain aside gently. He placed the muzzle of his rifle against Rich's right ear and worked the bolt to slide a bullet into the chamber.

"Good afternoon, Rich," he said pleasantly. "And how is your day?"

The huge body froze, massive arms rigidly gripping the steering wheel. Rich had clearly understood the significance of the "snick-snick" of the rifle bolt movement. Slowly, he turned his large head turned to the right, gently pressing his unshaven face against the rifle muzzle. He showed no emotion other than his eyes opening wide.

"You're supposed to be dead," said Rich. His voice was a notch higher than even his normal alto tone. Garry slowly increased the pressure of the rifle muzzle against the man's elephantine ear and Rich's stare returned to the front.

"I'm sorry to disappoint you," said Garry. "I woke up as you threw me overboard."

"Shit! I told him you needed another dose."

"Told who?"

Rich's heavy face was motionless.

"The same man who was late getting back with the boat?"

"Yeah."

"Stan Mortensen, in fact."

He received a stony silence, though the quick tightening of the hands on the steering wheel told Garry his bolt had hit home.

"And that bitch kept us back, too," Rich grunted.

The words took Garry by surprise. "What bitch?" he asked, feeling a tremble in his body as some unidentified memory screamed in horror within his mind.

"Dunno her name," muttered Rich. "Stan said she wanted to come along with us and see you get dropped overboard. She kept asking us to wait. I think she wanted to see you wake up before you went over. Eventually, I told her to shut up, and I threw you over the side."

Newman! Jesus Christ, it was Bridget Newman! Garry bit his tongue as the memory surfaced clearly in his mind. The dark face had watched him as he was carried out. Her eyes had feasted on his imminent death, like a vampire that fed on human souls rather than blood. Garry's hands sweated and he felt his face grow warm with fury. *What sort of creature was that woman?* he wondered. He realized that it was Newman's very lust to see him die with the knowledge of what was happening to him that had saved his life. He controlled the rage and returned to the immediate subject.

"And who's your little pal, Rich?" asked Garry, trying a new topic.

Rich was silent for a moment before he spoke, but when he did, it was not the answer that Garry wanted. "Is that thing loaded?" asked Rich. He seemed calm, as if asking the time of day.

"It surely is," said Garry, not liking the turn of the conversation.

"I don't think it is," said Rich, and started to move his face round again. Garry eased the muzzle away, moved it a few degrees to his left and aimed for the open window. The shot was thunderous in the enclosed cabin and the stink of explosive struggled to compete with the stench of stale ash.

"Jesus Christ!" roared Rich, and slammed his hands against his ears. The muzzle had been only inches away from his left ear. Garry had no sympathy for him at all, though his own head was ringing from the explosion. He rapidly worked the bolt again. The empty cartridge leaped out of the rifle and clattered against the windshield before falling on the floor by Rich's feet.

Carefully, Garry looked around the parking lot. The shot had been submerged beneath the rumble of several machines with their engines running, and any detected sound had probably been taken for a back-fire.

"Let me tell you a couple of facts of life," said Garry, feeling frustrated by the difficulties of extracting data from this large man. "That time you missed me in Chicago, I went back and found the people you and I both barged through running down the stairs." The lie came to him without difficulty, but he was in no mood to worry about morals. "They could easily identify you," he continued. "And of course, that time you attacked us in the garage, I have several witnesses to that. Which means a jury will easily believe that at some later time, you tried to kill me."

Rich shifted uneasily in his seat.

"So let's try again," said Garry. "Who's your pal?"

"His name's Don Wayland," muttered Rich.

"Good. And where is Don Wayland now?"

"On his way to Des Moines."

"And what's your second name?"

"Jenkins."

"Turn the engine off, Richard Jenkins," commanded Garry. Rich leaned forward and turned the key. Silence descended as the cabin stopped vibrating.

"And you killed Andrew Whittaker too, didn't you?" Gary continued.

"Don did that. He's the one who likes guns."

Garry let the information sink in then passed on to

other matters. "Let's continue with some home truths, Rich," he said into the calm. "You two kidnapped me once and did grievous bodily harm to me, and tried to repeat it on a second occasion. Then on yet another occasion, you attacked my fiancée and me. Do you think anyone would care if I blew your head off now?"

The rigidity in front of him told Garry he had made a point. He pushed the hot muzzle of the rifle a little harder into Rich's ear and the big man flinched. Garry took a grim pleasure from the movement.

"So have we made my point, Rich," he continued, "that a conviction for attempted murder is a dead cert for you and Mister Wayland?" He watched the side of Rich's face as the thought was evaluated and considered. He could almost hear the brain cells churning as they worked on a complex problem.

Rich finally nodded. "Yeah," he growled.

"Good, I'm glad you see that. And do you also see that the truth will come out about the shooting of Whittaker? I don't think Illinois still has the death penalty, but it would be a life sentence without parole for both of you, right?"

Rich swallowed hard. "Yeah," he said finally.

"Good," repeated Garry. "But of course, you were only following orders, weren't you?"

Rich was still for a few seconds as he considered this unexpected diversion then nodded again. "Right," he said.

"Mister Mortensen's orders?"

"Yeah."

"So a deal with the cops would probably keep your ass out of maximum security prison and give you a chance of seeing daylight again before you die, don't you think, Rich?"

The bovine eyes turned a little as Rich nodded once more. "Yeah," he said.

"Good. Turn on the CB, will you, Rich?"

Rich leaned forward, pressed a button on his dash, and Garry saw the red light come on under the handset of the radio.

Garry took a deep breath, trying to hide his tension from Rich. For all his outwardly calm control of the situation, Garry was struggling to stay in charge of himself. The trembling in his body which had begun when he heard Rich's cough had faded a little, but occasional small tremors ran through him, reminding Garry that he was talking to the man who had severely beaten him and tried to kill him, almost successfully.

Garry let out the breath slowly, took another one, and felt a measure of control. "Hand me the mike," he said. He kept the rifle firmly embedded in Rich's ear, but Rich handed the microphone behind him without any excess movement.

The loudspeaker was burbling with the chatter of other users, and Garry waited for a moment of silence. When it came, he pressed the button firmly and spoke. "This is an emergency. Is any police vehicle monitoring this transmission?"

The response was immediate. "This is the Michigan State Police," said a calm voice. It had an air of natural authority. "All CB users stay off the air until further notice. Caller, state your emergency and location."

Garry felt a load fall from him. "Michigan Police, please come to the truck stop at Dexter, just off

Interstate 94. The Mortensen Transport trailer. I am holding a wanted criminal."

"Identify yourself, caller," said the voice.

"Officer, I am holding a wanted killer at gun point. You had better get here fast because I can't be certain how long I can go without shooting him."

That did the trick and Garry was pleased to see the flinch of fear in Rick's heavy body.

"Stand by," said the voice. "Five minutes. CB users, you may resume use of this frequency.""

Garry dropped the microphone back on the front seat. "I think that will do it, Rich," he said. "You can switch off now."

Rich looked tired. He replaced the mike, switched off the radio and sat back. There seemed little life in him, but Garry took no chances. The rifle remained firmly embedded in the elephantine ear for the next few moments of quiet.

In the distance, the sound of a police siren grew into an audible wail. It grew louder and louder until it stopped abruptly and Garry saw the flashing lights of two patrol cars in the side mirrors of the truck. Both cars stopped, one on the left side of the cabin, the other across the front. Garry lowered his rifle and laid it on the bunk.

A door slammed and the cabin shook as someone climbed up the driver's side. A peaked hat looked in and stared at Rich then at Garry.

"This is Richard Jenkins," said Garry to the peaked hat. "Together with Don Wayland, he is wanted in Illinois for murder, attempted murder, assault and a few other things. My name is Garry Barton."

"Out," ordered the face below the cap.

"You heard the nicepoliceman," said Garry. "Move your butt, Rich."

With a sigh, Rich unfastened his straps and opened the door. He climbed out of his seat as if he had been driving for twenty hours, stiffly and seemingly exhausted. Garry waited for the shaking of the cabin to stop then eased himself out of the sleeping compartment to sit in the seat just vacated by Rich. He leaned back and took the rifle, opened the bolt, removed the bullet from the chamber and put it in his pocket. He unclipped the magazine, put that in his pocket also and opened the door. Carrying the rifle by the muzzle, he descended the ladder with only one free hand.

The police officer who had spoken to Garry was standing a few feet away. Another stood a little further back, both pairs of watchful eyes observing the scene, hands on the holsters of their pistols. The first one nodded at the rifle. "Put that thing on the ground, Mister Barton, and stand away," he said. His tone was calm and neutral. Garry obeyed and looked around.

Rich was seated in the rear of the cruiser parked in front of the truck, another officer with him. From the driver's side of that cruiser, one officer was watching Garry intently while using the radio.

The first officer pointed at Garry. "You said your name was Garry Barton?" he said abruptly.

Garry nodded. The officer said something to the driver. The words were inaudible to Garry.

Nobody moved until the officer replaced the radio and nodded at his partner. The driver gestured at Garry to approach.

"You're Garry Barton, and your home is in Wilmette?" he asked when Garry reached the car. Garry nodded again. The officer studied him carefully for a few moments, and got out of the car. "The story checks with the Illinois people," he said, addressing the other patrolmen. "The descriptions of both these two also check. The lieutenant says bring them both in. We'll sort it out at the station."

He turned to Garry. "There's a Detective Sergeant Burroughs in Chicago wants to talk to you real bad," he said.

"I'll bet he does," replied Garry.

"He'll call you when we get to the station," said the cop. "He sounded mad as hell."

"No doubt."

The cop grinned. "Where's your vehicle?" he asked. Garry pointed at the Grand Marquis. The officer gestured to follow him to the car. "We'll all go to the station," he said, "and get the paperwork done."

Garry reached into his pocket and took out the car keys. He was feeling deathly weary and small trembles were beginning in his legs. "Could one of you drive?" he asked. "I don't think I'm quite capable right now." He leaned against the side of the police cruiser, and then slumped to the ground in utter weariness.

Chapter 17

The atmosphere in the boardroom was peaceful, almost sad, the way a classroom is after final examinations have been taken and the school year is over. The four people seemed preoccupied with their own thoughts.

"It's done," said Newman. "There'll be no more interference from Garry Barton or HLM." Her face held softer lines than any of them had ever seen. She seemed a little dreamy and far away.

"How?" Petheram demanded. His face was pale, but his eyes showed a flash of excitement.

Newman looked briefly at him. "The men captured him outside Barrington," she said. "They held him until nightfall and then he was doped. They dropped him off Mortensen's boat in the middle of the lake." Her lips curved in a smile.

"Clever," said Trent. "That means he'll have genuinely drowned, water in the lungs and all that. When they find the body the authorities will assume a boating accident."

"That's why they undid his hands and feet before throwing him over," agreed Newman. "And they dropped him quite near the city. The body should be found in a day or two. I think Haywood's people will get the message." Her face showed animation. Petheram stared at her for a second or two then looked out of the window.

"And nothing can link us to these people?" asked Conway. He looked calm, a man who had accepted the necessity of drastic action, however much he might regret it.

"Nobody," said Newman. "Mortensen assures me these men have done similar work before. Even though I agree that they failed to perform properly in the past, they are completely trustworthy when it comes to silence."

"Good," said Conway. "Then it is surely time to leave these unpleasant matters behind and get on with the real business of our survival."

The room stirred a little, as four people shifted position and began to open files.

"Bill," asked Conway. "What have you done to restore our position?"

Trent looked up, swung his eyes briefly between Conway and Newman and looked down at his notes. "I've advised all clients of a fifteen percent reduction of fees for the coming year," he began. "And I've told all the clients that we'll be introducing advanced computer audit to them over the coming months, which will reduce the time taken for their audits and further reduce the costs."

"Good," said Conway. "But who's going to do this? Not George Elliot, surely?"

Trent grinned, and pushed his glasses back up his nose. "Elliot left yesterday," he said. "It took little persuasion on my part." He smiled at the small chuckle that ran round the room.

"Then who?" asked Petheram.

Trent opened a file and extracted a few sheets of paper. He passed a copy to each of the others. "Walter Martindale," he said. "That's his resume, and it's very impressive. He's moving over from Chalmers and North next week. He said he wanted a new challenge and this one sounded hard enough. He introduced computer audit there many years ago, and he's right up to date. A lot of people think he's the best there is in the business."

There was a rustle as each of the four studied the papers, emitting the odd grunt at various points.

"Very impressive, as you say," said Newman. "That deals with the technical side. What about the human side?"

Trent nodded vigorously as if expecting her question. "I've increased the staff pay levels by ten percent across the board," he said. "And I've promoted four new managers. They've been told that partnerships will be available as soon as business recovers to last year's level. They seem excited and the morale in the whole place is lifting."

"It eats into our cash reserves rather severely," Conway objected, but his words were refuted at once.

"Rather that than go out of business," said Petheram pounding the table. "I think Bill's done an excellent job and deserves our thanks."

"I agree," said Newman. "Our next objective is to recover our client base."

"Of course," agreed Petheram. "Meanwhile, what do we do about management consulting? We need somebody solid to head that up, too."

"Well for Christ's sake, get an accountant," growled Trent. "Somebody who understands the business at least."

"Sure," said Petheram with a grin. "Of course, the ideal man would be Garry Barton."

A small laugh ran round the room just as Garry walked in.

For a few moments, Garry said nothing and studied the room. Trent was staring open-mouthed at him, spectacles almost at the end of his nose. Conway was frozen and expressionless. Newman had turned round to see who the intruder was, and her face reflected rage. Only Petheram appeared to register the implications of Garry's presence. He was white-faced, and Garry heard a whispered "Oh Jesus Christ!" from him.

Conway was the first to speak out loud. "My God, Garry!" he said. "You're supposed to be dead."

Garry looked at him without warmth and walked to the table. He pulled a chair out between Newman and Petheram and sat down. The two partners shifted nervously away from him, and Garry smiled pleasantly at them.

"Funny thing that, Jack," he said, turning his face back to Conway. "You're the second person who's said that to me in the last twenty-four hours. The other guy was the one who thought he'd killed me."

He looked around the frozen scene then addressed Newman. "Did you enjoy watching me die, Bridget?"

he asked curiously. Her face went blank and Garry looked at each of the other partners in turn. "She didn't tell you?" he asked to the group at large. "She didn't mention that she just happened to be on the boat as I was dropped off the stern? Well, she was." He turned back to look at Newman. "And I can tell you, gentlemen, she was loving every second of it, weren't you, Bridget?"

The silence roared back at him.

"Come the trial, Bridget," Garry continued, "you may want to explore a plea of insanity. Just a friendly suggestion."

Garry looked hard at the three men staring at him. "I'm afraid you guys don't have that option," he said and turned back to the woman. "Those men you hired, Bridget," he said. "They were pretty incompetent. I expected better of you."

She glared at him with an expression of fury worse than anything Garry had ever seen. But it didn't generate the fear it would have done in the past. "You're talking garbage, Barton," she sneered. "It's become a habit of yours, it seems."

Garry grinned at her. "Remember that I told you one of them was called Rich?" he said, and ignored her glare. "Well, I learned yesterday that his name is Richard Jenkins. He told me that when I shoved a gun down his ear and he confirmed it when the cops arrested him a few minutes later."

The silence in the room was like a frozen Arctic dawn. Garry felt that he was the only living thing in the place.

"And he works for Stan Mortensen," he continued. "So does his little helper, a guy called Don Wayland.

He's the one I gave a high-pitched voice to in our last encounter. The police are picking him up about now near Des Moines. Isn't it interesting, Bridget, that they both work for a friend of yours? One who has both the morals of a sewer rat and a considerable debt to you?"

"How the hell would I know?" replied Newman tonelessly. "And why should I care?"

"Oh you should care, all right," said Garry as he looked round the room. "So should you all. Because Jenkins and Wayland have absolutely zero interest in taking an attempted murder rap when they were doing it for somebody else. Rich has already filed statements that Stan Mortensen ordered them to kill me, and I've no doubt Don Wayland will do the same."

"So?"

Garry had to admire Newman's strength. She was the only one still in control. Petheram was openly weeping now and Conway had dropped his hands to his lap and was staring at them like a small boy being chastised. Trent had placed one hand over his mouth and was staring at Garry with intense horror.

"So, Stan Mortensen isn't some Mafioso with a rule of strict silence," continued Garry. "He's not going to take it alone either. Why should he? He's never met me, knows nothing about me. I imagine the cops asked him some quite embarrassing questions on the subject of motive last night after they'd put Rich Jenkins away."

He looked around the room. "And while attempted murder is one thing," he said, "actual murder is another. Rich told me that Don Wayland pulled the trigger when Andrew was shot. So, of course, both he and Don would be guilty of Murder

One.   They don't want to face life in a maximum security block, and who can blame them?"

Garry smiled at them again. "A deal with the DA is their best chance on that, too. And Mortensen will want to do the same to stay out of the really nasty prisons. So it keeps coming back to you guys, doesn't it?"

He looked curiously at Newman. "You must have ordered the killing of Andrew Whittaker almost as soon as he left," he said.

She stared firmly back at him, all attempts to hide her involvement gone. "He would have talked," she replied. "And I knew this pathetic bunch..." She looked with contempt around the room. "This lot would never have gone along with it. They couldn't have handled it. They took a lot of leading by the nose until they were ready to have you killed."

"But it wasn't a problem for you, Bridget?" he asked, softly.

"Why should it be a problem?" she retorted coolly. "He was in the way, he was a risk. He had to go. The same with you."

"But you enjoyed it Bridget, that was the difference between you and your partners here. I wasn't completely knocked out, and I saw the look on your face as they were carrying me to the boat. You were turned on. Did you watch Andrew's death as well? Did you get an orgasm from either of us as we died?"

She glared, her black eyes like pools of black rage in her white face then she turned away from him.

Trent was moaning softly and Garry looked briefly at him. Petheram had put his head in his hands.

Conway hadn't moved except to raise his head and look at Garry.

Garry looked back, almost in sympathy. "Not quite what you expected, was it, Jack?" he said.

Conway shook his head. "It seemed to run away with us, Garry," he said. "I am most truly sorry."

"And so am I, Jack. You were the only one who seemed to realize that I actually had PAC's interests at heart when I criticized the firm."

"I know that," replied Conway. He seemed to recover his composure and looked like an aristocrat again. "I've been dreadfully weak," he continued. "I let the Philistines take over."

"Yes, you did," said Garry, and he looked at Newman. The power had gone out of her as if someone had pulled a plug. Her black stare had faded, her face falling into lines of old age that Garry had never seen before.

Conway was still talking softly, and Garry returned his attention to him, hearing something unexpected.

"You know, Garry," said Conway, talking as if he really didn't know or care if anyone could hear him, "I realized some time ago that Bridget had ordered the murder of Andrew Whittaker. It frightened me terribly. I wondered if she would do the same if any of the rest of us looked like withdrawing our support from her initiative."

Garry could think of nothing to say and merely looked sadly at his old chairman.

"I even bought a gun," said Conway, looking up at Garry with a tiny smile, "in case she thought I was pulling away and decided to do something unpleasant about it." He seemed to be sharing some small, final joke with Garry.

The joy of this triumph had gone, Garry realized. He was feeling sadness that came from the recognition that a proud firm of professionals had just collapsed. He felt most sorrow for the employees and, with a jolt, saw the opportunity. He felt a strong urge to get up, call Peter and start work on a proposal to take over the entire structure of PAC immediately. He knew the bank would support such a sweeping move, and the justice would be lyrically poetic.

He rose to his feet and moved to the door. "We won't see each other again," he said, "except, perhaps, at the trial. I won't wish you well."

He opened the heavy oak door, and let it close behind him.

"Thank you, Detective Sergeant Burroughs," said Garry. "I really appreciate the chance to talk to them first."

"I think they owed you that one, Mister Barton. So did I. I should have taken you more seriously at the beginning."

Garry smiled. "You've finally decided accountants can be as bad as lawyers?"

Burroughs gestured at the man with him, a large, muscular man with a hard, expressionless face. The two of them moved to the boardroom door. Burroughs paused and looked back at Garry. "Who'd a thunk it?" he asked, a small grin on his face. "Killer Accountants! Fuck a duck! Goddamm Certified Public Killer Accountants!"

"One of them's a lawyer," said Garry.

"Well, that's okay then," replied Burroughs and put his hand on the door.

The sudden shout from inside the boardroom froze all three of the men in the lobby. There was a hysterical quality to the voice, a man's voice almost breaking into a scream. Garry heard the voices of Petheram and Trent also raised in sudden alarm. The sharp explosion of a gunshot terminally punctuated the fear and broke the stasis of the two detectives. Both drew weapons from holsters under their jackets. Burroughs exchanged a look with his colleague then he surged the heavy door inward and ran in. The second man ducked low and threw himself just inside the door, his gun at the ready.

But as they moved, there was a second shot, the same calibre as the first. Too astounded to feel fear, Garry followed the second man into the boardroom and froze at the sight.

Bridget Newman was dead. There could be no doubt about that. She had collapsed backward in her chair and her face was a mass of blood. Her immaculate dark skirt was sprawled in an untidy mess over her thin legs, and brilliant red stains stood out garishly on her perfect silk blouse.

Conway was still sliding down the far wall of the boardroom, leaving a thick smear of blood on the dark wood. An automatic pistol was in his hand, and like Newman, his face was a mask of blood and distorted, unrecognizable flesh.

In complete silence, the only movement was that dreadful, bloody slide down the wall until Conway reached the ground. The stink of explosive mixed with the smell of wood-polish and the stench of fear.

"He... he shot her!" gasped Petheram. "He had the gun in his briefcase... he took it out and shot her...." Sweat poured down his face and his eyes were so wide that a complete ring of white was visible round his pupils. "Then he put the gun in his mouth, and...."

Slowly, Garry backed out of the room. In the lobby, a number of people had gathered, expressions of terror and bewilderment common to all of them.

Garry didn't wait to see any more. He was anxious to go, to get back to the office and get the plan in action to take over the shattered remnants of PAC. The numbness at what he had just seen shoved the horror of the event into some space where later he could retrieve it and sort it out. But for now, new corporate life needed tending to compensate for the deaths to which he had just been a witness.

Another thought gave him more warmth. British Airways had a 747 arriving at O'Hare that afternoon, and there was someone on that plane that he loved very much.

The elevator door opened, and Garry left to start rebuilding a small part of the world.